The Raven's Lady

THE RAVEN'S LADY

The Duke's Men Series

Kate Moore

The Raven's Lady
Copyright© 2024 Kate Moore
Tule Publishing First Printing, October 2024

The Tule Publishing, Inc.

ALL RIGHTS RESERVED

First Publication by Tule Publishing 2024

Cover design by Erin Dameron-Hill

No part of this book may be used or reproduced in any manner whatsoever without written permission except in the case of brief quotations embodied in critical articles and reviews.

This is a work of fiction. Names, characters, places, and incidents are products of the author's imagination or are used fictitiously. Any resemblance to actual events, locales, organizations, or persons, living or dead, is entirely coincidental.

AI was not used to create any part of this book and no part of this book may be used for generative training.

ISBN: 978-1-964703-62-6

"Anyone who had made money by any means, and was ambitious for himself and his family, automatically invested in a country estate…"

CHAPTER ONE

THE DOOR OF Verwood Hall, an old house of buff-colored Bath stone, built in the baroque style of Wren, stood open, admitting a sharp gust of wind which tugged at the hem of Lady Cassandra Lavenham's plain brown cloak. Through the open door, Cassie could see dark clouds rolling in above the chestnut trees lining the carriage drive. She accepted an umbrella thrust her way by William, Verwood's remaining footman and gathered her cloak about her.

Just as she prepared to step out, her aunt Honoria called down to her from the landing above the entrance hall. "Cassie, you'll be soaked to the skin before you're home again."

"Very likely, Aunt, but I won't mind. You do want your package, don't you?"

"Oh yes, I've been waiting so long." Honoria, her lace cap rakishly askew over graying red-gold curls, twisted the ends of a lovely, blue East India shawl draped over her shoulders. "Couldn't we send William or one of the lads from the stables? I'm certain that if we stressed the ... delicacy of the situation, William would be discreet."

"No doubt, Aunt, but then, I'd miss my walk, and you know how unreasonable I become when I've had no proper exercise in a day."

"You are never unreasonable, love, except in your deplorable tendency to self-reliance. Can you manage all that way? Your foot will hold up?"

Cassie smiled up at her worried relation. "My half boots are quite sturdy, and William has provided me with an umbrella."

"You will return in time for our meeting, won't you? I cannot manage the property agent alone."

"If I get behind hand, I'll stop at the Crown and get them to bring me in their gig. Don't worry. I will be here."

"Oh, good thought. The inn gig will be perfect for your foot."

Cassie offered a cheery wave to Honoria, and stepped resolutely through the door. As soon as it closed behind her, her spirits lifted. She managed the front steps as she had learned to do and headed up the carriage drive. She judged that she had two hours at least for her errand in the village before the rain truly set in. The property agent was expected in the afternoon, so she would have time to change and put herself to rights before meeting with him.

Of the three women living at Verwood, Cassie, at twenty-four was the youngest. She judged that she had the easiest means of escape from the demands of managing a large household on somewhat straightened means. She rarely let weather interfere with her daily walks and felt no need to conceal them from her neighbors, however eccentric such solitary rambles might appear. Cassie could lose herself in woods and sky for an hour or more each day and return to Verwood refreshed in spirits. Miss Honoria Thornhill was Cassie's mother's surviving sister, a single lady of some fifty-odd years, whose escape was writing novels, an occupation which she concealed from Cassie's grandmother on her father's side. Her Grace, the Dowager Duchess of Verwood, the third member of their female household, had no tolerance for *women scribblers* as she called them. And so, once again, today, Cassie had been dispatched to the village to retrieve the first copies of her aunt's latest book *Audacity and Ambition*.

A particularly strong gust caught her, and she quickened her steps, turning off the drive to strike out on a well-worn path through the woods. With any luck she would not only beat the rain, but when she returned, she and Honoria would secure a tenant for the house. It had become necessary to let the house due to Cassie's grandmother's passion for horses. At seventy-nine, Her Grace remained a remarkable horsewoman, and a demanding employer. No trainer satisfied the dowager's standards, and no Verwood horse had raced in three years, nor had any of their neighbors sent horses to be prepared at Verwood. With Verwood no longer functioning as a stud, the staggering costs of maintaining a score of horses in the style her grandmother considered worthy of Verwood Hall was draining their resources faster than Cassie's current allowance from her trustees or the proceeds from Honoria's pen could provide.

Cassie had high hopes for the afternoon's meeting with the property agent. His letter assured her that his wealthy client was determined to find a suitable house in the neighborhood for immediate occupancy. In Cassie's mind the deal was as good as done. Verwood was the only house for let in the area. True, the house had a few shortcomings that perhaps made *immediate* occupancy not quite practical, a leak in the library, a hearth in the best bed chamber that smoked when the wind was northerly, but she was sure that a properly eager tenant would see that such difficulties could be overcome. First impressions mattered, so they were to meet in the red drawing room with an excellent tea prepared by Cook, another woman who knew how to manage on slender means.

IN THE PRIVATE dining room of the Crown in Wormley, Sir Adrian Cole leaned one elbow on the sill of the old diamond-paned bay window and regarded his property agent, Jacob Trimley. Cole was becoming used to his new name and title, both of which had inspired the landlord of the Crown to put forth considerable effort to please. To those who truly knew him, he retained his boyhood name, Raven.

The Crown, where Raven and Trimley had taken refuge during an earlier deluge, served a decent roast fowl luncheon, the remains of which lay on the table next to the open ORDNANCE SURVEY map, sheet NUMBER 86.

The final gusts of the passing storm fluttered the frayed curtain at his elbow, and it occurred to Raven that the luncheon delay suited Trimley. There was something his agent wasn't telling him about the estate Raven intended to buy.

"You haven't made them an offer, have you?" he said.

The comment caught Trimley with his fork in the air. He stabbed a last bit of boiled potato, put his fork down, and raised his napkin to his mouth. From behind the cloth, he mumbled, "An offer to purchase would not be accepted."

"Why not? You told me the place has been advertised for months without drawing any takers. By now the owner must be in dire need of funds."

"They may have set the asking price a trifle high." Trimley reached for his tankard of the landlord's home-brewed.

"Why is that? I wonder." Raven raised a brow. He thought the asking rate rather low. "What are you not telling me, Trimley?"

Trimley took a swallow of his drink. "Well, it's possible that the place wants some attention."

Raven sat up. "You mean it's a bleeding ruin?"

"Nothing of the sort. Keep in mind, Sir Adrian, the location." Trimley set down his beer and tapped the map. "You will not find another property as good, or one nearer Lord Ramsbury's seat. The Verwood estate has a small park, to be sure, a thousand acres, but it's well laid out. The lake is lovely, and the house sizable, just right for your purpose I should say."

Raven looked at the map. In December he had marked out Lord Ramsbury's estate and instructed Trimley to find a property in the neighborhood suitable for a newly knighted, obscenely rich gentleman. Proximity to Ramsbury's estate was the key to Raven's hopes and plans. Now, when an available property had been found, Raven wanted no delays. "That's not the usual size for a duke's principal seat, is it?"

"Well, no," said Trimley.

The waiter entered and began to clear the table, and Trimley launched into a history of the dukes of Verwood, explaining how the title had passed from the last duke to his younger brother rather than to the son who had died in the Anglo-Burmese War.

Raven half listened as the waiter did his business. The leaded diamond panes of the window told the long history of the inn, the oldest panes made of broad glass, thick and uneven with surface scars from being ironed and a green tint from iron oxide, the newer panes with the smoother surface but the tell-tale concentrate ripples of crown glass. A freshening breeze through the open casement brought the sounds of ostlers tending to the horses of patrons impatient to be underway. Raven, too, was impatient, with dead dukes and their living offspring whose inability to hold onto a fortune now obliged them to let Verwood Park.

Raven knew toffs. He'd dealt with them in London and studied with them briefly at Cambridge. They'd been unavoidable in the few terms he'd spent at college. His tutor there, Mr. Clumber, an old fellow, had stretched his income by taking on private pupils preparing for a tripos or honors.

Raven had studied with those young men, ridden with them, drunk with them, and bowled them out on the cricket pitch. He had thought himself one of them until Mr. Clumber explained that there would be no tripos or honors for Raven. *I daresay you're a clever lad, Cole, but you're sadly out of place among your betters at college, boy. There's an order to be preserved after all.* Raven had been busy overturning the order of things ever since.

Only one of Clumber's pupils had remained a sort of careless friend over the years. Chance meetings with Ned Farrington in town had twice improved Raven's luck. Once when Ned told Raven to stay in the funds during a mild banking panic in London, and again when Ned had taken Raven to a rout party at Lord Ramsbury's London house to celebrate the knighthood his fire engine had earned him. A Cole-designed engine had been one of the engines deployed to save Westminster Hall from the October fire that had consumed the palace where Parliament met.

Trimley wrapped up his history with an explanation of how the unentailed property around the original site had been sold off, while the remaining thousand-acre estate had been preserved as a residence for the late duke's mother.

"She must be an ancient specimen. Make her an offer."

"Oh, she's an octogenarian to be sure, but it won't do to disturb the dowager. It's a matter of proceeding with some . . . delicacy and discretion. These old families, you know, they can't be seen to need to . . . retrench."

"Trimley, with whom are we actually dealing?"

Trimley shuffled some papers on the table. "We deal with C. J. Lavenham, who represents the dowager. A servant will meet us at the porter's lodge and escort us to the house. Where, I dare say, Lavenham will meet us."

A disturbance outside the window drew Raven's gaze. He glanced down into the courtyard, where a fine chestnut gelding whinnied piteously. A gentleman in a caped greatcoat and beaver hat at the horse's head handed the animal into an ostler's care and turned to a tall, sturdy youth in rough country dress, his hands outstretched in an apologetic manner. Every schoolboy who ever had a tyrant for a master knew that gesture, knew the stinging rebuke about to land on the youth's outstretched palms. Raven came to his feet without thinking.

The gentleman shouted, and raised his driving whip when a woman stepped between the two men. She spoke in a voice too low for Raven to hear. The whip remained raised. Raven tossed his purse on the table and headed for the door. "Pay the shot, will you, Trimley? I'll be in the yard."

In the courtyard the ostlers had stopped their work to gawk at the little drama underway. The angry gentleman in the greatcoat, flapped his whip arm up and down, ranting about his curricle. According to him, the vehicle had been reduced to a pile of kindling in a ditch and his horse irreparably injured through the boy's stupidity.

The youth was taller and more broad-shouldered than his accuser, but his posture was cringing, as if he would shrink into himself if he could. Raven guessed his age to be eighteen. At that age Raven would have knocked his opponent down and walked away, but the lad said nothing in self-defense as the gentleman's tirade blasted over him.

The boy's champion was a straight, slim woman in a plain brown cloak, her hem six-inches deep in mud, her face obscured by the brim of a serviceable country bonnet, a closed umbrella hooked over one arm, and a brown paper package clutched to her bosom.

"Are you quite finished, now, Hugh?" she asked the gentleman. Raven immediately revised his estimate of the woman's age and condition in life. He had assumed that she must be the boy's mother, but the voice was young, and the cool tone, unmistakably well-bred. He should walk away. A public row between a pair of strangers was no business of his. But the youth's anguished gaze, shifting back and forth between the two speakers held him there.

"What, are you his dry nurse, Cassie?" the angry gentleman continued. "The stupid lout is a menace. His people need to keep him confined at home. He has no business being on the public road, and you have no right to defend him."

"He's the best farrier in Wormley, Hugh, as you well know. He's on the road because his work is in demand. His cart is belled as a signal to other drivers, and, I dare say, with a little caution, you could have avoided the accident."

"I could have avoided? The great hulking slow top is supposed to pull aside for his betters. He can't even manage his donkey. The damned beast brayed at the worst possible moment."

"And Prince took exception to the donkey, did he? Let Grandmama look at him. I'm sure she has a poultice for that foreleg to keep Prince from being scarred." The woman stepped forward and laid a hand on the horse's nose, offering a soothing stroke.

"Damn your grandmother's poultice. It's compensation I want, and I'll have it, too. That rig was London made."

The woman's head came up. "Very well, Hugh, produce a witness to the event."

Raven shifted his position to see the lady's face, but the bonnet still hid her from him.

He had to admire the bold tilt of her head. She would not back down.

"What?" Hugh cried. "Are you doubting my word as a gentleman?"

"And your sense of fair play. If Dick Crockett truly is at

fault in the affair, then of course, compensation must be made."

"You're not listening, Cassie. You can tell old Crockett his son has cost him sixty guineas. If he can't pay for the damages, he'd best keep the idiot off the road."

"Hugh, stop calling him an idiot, for he is nothing of the sort."

The gentleman looked over her head at the youth. "I'll call the bacon-brained slow top what I like. He can't hear a word, can he?"

"Not with his ears, but he hears you. Make no mistake about that."

Raven glanced at the youth again. The intense concentration in the anguished face made sense now. The lad might not understand the words, but he knew Hugh was a threat. An argument between a pair of toffs, who appeared to know each other well, might be none of Raven's affair, but he didn't like a man who would callously reduce another man to beggary.

He stepped forward. "Sixty guineas, did you say?"

The gentleman and the woman turned to him. Raven caught his breath at the face previously hidden by the bonnet. The voice had prepared him for youth and refinement, but he'd had only a vague expectation of genteel womanliness. Now he saw smooth, rounded cheeks, above a wide bow of a mouth. Expressive gray eyes looked at him frankly from a countenance made uncompromising by a pair of definite dark brows.

"Who the devil are you?" the gentleman asked.

"A traveler delayed by your quarrel." Raven reached into

his coat and produced a wad of Bank of England notes. He counted out sixty guineas and held the notes aloft. "Yours," he said to the gentleman, "immediate compensation for your inconvenience…on one condition."

"Condition?" Hugh sneered, but his gaze remained locked on the notes in Raven's hand.

"Apologize to the lady and to her companion." Raven smiled at the gentleman, aware of enjoying himself for the first time since he and Trimley had left London. He might appear to be Sir Adrian Cole, newly knighted by his majesty, but inside he was his old self, Raven.

"Apologize!" Hugh raised his whip hand.

Raven lunged for Hugh's arm, grabbing it and twisting it behind his back. He wrenched the whip from Hugh's hand and with a shove sent Hugh staggering across the courtyard. Clumsily regaining his balance, Hugh turned to regard Raven with intense malice.

CHAPTER TWO

Cassie studied the stranger. Until he spoke, she had been unaware of his presence in the crowd of gawkers, most of them village lads. He was no doubt on his road and must have taken refuge from the storm in the inn. He was tall, athletically built, and plainly in command of an expensive tailor and deep pockets. His handsome face was marked by an easy authority. His elegance made her conscious of the plainness of her cloak and the mud on her skirts.

His gaze was fixed on Hugh. Again, he offered the bank notes. He appeared to recognize Hugh's nature, but not how dangerous it was to provoke him.

Hugh was breathing hard. "One … does … not … apologize to one's inferiors."

"But I understand that Mr. Crockett here"—the stranger indicated Dick, as if he meant to include him in the conversation—"is your superior in at least one respect, if he is, indeed, the best farrier in these parts."

"You, sir, are meddling in an affair that's none of your business."

"Alas, your quarrel has impeded my business, or I would gladly let you continue to waste your breath defending the indefensible."

"Indefensible!" Red splotches bloomed in Hugh's fair

cheeks. "This"—he pointed an accusing finger at Dick, then dropped it in the face of the stranger's forbidding countenance—"fellow has—"

The stranger held up his hand. "Spare me." He gave the bank notes a little shake. "Whatever the cause of your inconvenience, I suggest you cut your losses. Sixty guineas." He paused. "It's not difficult, really. A simple *I beg your pardon* will do."

There was a moment of frozen silence in the inn yard. Cassie realized she was desperately clutching her aunt's package, hoping that Hugh could behave with sense for once. She suspected that even the flies had suspended their buzzing waiting for his reply.

"Oh, very well then," Hugh said. He pivoted and executed a sloppy bow in Cassie's direction that slightly included Dick. "Cassie, Crockett, I beg your pardon."

He turned to the stranger with a smirk. "Satisfied?"

The stranger merely extended the hand with the bank notes. He let Hugh take them, careful that their hands did not touch, an insult that Cassie knew would not go unnoticed by Hugh, who stalked off, yelling at the yard boys to bring him a horse. The little drama ended, and the inn yard came back to life with ostlers hustling to hitch teams to carriages and bring saddled horses to their riders.

A tug on her sleeve made Cassie turn to Dick Crockett. His eyes were big with questions. The youth was deaf from an illness contracted when he was eight. His family spoke with him through signs they'd invented and through writing on slates. The boy was good at reading faces and doing sums. He knew how hard it was to come by ready cash.

Cassie tried to ease his fears. She had a little facility with the signs he used especially those that had to do with his work. It was harder to explain the role the stranger had played in pacifying Hugh. Dick mimed the counting of the bank notes. Cassie shook her head and told him not to worry. His gaze focused on her lips. She promised that she would talk with his parents later.

When she was able to turn her attention to the stranger, his chaise and four had been drawn up, and he was on the point of climbing aboard with another gentleman. Again, she got a sense of his wealth. Not only was he able to throw away what could be a year's income for the likes of Dick Crockett, he had a team of horses her grandmother would likely kill to possess.

"I fear you've made an enemy," Cassie told him, looking up into the strong, lean face. It was something to be the object of the stranger's intense gaze. As one of the neighborhood's eccentrics, she was used mainly to indifference from the male population around her. The stranger seemed really to see her.

"Will he bother you because of my interference?"

"Oh, I think not. He has little regard for my opinion."

"Yet, you've known him a long time?"

In the face of his alert, and she had to admit, admiring gaze, Cassie tried to return a light answer. "All my life. It's impossible to avoid knowing one's neighbors in the country."

"Ah," he said. A smile tugged at the corner of his fine mouth. "I'll have to remember that."

His companion stuck his head out of the carriage. "Sir

Adrian, we must be going."

The stranger turned to her one more time. "You're sure Hugh will not be a problem for you."

"I'm sure," she said. "I haven't thanked you properly. Thank you."

"No need to thank me. You seem to have had Hugh under control."

"Oh, I doubt that Hugh is ever under control exactly, but you knew what would turn him from his anger."

"Greed, you mean?" One of his dark brows lifted. "I've met his like before."

For a moment they stood looking at each other.

Then he offered her a brief bow, and climbed into the waiting carriage. As it pulled out of the inn yard, Cassie shivered in the breeze. She had vanished from the stranger's thoughts. The brief warmth of his regard had passed. He had returned to whatever pressing business the storm had interrupted. She looked for Jenkins, the head ostler, to procure her a ride home in the inn gig. Honoria must be worried by now.

CHAPTER THREE

Cassie set her package on the demi-lune table in the entrance hall and began to strip off her damp bonnet and muddied cloak. Her foot throbbed, but on the way home in the gig, she'd been thinking what a fine world it was with the spectacle of fleeing clouds overhead and the pleasing sensations that arose from the stranger's kindness. There were such people in the world after all, gentlemen even, who, seeing a fellow creature's distress, responded with kindness. The muffled sound of voices in the red drawing room caught her ear, and William appeared to take her cloak and bonnet.

"Who's here?" she asked.

"Two gentlemen, my lady. Arrived not ten minutes ago. Miss Honoria is with them."

Cassie glanced at the hall clock. The agent was early then, and not alone. She would have no chance to change, to arm herself a little, to shift her thinking to a more business-like mode. The old blue dress she'd worn for her ramble to the village would have to do. If it made her look like a village waif rather than a duke's daughter, so be it. Honoria needed her.

"And Her Grace?" Cassie tried not to betray any alarm at the prospect of an untimely visit from her grandmother. The lease arrangements were best concluded without her grandmother's interference.

"Still with her horses, my lady."

Cassie counted her blessings. Her Grace had agreed to the plan to lease Verwood, but maintained the view that doing so was an act of extraordinary benevolence for which any tenant must be excessively grateful. "Have refreshments been offered?"

William nodded. She thanked and dismissed him and paused only to square her shoulders before opening the old oak door.

"Cassie," her aunt sighed. "Thank heavens. You've come."

Cassie barely registered her aunt's agitated countenance. Two gentlemen rose and turned her way. It was the kind stranger and his companion. The man must be his agent.

"You? You wish to lease Verwood?" Cassie stepped forward with a warm smile even as a stern, unbending expression took over the face of the man whose kindness she'd been considering as an unexpected blessing.

"Oh no, Cassie dear," her aunt said. "I'm afraid there's been a terrible misunderstanding. Sir Adrian wants to buy Verwood."

The words stopped Cassie cold. Her smile died. Her bad foot sent a sharp twinge up her leg. "But we haven't offered to sell."

"You're C. J. Lavenham?" he asked.

"Lady Cassandra Jane Lavenham," Aunt Honoria confirmed.

Sir Adrian's frown deepened. Cassie could see he had some objection to her role in the matter. "Your father was the previous duke?"

"He was. I'm sorry that you've come all this way to be disappointed, and no doubt, inconvenienced, but really"—she cast a reproachful glance at the agent—"we made it quite clear in our notice that we were offering to lease not sell the property."

The agent cleared his throat. "Jacob Trimley, my lady, at your service. I believe we might yet reach an agreement, as Sir Adrian is keen to take up a residence in the neighborhood appropriate to his station."

Cassie regarded the gentleman apparently eager to take over her house. She felt foolish. In the gig on the way home, she'd been dwelling on the kindness and solicitude he'd shown to Dick Crockett and herself in the inn yard. Now she could see only the determined set of his jaw and something implacable in his gaze. Here was quite a different adversary from Hugh. His presence altered the room, made its little flourishes of gilt and brocade seem overdone and outmoded. She sensed that his sharp eye had already spotted how faded and threadbare the chairs were.

She offered her guests a thin smile and moved to take a seat. The little business of settling in a chair next to Aunt Honoria and allowing the gentlemen to be seated in turn created a pause for Cassie to gather her thoughts. Verwood Hall needed a tenant, and of one thing, she was sure, Sir Adrian had the funds to meet her grandmother's notion of a proper rent for the place.

She smoothed her skirts over her knees, considering how to proceed. "Thank you, Mr. Trimley," she said, looking at the agent, not his client. "Verwood cannot be sold while my grandmother, Her Grace, the Dowager Duchess, lives. But we remain pleased to consider an application to lease on behalf of Sir Adrian, and hope that the established usages between landlord and tenant may yet offer some way to an agreement as you suggest."

"Very good of you, miss... that is, my lady," said Trimley. "To Sir Adrian, establishing himself with credit in the neighborhood is of pressing importance, so perhaps you would agree to his immediate occupancy and a lease, of say, three years at the rate previously mentioned."

Beside Cassie, Honoria gasped. Sir Adrian appeared unmoved.

"Immediate occupancy?" Cassie asked, seeing ledger books that had been against her for months turn and go her way.

"Within a fortnight, say." Trimley glanced at the closed face of his employer.

"A fortnight! How could we, Cassie?" Honoria exclaimed. "The dower house could hardly be readied in such a span, and the duchess..." Her aunt was beginning to babble. There was no other word for it. Her poor shawl would soon be in knots. Cassie put a hand on Honoria's to calm her.

She studied Sir Adrian's stern countenance. His desire to have Verwood without poking into any of its rooms or considering its limitations, and there was one very large limitation her grandmother would impose, could only mean that he had some personal motive or design in mind.

"Are there no other properties in the district that would suit?"

Sir Adrian turned to her, cool and unyielding. "None. I

can arrange assistance for you to move household if you like."

Facing that unshakable determination, Cassie had a sudden flash of sympathy for Hugh. Sir Adrian Cole was a man who would impose his will on the world. She was saved from the intemperate reply that sprang to her lips by the opening of the drawing room door.

RAVEN ROSE, AND half a beat behind him, Trimley popped to his feet. There was no mistaking the woman who entered the room as anyone other than a duchess. In a riding habit of midnight blue, silver hair framing a face pared down to its elegant bone structure, startling blue eyes above an aquiline nose and a mouth drawn into a tight bow of disapproval, she appeared an icy shard of pure will. From the tips of her York tan-gloved fingers, she dangled a brown paper package. The young footman who'd opened the door, stood to attention behind her.

"What is the meaning of this rubbish?" she asked, fixing a contemptuous gaze on her granddaughter. "Murray's publishing house?"

Raven heard a soft moan from the dithering aunt before Cassandra Lavenham stepped forward to take the package from her grandmother's hand. "Oh, Grandmama, it's just a novel I ordered from London. I beg your pardon for leaving it in the hall, but you see, Sir Adrian and Mr. Trimley are here to discuss the lease arrangements."

The duchess turned to Raven, and he met her fierce scrutiny. There was little she could see in him but the careful work of an excellent tailor. She could hardly read his past history as Raven, one of the Duke of Wenlocke's lost boys, or his more recent history as his grandfather Jedediah Cole's heir. The brand-new *sir* of his knighthood would hardly impress her either. He met her stare, and let her size him up however she meant to rate him.

"Who are you? Who are your people? Cole, that's your name is it?" she demanded.

"It is, your grace."

"Not a name of distinction, is it?"

"We Coles have had our share of the world's notice, your grace." Adrian found himself revising his estimate of Cassandra Lavenham's courage. The woman who had faced down Hugh had apparently learned from dealing with the dowager duchess, who looked capable of staring down giants.

"What is your family's trade, young man?"

"Iron and glass, your grace. Cannons for Wellington. Fire engines for London."

"And, no doubt, glass for shop windows! You expect to enjoy the rights and privileges of Verwood?"

"I expect to pay for them, your grace."

"To be sure. I may have been induced to let my house, but as to compromising its dignity by permitting any trumped-up nonentity to—"

"Grandmama, remember our purpose," Lady Cassandra interjected, drawing the duchess's gaze. "You may trust me to make all the terms and conditions regarding your stables clear to Sir Adrian."

Lady Cassandra held her grandmother's gaze for a long

moment before the older woman turned back to Raven. "That's your chaise in the drive?"

"It is."

"A neat turnout. And your man, he knows how to handle his cattle?"

"He does, your grace."

"Best to have him see my man Snell about your horses then. There's a sharp wind blowing."

"Thank you, your grace."

The duchess's gaze swung to Honoria, still twisting the ends of her shawl. "Honoria, whatever are you in a quake about?"

Honoria's gaze darted from Lady Cassandra back to the duchess. "There's been a terrible mistake, Lottie. Sir Adrian wishes to *buy* Verwood."

The unblinking icy-blue gaze turned from Honoria back to Raven. Cassandra Lavenham's shoulders slumped.

"Then he'd best be on his way," the dowager announced. "All the iron and glass in England can't buy Verwood. It is not for sale. This house has belonged to the Lavenhams since 1485. Honoria, Cassie, bid the man good day." The duchess turned. The young footman sprang forward to open the door, and the dowager swept out. Honoria rose and scuttled after her.

The door closed behind her, leaving Adrian, Trimley, and Lady Cassandra in the room with its crimson silk walls and gilt furnishings. Lady Cassandra had not hurried after her relations. Adrian took that as a favorable sign.

Somewhere beyond the red room another door banged shut, and Lady Cassandra Lavenham came to her feet. Raven took in her appearance again. The long-sleeved pale-blue gown was several years out-of-date to his London-trained eye, and well-worn. Its only claim to fashion a strip of gold velvet trim at the waist. An incongruous pair of sturdy boots, still showing bits of mud, peeked from under the hem. It was plain that she was in dire need of funds.

"I'm sorry for any inconvenience we may have caused you, Sir Adrian," she said. "I thank you again for your intervention on behalf of Dick Crockett earlier. It was most kindly done. Good day to you." With a nod she turned away.

"Wait," he said. "I am still very interested in the lease of Verwood."

She stopped and glanced back at him. Her dark straight brows went up. "Did you miss how highly offended my grandmother is?"

"But you," he said, "are of a more practical turn of mind. If I can convince her to reconsider, may I have your support?"

"You think you can appease my grandmother? You can't simply wave Bank of England notes at her."

"I wouldn't dream of it."

She regarded him with frank puzzlement. "Why, may I ask, are you so interested in Verwood?"

He did not intend to tell her that, at least not just yet. It would all come out when he'd succeeded in his purpose, when his triumph was complete. "It is exactly the sort of property I've been looking for since I came into my ... inheritance. It will suit me perfectly to establish myself in a neighborhood among country families. You said earlier that in the country one knows one's neighbors."

FROM THE TOP of Verwood's south steps Raven looked down the long, straight, chestnut-lined avenue. The trees were newly in leaf, sparkling in the rain's aftermath. The tall spikes of bloom that would produce chestnuts in the fall, swayed in the last of the breeze. In the distance, the avenue passed a smallish lake on its way to the lodge with its Lion Gates. He could not fault the taste of the dead dukes of Verwood, nor did he wonder at the dowager for clinging to her horses when she could no longer afford them. Verwood was not a place to relinquish easily.

In the end, Raven believed Lady Cassandra would come to terms. Plainly, she was the practical one of the three. While her aunt dithered and wrung her hands over the difficulties of moving household, and her grandmother waved away what was beneath her notice, Lady Cassandra would accept the inevitable. Raven would have his lease, and an option to purchase the entire estate should the duchess pass away. In time, he knew, Verwood would be his. He could sense it as he had always sensed opportunity.

He never doubted his luck. Even when the Reverend Clumber had pronounced Raven unworthy of a place at college, Raven had known that he would move freely in a world far beyond the banks of the Thames or the Cam. And Clumber, for all his self-appointed role as guardian at the gates of rank, had indirectly shown Raven the way.

It had been Clumber's practice to take his pupils on

walking tours of ancient Britain, to the ruins of Roman and Saxon settlements. The one summer that Raven had been admitted to the group, he and the others had scrambled over the shale rocks of the coast west of Poole and come upon bronze Roman arm bands and the substantial remains of an ambitious seventeenth century glassworks. Raven had seen at once what held no interest for the others. The old glassworks might be a ruin, but the man of vision who built it had risen in the world and set his heirs on a path to become *sirs* and *lords*, men of influence and consideration in the world.

When Raven left college, he talked his grandfather into buying a bankrupt glassworks in Shoreditch. Making the old glassworks profitable, he told his grandfather, would be his education, not Cambridge.

Reluctantly, his grandfather had agreed. Raven bought the existing inventory and machinery at auction, tracked down and hired the out-of-work artisans, and established the new works on seven acres of vacant land on the river. At first the business supplied mirrors to cabinet makers, but in an age of vanity and fashion, Raven's mirrors had drawn the king's notice and a royal patent. Raven had expanded the business, shipping glass ingots around the world to places starved for English goods, and experimenting with mechanical presses. In time, he was sure, London shopkeepers would fuel a demand for plate glass in ever larger smooth panes through which passing patrons could view the goods for sale. Cole's Cast Plate and Glass Manufacturers was ready. Soon his glassworks would produce a million square feet of plate glass a year.

That was before the fire. Since the burning of the Houses

of Parliament, with the role of a Cole fire engine in the saving of Westminster Hall and his own knighthood, both the original Cole iron works and the new glass manufactory had been flooded with orders.

The carriage rumbled through the iron gates from the stable complex. Trimley, when pressed, had admitted that the stables were a separate piece of the estate, the use of any part of them to be negotiated separately. Trimley had been eloquent about the grandeur of the facilities. Raven had seen for himself the duchess in finery and her granddaughter in near rags. What Raven meant to determine was why the Verwood stables were draining money from the estate, not paying their way. He knew just the man to get to the bottom of that little mystery.

He would send Trimley back to London with his instructions, but Raven would put up at the Crown.

His carriage pulled to a stop at the foot of the stairs. Raven was getting ahead of himself, and he knew better. Once the ladies removed to the dower house, he would bring in an army of carpenters, plasterers, and painters until he had Verwood the way he wanted it. He knew there had been neglect and suspected there would be surprises—leaks, wood rot, crumbling mortar—but he had the blunt for anything the old house had to offer, and he knew how to manage men to get things done. For the first time since he had begun his search for a property, he allowed himself to think of what it all meant.

By midsummer he could step out of these doors, stroll to the stables, mount a horse, and be at Lord Ramsbury's door within an hour. What had been beyond his reach from those

London rooftops he had roamed as a boy with Jay and Lark, Rook, Finch, Swallow, and Robin was no more than a short ride away, Ramsbury's daughter, Lady Amabel Haydon.

CHAPTER FOUR

A BRILLIANT SPRING morning followed the rain of the day before. The birds started up shortly before first light, and by the time the kitchen fires were lit and the chocolate brewed, Cassie had escaped with a set of keys to the dower house. No one except William observed her leaving. Honoria was at her writing desk and Grandmama was riding.

There was nothing like the clear light of day to reveal truths one would rather not face. They were quite out of money, and Sir Adrian was their best hope of providing a respectable means of keeping Verwood solvent. He would be back, and Cassie wanted to be prepared for his return.

He had no idea what an immovable object her grandmama could be, but Cassie sensed that Sir Adrian was not easily swayed from his course. She had changed her opinion of him since their first meeting. What had seemed like kindness to Dick Crockett was perhaps mere annoyance at the inconvenience of the scene in the inn yard. Sir Adrian clearly had money to toss at problems to make them go away. The question that puzzled Cassie was why he wanted to toss money at Verwood. It seemed odd to her that he had fixed his attention on a small, relatively obscure Hampshire property at an inconvenient distance from London. If she understood his motive, she felt sure her position would be stronger. As it was, he had seen her true circumstances, the worn furnishings, old gown, and muddied boots. It irked her to think he was right. She had to be practical.

She crossed the drive and followed the narrow carriage way through the woods. Weeds sprouted through the gravel, and when she reached the yellow stone dower house, all she saw was neglect, an overgrown lawn, sprawling shrubs, and drooping vines. Cassie tried to remember the house's better days in her childhood when Grandmama lived there before the deaths of Cassie's older brother Edward, and shortly after, her father. When her uncle became duke, he chose a rather larger estate in Kent to be his principal seat, selling to their neighbor Lord Ramsbury much of the unentailed land of Verwood, leaving the hall to be Grandmama's residence.

Cassie thrust her key in the lock. The door yielded with a crack, and she entered, immediately shivering at the cold and wrinkling her nose at damp and dust and, she suspected, mice. Sir Adrian had offered to help them move households, and she wondered what other help he might agree to give in his determination to strike a deal.

In the ground floor rooms, she found the furnishings swathed in holland covers, dust, and cobwebs. The drapery had long since been removed from the windows and reused in the main house. Mice had definitely taken over in the kitchen. Only when she climbed the stairs, did her impression of the house improve. The bedrooms, though empty of furnishings, were bright and airy in the morning light, looking out past the kitchen garden over a stone wall into a small open field. A brief childhood memory made her smile.

It was a rabbit field. Perhaps, in spite of Honoria's fears, the house could be made livable. Cassie knew which rooms Grandmama would claim, and which would suit Honoria. Cassie would settle in the middle, between her two relations, where she usually found herself.

She finished her tour of the rooms. If Sir Adrian wanted them to move to the dower house, she would hand him a list of needed repairs.

AFTER BREAKFAST RAVEN sent a bewildered Trimley off to London with instructions, and set out for the village smithy. The landlord at the Crown directed him to George Crockett's establishment, a long, low, whitewashed building with a thatched roof, darkened and bowed by weather, standing at the lower end of the village. In the yard a chestnut tree towered over a rustic table and chairs, and chickens scratched about, under and around a farmer's cart without a wheel. A pair of sturdy russet-haired boys tended a smoking bed of coals. Ten feet from the boys stood a wooden framework like a perfect spider's web surrounded by a ring of leather buckets filled with water. A red setter lounging at the threshold of the open door rose and came to give Raven a greeting, his plume of a tail wagging. From inside came a rapid series of blows of a heavy hammer on wood.

As Raven ruffled the dog's silky ears, one of the lads dashed into the shop, and the hammering stopped, followed by a quick exchange of male voices. Then the lad reappeared. He halted in front of Raven. "If ye be needin' me Da, sir, he asks ye t' wait a tick while he sets a wheel for farmer Hewitt. Me mum has coffee and cake if ye like."

"Thank you. And you are?" Raven asked.

"Ned Crockett, sir. If ye'll follow me, sir."

Raven nodded, and the boy turned and led him into the smithy, dark and warm, and lit by the glow of the forge. The room smelled of iron and horse and burning coke. As Raven's eyes adjusted to the gloom, he took in Crockett's arrangements. The long, narrow shop was divided into three areas, at one end a nook under a window with a bench for waiting customers, the main area dominated by the forge against the rear brick wall and the anvil on its stump, and at the end, where Raven had entered, an enclosure for horse-shoeing.

Crockett stood, mallet in hand, contemplating a large wooden cart wheel, assessing whatever repairs he'd made. He was tall and rather wiry, wrapped in the leather apron of his trade, with the muscled forearms of a man who hammered and bent iron into shape. He had a head of shaggy russet hair and a beard to match. Standing opposite him was Dick, the youth Raven had met at the inn the day before. A clear resemblance marked them as father and son, though the youth was the brawnier of the two men. When Dick Crockett spotted Raven, he signaled his father with a quick series of hand motions.

Crockett turned to Raven at once. "So yer the gentleman that stood up for my lad."

Raven nodded.

"Thank you, sir. If there's aught I can do for ye, just say the word."

"There is something, when you can spare the time. But you must know that your son's first defender was Lady Cassandra Lavenham."

Crockett glanced at his son. The youth seemed to follow the conversation without the cringing anxiety he had shown the day before. "So our Dick tells us. Still, we are indebted to you, sir. Let my good wife get you some coffee or a pint if you prefer, and you can tell me what it is. First, I must set this wheel for neighbor Hewitt." Crockett indicated a fair-haired man in a neat brown suit and a straw hat, sitting by the window.

Raven nodded, and Crockett sent Ned through the far door of the shop. A woman appeared, drying her hands on an apron, and bustled up to Raven.

"Sir, good morning. You're most welcome here. Will you have a pint or some coffee and cake?"

"Coffee," said Raven, "if I may take a mug outside. I'd like to watch the wheel setting."

Mrs. Crockett, dark-haired, round, and rosy-cheeked, beamed at him. "There's a bench against the wall."

Raven followed Crockett and Dick as they carried the wheel, which Raven guessed must weigh at least two hundred pounds. When the Crocketts lowered the wheel onto the webbed framework in the yard, the Crockett boy Raven had not yet met walked round it, dousing the rim with water. Then the elder Crocketts took up their tongs and moved to the smoldering fire. Watching each other, they lifted from the heat a perfect hoop of iron, flat like a ribbon. They moved in step and positioned the hoop over the waiting wheel. At a nod from Crockett senior, they lowered the heated iron onto the wooden rim. The second boy and Ned sprang into action pouring water around the rim where iron and wood met. Hissing clouds of steam rose into the morning air. Crockett moved in the wake of the boys, hammering metal and wood together as the cold water tightened the iron hoop around the wooden rim. The whole operation was quick and smooth, and Raven could see that Crockett knew his business, and had trained his sons to do their part. It no longer seemed odd that Dick Crockett had found employment with the imperious old duchess.

While Crockett senior and Dick lifted the cooled wheel from the web-like frame, Mrs. Crockett brought Raven a mug of coffee, which he drank, admiring the way father and son worked together. When they needed words, both men used hand gestures. They set the wheel on the wagon axle, and the younger boys brought a sleek and sturdy horse around from the back of the smithy. The farmer, Hewitt, reappeared and hitched his animal to the cart. Civilities were exchanged, and off he drove.

Raven rose from the bench. Crockett came his way, and Mrs. Crockett emerged from her kitchen again to offer her husband a pint. He removed his heavy gloves and took a long pull on his drink.

"Now, sir, what can I do for ye?"

"I won't keep you long. I am looking to … lease the Verwood property, and I understand that your son works for the dowager duchess."

"Does all the shoeing for her," said Crockett.

"Then you must have an idea of the scale and state of the operations at Verwood. I understand the stables will not be included in the facilities a tenant may use."

"Wondering why that is, are ye?" Crockett asked.

Raven nodded. "I thought you might be able to enlighten me. Is it a working stud?"

Crockett appeared to consider Raven's question. "I'm that glad ye helped our Dick yesterday." He regarded Raven with a measuring glance. "Ye kicked a hornet's nest with that Hugh. He's a wrong one. Ah well, it's like he's gone back to town with yer blunt."

"So, he'll not trouble your lad?"

"Oh, Hugh will turn up again when he runs out of money. When he does, I'm thinking to send Ned with Dick on his rounds, to be safe. Ye'd best have a sit down."

Crockett led the way to the table and chairs under the chestnut tree. When they'd settled, Mrs. Crockett came and placed a plate of hard eggs, pickles, and cheese on the table.

Crockett built himself a stack of the edibles. "You asked the size of the place. Verwood is quite grand. Some are like to say it's too grand for three women." George Crockett shrugged and took a swallow of his drink. "There are twelve stalls, three foaling boxes, eight loose boxes for riding horses, and six for the farm's workhorses. There's a four-bay coach house, though the dowager uses but the one coach, and that not often. As to the managing of Verwood, her grace is quite particular and takes it all on herself."

Raven did some quick mental calculations. The cost of such an operation hardly made sense for a household of three women with little acreage to supply rents. "But it's not a working stud?"

Crockett took another pull of his drink. "Was once, but

the duchess doesn't keep trainers. She hires 'em, but they never stay. The last one left three years ago when there was a promising young stallion. In those days there was a steady queue for services. Then it all stopped."

"Do you know why?"

A guarded look came into Crockett's face. "It's not my place to say. Toffs, beggin' yer pardon, sir, are a different sort from us plain folk."

"Well, I can say," said his wife appearing again and setting a fragrant slice of bread on her husband's plate.

"Now, Mary," Crockett began.

"Don't *now Mary* me, husband. If Sir Adrian here is going to have aught to do with Verwood, he should know what's what. There's been no trainer there, since Lady Cassandra had her accident."

Raven was sure that his face betrayed surprise. He had an instant recollection of Lady Cassandra's muddied boots under a worn gown, and her slumping shoulders.

"Now Mary," said her husband again. "Ye don't know for a fact that Lady Cassandra's accident made her grace close the stud."

Mary Crockett, hands on hips, met her husband's frown without blinking. "What I do know is that Lady Cassandra went to London and came back changed. She rode that horse of Her Grace's that people say is unmanageable. Now Lady Cassandra doesn't ride, doesn't go about to assemblies and balls and the like. You've seen the poor girl's limp. And Her Grace doesn't race her horses or do foaling or training. Mind you, Her Grace will have to sell a horse or two if things don't change."

Raven watched the frown deepen on Crockett's brow. "Her Grace is good to us, woman. It's not our place to judge how she runs Verwood. Nor to be speculating on what happened to a young lady of quality in London."

Raven rose. He had no desire to start a quarrel between husband and wife. "I beg your pardon, Crockett, Mrs. Crockett." He had learned a good bit more than he'd expected, but the mystery of the lease opportunity had deepened. Apparently, there was more to the leasing plan than mere economy. "I didn't mean to pry, only to understand the business end of things."

"Well," said the unrepentant Mrs. Crockett. "You'll be doing Lady Cassandra a favor if you lease that house, take the burden of paying the bills right off those shoulders of hers."

"Ma'am, I hope I may, and you may trust me not to spread idle talk about the ladies of Verwood."

"Are you going out there today?" Mrs. Crockett asked.

Raven smiled to himself. It appeared that whatever he did in the neighborhood would soon be known to everyone in the village. "Directly," he said.

"May I trouble you to take some honey to Lady Cassandra?"

"Now Mary," began her frowning husband.

"I'm happy to take honey to her ladyship." At least the honey would give him an opening for a conversation.

ON THE ROAD to Verwood, Raven thought about the

practical woman he meant to win over as an ally. Everything he'd heard from the Crocketts confirmed his plan of appeasing the duchess through her horses, but now there was this mystery about Lady Cassandra Lavenham. The footman who answered the door claimed to have no knowledge of her whereabouts.

"She walks a great deal, sir," he told Raven with a shrug. "Shall I see to your horse, sir?"

"Her Grace won't object?"

"Not to Apollo, sir, he's a favorite, born and bred here."

Raven smiled and handed the reins and a coin to the youth. His luck was holding. He stood on the steps and surveyed the long drive as he had done the day before, trying to imagine where Lady Cassandra might have gone. He had not passed her on his way from the village. Then he spotted her at an opening in the chestnut trees lining the drive. She emerged from a faint track that led into the woods, dressed plainly again, in a hooded cloak, and those boots. Since being knighted, he had become accustomed to females in glittering finery, floating or gliding effortlessly around the ballrooms and parks of London. It seemed improbable that Lady Cassandra, with her feet firmly on the ground, had ever been one of them as Mrs. Crockett had suggested.

Lady Cassandra saw him and halted, frozen for a moment, frowning. He came down the steps and strode her way. When she moved to meet him, he kept his gaze on her face. If she limped, he would see the limp soon enough. They met at the edge of the carriage drive.

"Good morning," he said.

"You persist I see. May I remind you that Verwood is not

for sale?"

"It is a lease I'm after, and I find persistence generally yields results. Did you walk far this morning?"

"Just to the dower house."

He glanced down the track into the woods from which she had come. He suspected that her little jaunt to the dower house meant that she had been thinking practically, as he'd hoped she would. "Ah, how does it look?"

"Neglected."

"Can you picture yourself living there?"

"That is not the right question."

"No?"

"You mean can I picture my grandmother and my aunt living there?"

"My offer to help with the move still stands."

"Sadly, such an offer is of no use with the house in its current state."

He laughed. He recognized a negotiating tactic when he saw one. "We do want the same thing, you know," he said.

"Do we? And what is that?" she asked.

"A signed lease for Verwood." He offered her his arm. "Show me what needs to be done to this dower house of yours."

She glanced at his arm, and gave a little shake of her head, clearly unwilling to accept his help. He didn't know what to make of her refusal. Resistance or defiance? He doubted that she was as lofty as her grandmother, but he could not be sure. She turned and took the path into the woods, and he fell into step beside her.

When the house came into view around a curve in the

gravel drive, she stopped and looked up at him, her expression amused, irked, and above all, intelligent. "Do you always get what you want?" she asked.

"I like to think I choose the objects of my pursuit carefully." Her nose distracted him briefly. A smooth, straight, slightly upturned nose of the feminine sort, it had a flat, shallow dent along the ridge, as if broken at some time. Her accident must have been serious.

"An obscure estate in Hampshire is a careful choice?"

"You won't deny that Verwood is a fine house."

"But it's not for sale."

"A lease will do … for now."

"You are provokingly confident. I spent months persuading my grandmama that leasing Verwood is absolutely necessary if she—"

"—does not wish to part with any of her horses," he finished for her "And then one unguarded remark from your aunt Honoria set your grandmother off. What if, instead of draining Verwood's coffers, the stables paid for themselves? They used to, did they not?"

Her expression changed. "How do you know that? Who told you?"

"I spoke with the Crocketts this morning." Raven produced the honey jar from his pocket. "Mrs. Crockett sends you some of her honey."

Her gaze dropped to the jar wrapped in linen and tied with blue bow. "Mary Crockett is a kind neighbor, but you must not credit everything she says."

Plainly, Lady Cassandra was aware of her neighbors' speculation about her. Raven thought her cheek flushed, but it might only be the coolness of the morning and the exercise. He waited for her to take the honey. The sun hung above the trees. The raucous bird song had died down a little. A hint of warmth was in the air. In London, in his grandfather's grand Italianate villa, Raven rarely heard birds. Bells ringing the hour and carts and wagons of every sort made the swelling predawn sound of the city waking. Not that he had awakened at dawn recently. For months, he had been dancing late into the night, coming home at first light.

Just when his holding out the honey jar grew awkward, she took it.

"Thank you." She began walking toward the dower house again, and this time he caught the hitch in her stride. She made no effort to conceal it, and it didn't slow her down. Still, Raven thought, much walking must lead to pain. The house came into view, two stories of yellow stone with a steep slate roof and a blue door. It looked neglected, but sturdy and well-situated. They approached the door.

"Crockett told me that her grace won't keep a trainer. Do you know why?"

She reached into a pocket. "Grandmama has definite opinions about the training of horses, no sweating, no stoving. Men are often surprised that ... a woman has any knowledge of the field."

"Yet, her horses no longer race in spite of her notable past success."

Lady Cassandra stopped abruptly on the threshold. "You must have had quite a conversation with the Crocketts."

"They are grateful to Her Grace, and who better than those who know her ways to help me understand her."

"Crockett never suggested that you offer Grandmama a trainer."

"He did not. It happens that I know an unusual one."

"Remind me again why you are so keen to lease Verwood."

"Doesn't everyone who makes a fortune, want a house?" He spoke lightly.

She thrust her key in the lock, and pushed the door open. He followed her in, noting the cold, and the faint odors of damp and dust. A small entry led to a good-sized parlor, cold and empty of color, with a circle of shrouded furnishings in front of a substantial stone fireplace. The house had none of the grandeur of Verwood, and he guessed the move would be a blow to the ladies' pride. Their debts must be pressing.

"A good blaze will help this room," he said. He pulled the holland cover off a chair, and under the rustling of the cloth, she murmured something he didn't quite catch. He uncovered another chair.

"Stop." She sneezed, and he handed her his handkerchief. "You are getting ahead of yourself," she said. "Even if this house can be made livable, to get your lease you have to find your way into Grandmama's good graces first."

"You don't think offering her a trainer will help?"

"It might, but perhaps there's something else about you that would…"

"Overcome the taint of trade in iron and glass? I assure you I have been welcome this winter in all the loftiest houses in Mayfair."

"Have you?" Her dark brows went up. "Somehow I don't

think unbridled conceit will be a winning strategy with Grandmama."

Raven choked. "Unbridled conceit?"

"Apparently, you have acquired boundless confidence along with your fortune. Is that how you earned your knighthood?"

"I earned…"

She sneezed again, and Raven took hold of her elbow and led her through the house and out a door in the kitchen into a small courtyard. She leaned against a low stone wall overlooking a field, and sneezed a few more times. He waited.

"Speaking of conceit…" he began. "I wager there's plenty of conceit in a household that can't afford coal or servants or new gowns for a lady, but that pretends to be above leasing a portion of the property to a respectable man of means."

Her eyes flashed up at him. She was taller than Amabel, and fearless and frank in her bearing with no illusion of feminine frailty, and, he suspected, she was about to let him have it. Then another sneeze took her.

"Oh bother," she said, recovering. "It's no use getting angry. The truth is that leasing Verwood is the practical solution to our family's dilemma. It is just that the littleness of a drawing room only twenty feet across is a strong a reminder of our circumstances."

"Will her grace care so very much about the house if the stables prosper?"

"No," she admitted with a laugh. "You're right. She will hardly spend any time here. But first we have to reconcile Grandmama to you as a tenant."

Raven liked that *we*. It meant she was going to be practical. But he didn't understand the problem exactly. "My money's not suitable for the ladies of Verwood?"

"Your money's fine. It's you. You aren't what we…" She waved a hand over his person. Even without a valet Raven had dressed himself to exacting London standards, so he couldn't think what caused her to object to him.

"What?"

"Expected." She blew out a sigh. "The tenant we imagined was … old, quiet, settled … married, content to drive a gig about the lanes or shoot a few pheasants in season. You'll be noticed."

"You didn't tell Trimley that you required any of these qualities in a tenant."

"That's because the *sir* misled me. I thought *Sir* Adrian Cole must be a merry old nabob returned from India, or a mill owner bringing his wife and daughters from some blighted northern town to live in the healthful south. How did you acquire a 'sir' at your age?"

"My age?" He no longer thought of himself as a youth. Dick Crockett was a youth.

"I was knighted for making fire engines."

"Fire engines?"

The perplexed look on her face made him laugh. "When I joined my grandfather's business, he asked me what I wanted to make. His fortune came from cannons for the army and the navy, but demand had slowed. I started with glass. Glass makes money, but it doesn't excite my grandfather. Then I suggested we make better fire engines, engines that can pump more water, at a faster rate. He liked that idea."

"And a better fire engine led to a knighthood?"

"Five engines. Ours were deployed against the fire in the Houses of Parliament last October."

"You were there, fighting the fire?"

"Yes." His reputation as a man who fought the palace blaze meant he'd been pointed out in ballrooms all winter. Whispers had followed him. Women had looked at him with a sort of awe, and some women, with a kind of hunger.

Lady Cassandra gave him a shrewd assessing glance. Plainly, his firefighting did not stir any particular admiration in her.

He laughed and pushed away from the wall. "Not impressed? What about showing gratitude for sending disagreeable Hugh on his way?"

"I am grateful. Whatever your motive for that act, it was a kindness to Dick Crockett."

"*Motive?* You suspect me of having a *motive* for helping a fellow who was getting the wrong end of an unfair fight?"

"You threw money at a problem and made it go away. That's hardly heroic."

"Does my money have to be heroic to rescue Verwood from insolvency?"

She took a deep breath. "As I said before, it's not the money, it's you we need to present as an unobjectionable tenant."

He shook his head. "You would prefer a tenant in his dotage who fought at Trafalgar or Waterloo?"

She grinned at him and shrugged her shoulders. "Even a minor victory like Navarino would do. Mostly, it would help if you could manage to be forty or fifty and a bit more … staid."

"That," he said, "is beyond my power. I am staying at the Crown and can return directly if you think of any way of gaining Her Grace's approval."

"Oh, the Crown. Which horse did they give you?"

"Apollo."

Her brows went up again. "Then you have made an impression. Apollo is the Crown's best horse, and Grandmama likes him. You must come for tea."

"Tea? Why isn't your solicitor handling the lease for you?"

"Because women can manage their own affairs," she snapped.

"Tea it is, then, if you agree to support me as an acceptable tenant for Verwood, for my service to the nation." Raven stuck out his hand to seal the bargain. He would have Trimley seek out Verwood's solicitor and find out the reason for leaving him out of the lease plans.

She cast him a brief puzzled glance, then her hand met his. The sensation of it brought him up short, her small delicate hand in his larger one. He had been thinking of her as this forthright, strong-willed person, managing business affairs women usually left to men. The soft hand threw him off for a moment.

She withdrew her hand, and he recovered. It was Amabel he should be thinking of, not this odd, prickly independent woman.

Cassie knocked on Honoria's door, received no answer, and pushed the door open. Honoria sat hunched over her desk, wrapped in her favorite shawl, pen in hand, staring out the window.

"Honoria." Cassie waited for her aunt to return from whatever fictional scene absorbed her.

"Oh, Cassie," Honoria said at last. "Have you been standing there an age?"

"Only a minute. Can we talk?"

"Of course, dear." Honoria put down her pen, covered her writing with a cloth, and turned her chair to face Cassie.

"He's coming for tea." Cassie moved about the room, picking her way among stacks of books on the floor, pages of *The Times*, and a basket of rolled-up maps. There was, as usual, no place to sit, a sign that her aunt was deep in a story. Cassie had left her boots with William and wore a pair of light slippers. Her foot ached. She had not taken Sir Adrian's arm, but of course, he had noticed her lurching gait. To his credit he was not so tactless as to ask her about it. Her limp was such a familiar part of the way she moved about at home and in the village that she had forgotten the curiosity it could arouse in a stranger.

"Who is coming to tea?"

"Sir Adrian, and we have to convince Grandmama that he is a worthy tenant."

Honoria twisted the ends of her shawl. "This is my fault, isn't it? If I hadn't mentioned his desire to buy Verwood, Lottie would not have taken offense."

"Please don't blame yourself, Aunt. He still wishes to lease Verwood, but we have to convince Grandmama to accept him as a tenant."

"Is he really our last hope?"

"He is the only one who's shown an interest in the property."

"It's odd, isn't it? How do you account for his interest in Verwood? He doesn't seem the sort to bury himself in the country. Didn't you tell Lottie that our tenant would be a quiet, older gentleman?"

That had been Cassie's mistake. She had assumed any man with a *sir* before his name must be old. Like Honoria, she couldn't account for his interest in the hall. "I think we have to take advantage of that interest whatever the motive behind it. I agreed to support his bid for Verwood."

"Is that wise? Lottie thinks he's presumptuous."

"He is rich and willing to make the dower house livable for us, and he's ready to act now." Once they were relocated, Cassie told herself, they would hardly see him.

"But what will you tell Lottie?"

"I'm working on that. He's done two things that might change her mind about him."

Honoria straightened in her chair. "Tell me."

"At the Crown yesterday…"

Honoria looked confused.

"When I stopped to get a ride home, Hugh was in the yard, berating Dick Crockett for an accident, which was most likely Hugh's fault as you know how recklessly Hugh drives. I couldn't let Hugh bully Dick, but then Sir Adrian, though I didn't know it was he, intervened and sent Hugh on his way."

"Intervened how?" Honoria asked.

"He offered Hugh sixty guineas for the damage to his curricle."

"Sixty guineas! Oh my! And Horrible Hugh took the money and left."

"More or less."

Honoria righted her tilting cap. "My dear, what are you not telling me?"

"It was the way that Sir Adrian handled Hugh with such assurance." Cassie was understating the scene. Sir Adrian had simply dominated everyone's attention, including hers. To have a man like that living at Verwood would change everything.

Honoria nodded. "He sounds like Lofty Lottie."

Cassie stopped her wandering. Honoria was right. Sir Adrian had that force of character that marked her grandmother, and the same singlemindedness. It puzzled her that he was directing all that energy and purpose toward Verwood.

"And the second thing, dear?"

"He makes fire engines."

"How thoroughly modern! Do you suppose his engines use steam?"

"I didn't ask." She was out of practice with meeting people outside her own small circle, being curious about them. He claimed to make *better* fire engines. He had been in the midst of the great fire at the Houses of Parliament. He was truly active in the world, trying to change it, drawing its notice and unafraid of that notice when it came. They could not be more opposite. Perhaps that was why it was so unsettling to be near him. Still, once she and her aunt and grandmother removed to the dower house, she would likely see little of him. Verwood would keep him quite busy.

A sharp rap on Honoria's door interrupted Cassie's thoughts. Honoria started and glanced at the cloth covering her desk.

The door opened and the duchess walked in, still in her riding habit. "So here's where you two are hiding."

"Not hiding, Grandmama." Cassie gave her grandmother a quick kiss on the cheek.

"No? More likely plotting. Have you heard what that man has done?"

"You mean our new … tenant?" Honoria asked.

"Our tenant? He wishes he had such a privilege."

"Has he given you some new offense, Grandmama?" Cassie asked.

"Offense? Not at all." The duchess looked round the room for a place to sit. "Honoria, what is this clutter? I know you're bookish, but this is taking the whole thing too far."

Cassie stepped in and removed the books from the bench at the end of Honoria's bed. The duchess sat, and pulled off her gloves.

"Grandmama, you were saying Sir Adrian did something?"

"It's the talk of my stables. Yesterday he saved Dick Crockett from that wretched boy of Ramsbury's."

"Horrible Hugh," said Honoria.

The duchess shot her a quelling look and turned to Cassie. "If he thinks, he can insinuate his way into my favor by—"

"Doing a kindness to Dick Crockett? He had no

knowledge of Dick's connection to Verwood."

"But I don't doubt he'll take advantage of it. Sir Adrian was here this morning, was he not? On Apollo."

Cassie drew herself up and met her grandmother's sharp gaze. She suspected there was truth in her grandmother's assessment of Sir Adrian, but that didn't change the facts. "Yes, he was here. He remains interested in a lease. I've invited him for tea."

"Tea? A man like that doesn't want tea, little cakes and dabs of sandwich. He wants substantial fare."

"We should have a picnic," suggested Honoria.

"It doesn't matter what we offer him," said Cassie. "What matters, Grandmama, is whether you are willing to have him as a tenant."

"What do we know about this fellow? Who are his people? For what did he earn a frippery knighthood? I suppose he thinks a trip to St. James and being knocked on the shoulder by the king makes him very grand."

"Sir Adrian makes fire engines, and he brought a pair of engines to the fire at the Houses of Parliament."

"Did he? So he is not purely decorative then, but useful. Still, for an ironmonger, he aims above himself. Are we to let a duke's house be polluted by a common tradesman?"

Cassie took a deep breath. Her grandmother might rail about Sir Adrian's origins, but Cassie suspected that her real objection to the man was to his force of personality. "A modest country estate, discarded by the present title holder, and very much in need of an infusion of cash can hardly be polluted by a man who can afford it."

Honoria's eyes went wide at Cassie's boldness.

The duchess laughed. "Very well, Cassie. I will meet this fellow again, if only to make it clear to him what is permitted and what is not."

CHAPTER FIVE

At Verwood at four, a stable boy came running to take Raven's horse while William the footman led Raven through a courtyard on the west side of the house. A wide vista of lawn and gardens opened up, and Raven imagined strolling the grounds with Amabel on his arm. Somewhere in this garden he would find a place to ask for her hand in marriage. He simply needed to secure the lease to bring his plan to completion. William pointed to a path, and Raven set out.

This afternoon was some kind of test. He believed he was ready for objections to his birth and background, objections he understood all too well. Her Grace had a value for rank, for keeping property in the hands of those who inherited it, not those who currently moved the nation forward by their energy and exertion.

The path skirted a line of trees and looked out over a sunken Italianate garden of clipped hedges and tall blooms. Beyond the garden with its central fountain, the ladies, in bonnets and pale gowns, sat in wicker chairs around a linen-draped table laid out for tea. A breeze ruffled the edges of the tablecloth and scattered drops from the fountain. The splash of water and drone of bees mingled with female voices.

He was conscious of their scrutiny as he approached. The

duchess, with her rigid posture, had rallied her troops for battle. They might not wear the red jackets of Wellington's army, but they were as close a rank as any square of infantry that faced Napoleon. In their finery, dove gray for the duchess, lavender for the aunt, and that eggshell blue for Lady Cassandra, the ladies made a pastoral portrait of ease and elegance. He reminded himself that gardens where ladies' hat ribbons could flutter in a gentle breeze existed because men of vision and energy once shaped England as his generation would shape it now. He slowed his pace. The duchess had chosen her ground well.

At the tea table Raven bowed. "Good afternoon, ma'am, Miss Honoria, Lady Cassandra."

The duchess waved him into a chair next to Lady Cassandra and across from Honoria. "Where did you get such airs and pretty ways? They won't get you your lease, young man."

"Grandmama," Lady Cassandra chided.

"I hope," said Raven, taking a seat, "that plain dealing will bring us to terms."

"Tea, Sir Adrian?" asked Honoria. She began to pour.

"Not tea, Honoria," said the duchess. "Wine."

"Oh dear," said Honoria, rattling the teacup, "we did say we would serve wine, didn't we? Wine, Sir Adrian?"

"Tea suits me." Raven smiled at Honoria and took the cup from her trembling hand.

"Cream?" asked Lady Cassandra.

Raven turned and accepted her steady pour. It was plain that she was a calming influence on her companions. He swallowed some tea and put the cup aside. He would fire the first salvo in the battle. "Actually, your grace," he said to the duchess, "I am willing to lease Verwood only if I may be permitted to make some improvements."

"Improvements?" The duchess scoffed. "That's hardly your business, young man."

"I believe, ma'am, that you've made improvements to the stables. I will bring the hall up to your standards."

"Who are you to speak of the standards of a noble hall like Verwood?"

Raven met her fierce gaze. "A man who knows what damp and dry rot, crumbling mortar and failing glazing can do."

"You get ahead of yourself. What are your intentions for the hall? I suppose you mean to play the grand host. I must tell you that Verwood has welcomed royal visitors."

"Has it? As I understand it, the most frequent visitor to Verwood is Dick Crockett, a humble blacksmith's son."

"Dick is a man who knows his place. I won't have some upstart mushroom coming and going from my stables at all hours."

Raven's jaw tightened at the term *mushroom*. It was a slight his grandfather particularly disliked. "You wish me to send notice in advance when I require a horse or a vehicle."

"I wish my horses not to be disturbed," the duchess snapped.

"Cake?" said Honoria, offering Raven a delicate plate with a large slab of golden-yellow sponge.

Raven took the offered cake. "It is difficult to introduce new horses into an established group. My dealers, Kydd Brothers, have experience in these matters. They can smooth the way."

A little pause followed. On Raven's left, Lady Cassandra tried to subdue the fluttering ribbons of her bonnet.

Her grace spoke again. "I know Kydd, but we stray from the point, young man. How do you mean to comport yourself in the hall?"

"As a gentleman." Raven stuck his fork into the cake and pried off a corner piece.

"Hah! A gentleman you say! Cole is no surname of dignity. A bit of metal and ribbon pinned to your chest hardly raises you from obscurity. Who are your people?"

"My grandfather, Jedediah Cole, is an alderman in London." Raven's grandfather took great pride in being a *city* man, active in London affairs. He had an open contempt for aristocratic layabouts who spent their days in clubs gaming away fortunes acquired by their ancestors. Raven had yet to tell the old man about Lady Amabel. But once he made something of Verwood, it would be the perfect setting to introduce his love to his grandfather.

"An alderman, is he? Then I'm sure he won't wish to quit his sphere," began the duchess. "I won't have you polluting the house with … brash London types. Who are your mother's people?"

Next to Raven, Lady Cassandra failed to subdue her bonnet ribbons, and the bonnet tumbled to the grass. A sudden gust lifted it and sent it scudding over the lawn. A look passed between the lady and her aunt.

"Oh dear, Cassie," her aunt cried, "your bonnet is heading for the water."

Raven almost laughed. The ploy was hardly subtle. He

wasn't sure whether the lady wished to protect him from the duchess's insults or to stop him from making a rash reply.

Lady Cassandra tried to rise from her chair. Raven put a hand over hers. He leaned in close and whispered in her ear, "I believe that's my cue." In a louder voice, he said, "Let me." He rose and strode across the lawn. A fitful gust lifted the straw hat and sent it over the low lip of the sunken fountain into the water. He looked for a stick or a rake, something with which to snag the floating bonnet before it went under.

Lady Cassandra appeared beside him. She handed him a thin pole. "A stake from the foxgloves. I don't expect you to sacrifice your boots for a very old bonnet."

He took the pole and braced himself, leaning out over the water to catch the bonnet. Cold spray hit his face. He blinked, steadied his grip and slid the tip of the stake under the crown of the bonnet. With a quick tilt of the stake, he secured the hat and drew it to the fountain's edge.

Lady Cassandra knelt and took hold of one of the drowned ribbons, pulling the hat from the water. She started to rise, but her leg buckled under her, pitching her forward. She gripped the stone edge of the fountain. Raven caught her elbow, and helped her to her feet.

"Thank you," she said. "For saving my hat."

"Was it necessary to risk it? Are you afraid your grandmother's insults will drive me off?"

She raised a brow. The breeze molded her gown to her figure and whipped strands of dark hair across her cheeks. "Hardly, though you seem to have a knack for drawing her fire. I just prefer that no actual blood be shed."

He laughed. "What do you advise then?"

She took a deep breath. "Tell her that she may revoke the lease at any time if you violate its terms."

Raven sobered. It wasn't a game he played. His plans depended upon securing Verwood, and he would not be driven off by a woman who insisted on the ancient privileges of her birth. "That would be most inconvenient."

"She won't do it. She won't pay the least attention to the hall once … you're in residence. She simply wants to … hold onto a certain sort of power in her world."

If Lady Cassandra wanted him to sympathize with her domineering grandmother, she would be disappointed. "The power of rank? If I invite my grandfather to *pollute* the hall, will that violate her terms?"

"I hope you will invite him. The terms can be … managed. Try not to be stiff-necked about it."

"You think I'm stiff-necked!" He glanced over at the dowager duchess.

She laughed, and her eyes brightened. "Exactly. And do try the sponge."

He offered his arm, and this time she took it. They returned to the tea table. The duchess was standing. Honoria was stabbing a large piece of sponge with a tiny fork.

"What have you two been talking about?"

"Lady Cassandra has pointed out some terms that may make the lease more acceptable to you, ma'am."

"Has she?" The duchess shot a sharp glance at her granddaughter. "Don't imagine, young man, that I don't know my way around a covenant. You will occupy Verwood by permission and under such terms as I approve."

Raven's jaw was tight, but the dowager's pride wouldn't matter next to Amabel's delight. "I would not have it otherwise."

"Very well. Have your man make the additions to the agreement."

"Once Trimley has modified the covenant, and once you've had a chance to read it over and sign—"

The duchess waved away his words. "Just remember, young man, that Verwood will never make you a gentleman. And you must get Cassie's approval for any renovations. I want that in the covenant."

"Grandmama, are you sure?"

The duchess turned back. "Of course, I'm sure. I'll be off now. You've kept me from my horses long enough." She turned to Honoria. "And you have had quite enough cake, Honoria. *Come with me.*"

Honoria dropped her fork and rose to follow the duchess.

When the other two were out of earshot, Lady Cassandra turned to Raven. The breeze still tugged at her skirts and blew her dark hair about. "Satisfied?"

"Impatient."

Her gaze flashed up to his. "When do you expect to occupy the hall?"

"First, you want to be settled in the dower house. I can have people begin work on it by Tuesday next."

"And the papers?"

"Will tomorrow suit?"

"So soon?"

"You need funds, don't you?"

She nodded, her eyes searching his. He supposed his impatience made no sense. Maybe she'd never been in love. He looked out over the garden, already seeing Amabel there.

"Tomorrow then." He bowed and offered his arm.

"You needn't, you know. We're not … friends."

"Perhaps, but I won't be browbeaten out of gentlemanly behavior by your grandmother."

She turned to the table and wrapped a piece of cake in a bit of linen. "Have some cake then, a first taste of Verwood."

CHAPTER SIX

THERE WAS A day's delay before Her Grace the Dowager Duchess of Verwood signed Sir Adrian's lease agreement. Further issues had arisen regarding which furnishings were to remain in the house and precisely which stalls in the stables were to be available for Sir Adrian's horses. In the end the ladies were to leave the public rooms furnished and to take only the items most personal to them to the dower house along with her grandmother's prized paintings of her horses.

Mr. Trimley, a notary, Cassie, and the duchess gathered in the red drawing room at noon. There was no sign of Sir Adrian, though his bold signature appeared on the document. The duchess took a seat at the console table and asked to see the clauses about renovation, the use of her stables, and her right to terminate the lease.

When she had reviewed those items, she said to Trimley, "Let's get on with it then."

As Trimley pointed out the places where she was to sign, the duchess batted away his hand, but she signed.

Cassie, who had spent the morning reading the document in all its legal detail, did not know whether she felt more relieved or more anxious about the move. There was a great deal to do in a short time, for which she was grateful.

With cataloging what was to remain and packing what was to go, and with determining where things from the hall would find a place in the dower house, she would have little time to feel any sadness over leaving what had been her only home. It might be hard to see that home in the hands of another, but she supposed that in time she would become accustomed to the change. One could become accustomed to difficult things.

When Trimley indicated that the signing was complete, the duchess put aside the pen, and stood. "We're done, are we?" she asked.

Trimley grinned broadly. "I assure you, ma'am, you could not entrust Verwood into more capable hands than Sir Adrian's. Everything will be preserved and looked after with scrupulous care."

ON THE MORNING after the signing of the lease, the first carts rumbled up the drive and turned down the lane to the dower house. A boy came running to the hall for the key, and handed Cassie a note from Sir Adrian. The note laid out a brief plan for cleaning the dower house and asked if she had color preferences for the rooms.

Cassie put aside the list she was making, took up the keys, and put on her cloak. Sir Adrian was not going to paint her house without her approval. She sent the boy ahead to say she was coming, and a quick walk took her to the lane. At the dower house, a group of workmen unloaded ladders, brooms, and buckets from one of the carts, and a man with a scythe was at work on the grass. Sir Adrian stood at the back of another cart conferring over some papers with George Dawes, the building surveyor who had supervised the repairs to the roof of the village church.

No one observed her approach until the boy came to a stop before Sir Adrian. All heads turned her way as she sank into the low point of her uneven stride. She halted and straightened, and Sir Adrian stepped forward. He had changed from the polished London gentleman she'd first met to a man more comfortably attired for the country in brown wool and a plain cotton waistcoat.

"I didn't mean to interrupt your morning," he said.

"Didn't you? With such provocation as this?" She held up the little note. "What woman does not have an opinion about the color of her walls?"

He laughed. "I had to ask."

"The ink is hardly dry on the lease," she said, looking at the bustle of activity around her. He must have believed all along that he'd gain the lease for he could not have organized such a work party in a day.

"As I told you, I am impatient." His gaze did not meet hers.

"For the joys of discovering dust and damp?"

"If you'll open the house for them, these fellows will begin."

He stepped aside, and Cassie moved to open the door. Then the workers filed past, each with a little nod. She followed and peered into the drawing room. As she looked around, conscious of the gloom, Sir Adrian entered with his papers. "You think the place needs painting?" she asked.

"Cleaning first, but a little fresh paint never hurts. I have some samples for you to look at if you can spare the time. Your opinion counts."

"I hope so." To have her opinion solicited was something of a novel experience. She and Honoria and Grandmama lived such separate lives in the hall that there had been little occasion for her opinion to matter. It was only as they faced the prospect of leasing the hall that Grandmama had consulted her. Once again the details had been left to Cassie. Honoria and Grandmama had returned to their separate spheres, Honoria to her books, Grandmama to her horses.

Sir Adrian opened his sheaf of papers on top of a cloth-draped table. She was surprised to see the floor plan of the dower house.

"You have been busy. Where did you get this?"

"I have my sources." He laid some square chips of color on each of the rooms. "What do you think? Will any of these colors suit?"

He had chosen warm reds and golds for the lower rooms of the house and cooler shades for the bedrooms. For the bedroom she had imagined would be hers, he had chosen a pale thrush-egg blue. She picked up the little square. He did not know her taste. It was just an accident that the blue chip lay where it did, like a dealing of the cards for a game of Commerce.

"The colors are lovely," she said.

"Have I your permission to paint then?" he asked.

"You may paint," she said airily, putting down the blue chip.

"You liked that," he said with a grin.

It surprised her, but she did enjoy it. "Yes, this *giving permission* thing might grow on me."

"May I ask one more thing then?"

She waited.

"May I have Dawes inspect the hall for any signs of ... decay?"

A crash from the kitchen interrupted him, and Sir Adrian strode toward the sound. Cassie followed. Two men emerged into the hall coughing and covered with soot.

"Dead bird in the chimney, sir," one of them managed to say, his eyes and teeth white in his blackened face.

"Clinker everywhere, sir," said the other man.

"Clinker?" she asked Sir Adrian.

He turned to her with one of his dark frowns. "Creosote from incomplete burning. If you'll pardon me, I'd best take a look."

She nodded. He simply stated a fact, but she knew what that creosote meant—neglect, years of putting off needed work, and getting by. "You'd best prepare Mr. Dawes for the worst."

She handed him her keys.

Two days before they were to remove from the hall to the dower house, Miss Pindock, her grandmother's able assistant, alerted Cassie that Miss Honoria had not completed her packing. Much as Cassie disliked Pindock's manner of telling tales, a visit to Honoria's room confirmed that Honoria was mired in book packing and had yet to tackle her clothes.

Cassie offered to help.

She peered into the tall mahogany wardrobe where her aunt's clothes hung. Honoria sat on the bench at the foot of her bed her nose in a book, a packing case open on the floor beside her. Cassie had forgotten that her aunt had so many gowns. She pulled two from the wardrobe and held them up for Honoria's inspection. One was a leaf-green muslin with holes at the elbows and a frayed hem. The other was a gray silk gown in excellent condition, from the half-mourning period for Cassie's father.

Honoria looked up. "Oh, the green is a writing frock. Keep that. I must have my writing clothes."

"Aunt, it's falling apart."

Honoria shrugged and turned back to her book. "Nobody sees me."

"I see you."

"What dear?" Honoria mumbled.

"I see you." Cassie made a new pile on the bed for the faded green gown. Her aunt was not vain about her appearance, and it was certainly frugal to get the most wear out of one's clothes, but something in Cassie rebelled against her aunt's accepting invisibility. "I thought we might go to London for a fortnight."

"London? But you had a dismal time there." Honoria closed her book.

"I did, but that was during the Season. We won't go for the Season." At the moment, the Season was at its frantic peak, which Cassie remembered well. Packing her own gowns, now long out of fashion, had recalled that unhappy time. Each item came with a history that revived feelings she thought forever buried. "We could go in September. You might enjoy visiting the bookstores, meeting your publisher, and maybe seeing some of the settings you've used in your books."

Honoria sighed. "I would like to see Lackington's and Hatchford's. Will we have the funds for a jaunt?"

"I think so."

"Sir Adrian *is* shaking things up, isn't he? Like an earthquake. Makes me think I ought to put something of the kind in my new book. It's set in Lisbon after all. How much money do you think he's spending?"

"I have no idea." Cassie had tried not to notice, but with Dawes's fees and workers' daily wages and with the needed repairs to the hall that Dawes had already recommended, Sir Adrian's bills must be mounting. And yet he remained unstoppable. That was the thing one noticed most about him, his energy. All the activity around her made her restless, too. But in two days they would be moved, and she could settle into her old ways.

As Cassie lay the gray silk on the *save* pile, William appeared with one of Sir Adrian's boy messengers.

"My lady," said the boy, red-faced from his run. "Sir A wants to know if ye'll approve the new paint color for the kitchen."

"Did he send a paint chip?" Cassie asked. He was testing her. She had no time to tramp over to the dower house to look at paint samples.

The boy shook his head.

"Can you say what color it is?" She pulled a lovely lavender muslin from the wardrobe. She'd not seen Honoria wear it, but it might do for a Sunday.

The boy twisted the cap in his hands, his lips pursed tight. "It's an animal, miss."

"An animal?"

The boy, his brow furrowed, looked anguished. "I said it to meself three times to remember."

"How very odd," said Honoria. "An animal, you say? Like a bear or a badger or a Bengal tiger?"

The boy gave another shake of his head.

"Do you see the color anywhere in this room?" Cassie asked.

The boy looked around at the stacks of books and piles of linens and clothes. "There, miss," he said, pointing to the gray silk on the bed. "It's an elephant, miss."

"Sir Adrian wants to paint the kitchen, gray!" said Honoria. "How singular!"

The boy looked crushed. "That can't be right, can it, miss?" he asked Cassie.

"Take a deep breath. It will come to you."

He closed his eyes and inhaled noisily. Cassie waited until his eyes popped open, and he released a gust of breath. She offered an encouraging smile.

"Now I remember, miss. The color is called *elephant's teeth*."

"Do elephants have teeth?" asked Honoria.

"Great long ones, ma'am." The boy nodded solemnly.

Cassie smiled at him. "Exactly. And they're called *tusks*."

She should have a coin with which to reward his efforts, but she had not yet dipped into the funds available from the lease. "Well-done," she said. "Let me write Sir A a note of approval, and then, on your way back to the dower house, you may stop in the kitchen and let Cook give you some cake and lemonade."

She lifted the covering over Honoria's writing and found a pencil and paper.

Dear Sir A,

Did you know that your minions have taken to calling you 'Sir A'?

"Elephant's Tusk" sounds a perfect, if fanciful, shade for the kitchen. You have my entire approval. Please reward your young lieutenant handsomely for the difficulty he endured in conveying your message to me.

Sincerely, C. L.

She folded her note and sent the boy off. Honoria had put her book aside and now watched Cassie.

"You're smiling," said Honoria.

"Am I?" Cassie asked. "I suppose the boy's earnestness amused me."

Honoria was watching her, really watching. "You know, dear, I think this move is good for you."

"For me?" Cassie took another muslin out of the wardrobe, a chocolate brown with a small purple sprig and the worn elbows and frayed hem of one of Honoria's writing gowns. She tossed it on the appropriate pile.

"Verwood is lovely, and no one appreciates it more than you do, but consider how refreshing new scenes are," Honoria suggested.

"I never tire of the woods and gardens."

"But you must admit that Verwood is a place of … loss."

Cassie could not deny it. Her mother had died giving birth to her. The news of her brother's death in the Anglo-Burmese War had reached Verwood in her thirteenth year. After that her father had lost all interest in the estate. In three years, he had wasted away. And when she emerged from mourning him, she met Oliver Torrington, Viscount Wycombe in London. For a few mad weeks in her abbreviated Season, Torrington had been her life. Then he had married another, and Cassie returned brokenhearted to Verwood and had her accident.

"I suppose one might associate Verwood with melancholy events, but I think of it as a safe, comforting place," she said.

"Safe, but … dull. You were never dull in London." Honoria began to twist the ends of her shawl. "I should have kept you safe, and now I make you dull here. It's my fault, isn't it?"

Cassie sat on the bench beside her aunt and took Honoria's hands in hers. "You must not blame yourself for what happened in London."

"I was your chaperone. I was supposed to protect you from men like Torrington."

"You could not have saved me from my folly. I was nineteen and smitten. There were warning signs, and I rushed right past them."

"You wouldn't be afraid to go to London again in my company?"

"I am no longer that green girl." She was also no longer a prize. Then she had been a duke's daughter with youth and looks and a fat dowry. "In any case, this time we will be sensible London visitors. We'll go to concerts and the theater and museums and bookstores, not balls and routs and pleasure gardens. We'll take long walks. Shall we go when your book is finished?"

"Who will put us up? We won't want to stay with your uncle Verwood."

"No. What about your Thornhill cousins in Brunswick Square? Might they take us in for a week or a fortnight?"

"A fortnight!" Honoria stood. "Perhaps I do need to keep some of these frocks."

"And wear them, too, Aunt!"

CHAPTER SEVEN

The Crown's private dining room now served as Raven's temporary office. There, his lifelong friend Jay Kydd pushed back from a hearty luncheon and raised a mug of the landlord's home-brewed. "You've done well, Rav."

Raven raised a glass in return. Now that the ladies had removed to the dower house, he had invited Jay down from London to help with the business of getting Raven's horses settled in Verwood's stables.

As boys in the duke's gang, they had been a matched pair, similar in size and dark coloring until at seventeen Raven shot up to his present height, while Jay remained short and wiry. Then the duke's discoveries about their parentage had further separated them. Raven had gone to his wealthy ironmonger grandfather while Jay had gone to an uncle who was a partner in a horse auction house in the East End. Jay had jumped at the chance to learn his family's trade. He had to be around horses, and he liked the company of jockeys and touts, trainers and breeders.

Jay drained his pint and set down the mug. "What I don't understand is why you want to bury yourself in the country and leave London's ladies pining. I'll grant you Verwood is a pretty piece of land."

"You saw the stables?"

"Aye, and met your lady landlord. Her Grace is a haughty piece of work. Good thing you saved Dick Crockett's bacon."

"You heard about that?"

Jay counted on his fingers. "From our host Higgins, from Mrs. Crockett, from Her Grace's head groom, from the lowliest stable boy. Saving Westminster Hall from the inferno was a mere nothing. Standing up for the best farrier in Wormley, now that makes you everybody's hero."

Raven laughed. "Stop."

"Crockett's well worth saving. I've seen the lad at work. He's got the touch. Calms his animals down. They trust him."

"What do you think then? Can I move my horses to Verwood without causing trouble among Her Grace's animals?" If anyone knew how to keep horses steady around new neighbors, it was Jay.

Jay turned serious. "I'd say bring your carriage horses in first, unless you need a hack. My uncle can get you one that won't embarrass you with the duchess or make trouble with her animals."

"I'll take you up on that offer when I'm settled. For now, I'm riding Apollo from the inn. He's well-known at Verwood and approved."

"When do you move to the hall?"

"Within the week."

"I thought you said it needed work."

"It does, but there are a few decent rooms." Raven knew the history of the hall now. When the old duke died and most of the unentailed lands were sold to pay death taxes,

Verwood's rents disappeared. Furthermore, the duchess kept much of her land in pasture for her horses. The three ladies had only their portions to keep the hall going, and the estate soaked up money like a sponge.

"Sounds mad to me. You already repaired the dower house for your lady landlord, and now as a tenant you're going to drop more of your blunt into the hall? What's this all about?"

Raven took a drink of ale. He could not hold in a grin. "A man needs a house if he's to marry."

"Marry?" Jay shuddered. "You've done the bended knee thing?"

"Not yet. Verwood's the proper setting for a proposal I think."

"Nothing shabby for you, mate."

The duke's lost boys had been taught to speak like the duke himself, but Jay preferred the cant of the horse world. He was a charmer with the sort of woman who liked a handsome face and a bit of swagger. He sported a dotted blue handkerchief instead of a silk tie, and top boots instead of Hessians, and a tweed riding coat. Raven supposed that if they'd remained the same in any way, it was in energy. Jay was as quick and as impatient as ever.

Now Jay leaned his elbows on the table. "So who is this damsel that's got you blowing a fortune on an ancient pile in the middle of nowhere?"

Raven shook his head. "When she says *yes*, I'll tell you who she is. I can't have you cutting me out."

Jay shot him a shrewd glance. "She's a lady, then?"

"An earl's daughter," Raven admitted.

"Glad to hear it. That leaves the village girls for me. Tell me I'm free to charm all the pretty ones."

Raven laughed. "As long as you don't break any hearts. Remember, Verwood is going to be my home."

Jay shook his head. "I'll wager you a pony that you'll be back in London by Michaelmas."

Raven whistled. "I won't be if you get my horses settled without offending Her Grace."

Jay tossed his napkin on the table and stood. "Afraid to take the bet?"

"Not at all. You're on for a pony."

"I'll stay the week. More if you need me," Jay assured him. "There's a little mystery I'd like to clear up."

"Mystery?"

"Well, I'd like to know why the duchess quit running a profitable stud."

"Ah," said Raven. "I've wondered that, too. Crockett told me that three, maybe four years ago, her grace had a promising horse."

Jay nodded. "My uncle said as much. My hunch is that whatever caused Her Grace to shut the stud down has to do with one fellow. He's the one that might cause trouble when you bring in your cattle. A bay with black points and an irregular star, almost a crescent, on his forehead. He's called Hermes. Something happened to make him difficult."

OUTSIDE CASSIE'S WINDOW, a rabbit sat on a mound of red earth nibbling new grass. Everyone, including the rabbit, was occupied except Cassie herself. Grandmama was with her horses, preparing the stables for the arrival of Sir Adrian's cattle. Honoria was writing. Only Cassie was idle. For more than two years, she had simply turned her mind to whatever next thing required doing to keep Verwood going. Now Verwood's books were in order. With the bills owing paid, she had nothing to dread from the arrival of another quarter day. Sir Adrian had firmly grasped the reins of the hall's upkeep. She was free.

To do what? she asked herself. *Find a husband* was the obvious answer. Husband hunting was the task of the gently bred maiden who wished to secure a respectable future for herself. But Cassie had tried and failed spectacularly in her one Season. She did not know if she could love another gentleman. The impression Oliver Torrington had made on her mind and heart had been a strong one.

She had for a time been intoxicated by his regard. In a crowded room, his gaze found her at once. He abandoned other companions with scant courtesy to reach her side. No evening ended without his seeking her for a last dance, or if they had crossed the bounds of an acceptable number of dances, he simply stood with her through the final set. If they parted at two, he met her at dawn for dashing rides in the park.

When his attentions ended, London seemed empty and life, flat. For two weeks, invitations still came, and she went through the motions of going to routs and suppers, boating parties and plays. He was nowhere to be seen, and no one else sought her company. She discovered that she had made few acquaintances outside of Torrington. Letters to him went unanswered. Then he returned. *Wed!*

She learned that his marriage had been expected by all who knew him. The attentions that she thought she had inspired now belonged to his glittering golden bride. The same way of turning to speak in the girl's ear, the same way of ignoring others to focus on her, the same way of laughing at something she said. The shock of it momentarily overcame all sense of propriety and decorum. Cassie simply marched up to him and called his name, and when he turned to her as if to a complete stranger, she slapped him, the way a man would slap another man for an insult. Her slap rocked him back on his heels. He gathered himself, looked through her, and turned back to his trembling bride. From that moment, everywhere she went, the notice of others was like a mirror in which she saw herself freakish and ugly. She could neither eat nor sleep. In a week, she and Honoria left London.

Recalling the debacle even now filled her with mortification. But she had fought back. She had discovered her capacity for endurance. Activity had been part of the cure, and it was only this unexpected idleness that lowered her spirits. The best thing to do was to get busy. She would write a note to her mother's cousins to inquire whether they could receive Cassie and Honoria in Brunswick Square in September. London was vast. She need not return to scenes of her former humiliation. A walk to the village to post her letter would dissipate the last of the dismals. She would be herself again in no time.

A CONVERSATION WITH Pindock about procuring an additional wardrobe for the duchess's riding habits caused an unanticipated delay in Cassie's plan to walk to the village. She would have to hurry not to miss the post. She tied the blue ribbons on an old straw bonnet she liked to wear for berry picking, tucked her letter in a basket, and set off through the woods for Wormley.

At once she felt her mind ease. The hawthorns were white with blossoms. Buttercups and blue speedwell bloomed underfoot, pushing up through the dead leaves of the old year. She had no trouble walking, and only stopped at the two-step stile where the public path crossed a strip of Ramsbury land. There, as she gathered up her skirts, the boot on her lame foot sank in a few inches of mud. She tugged, but the mud refused to let go. She set her basket on the lower step of the stile, hitched up her skirts farther, and gripped the fence rail to pull.

"May I help you, miss?" a low male voice asked.

Cassie looked around. Behind her on the path stood a jaunty stranger, his tan beaver hat at an angle on glossy black curls. He wore a flashy checked waistcoat under a brown tweed coat, top boots that had somehow avoided the mud, and pristine buff breeches.

As awkward as it was to be caught with her skirts around her knees, it would be silly to refuse his aid. "Yes, thank you."

He sidestepped the mud, picked up her basket, and leapt to the first step of the stile. Setting her basket on the upper step, he gave her a cheeky grin. "Ready?"

"What is your plan?" She distrusted that grin.

He leaned down. "Put your arms around my neck."

She shook her head.

"Really," he said. "If you're going to be missish, I'll have to leave you stuck in the mud."

"I don't know you," she said.

"Well, I don't know you. You're not an earl's daughter, are you?"

"No."

He grinned at that. "Good. Shall we have a get-acquainted chat while you decide whether to accept my help? Care to tell me your name?"

"I do not."

"I'll have to choose one for you then. Are you an Artemis? An Arabella? A Clover? A Dandelion? A Thistle?"

She shook her head, but couldn't help the laugh that escaped her. "I'm not a horse."

"Sorry, an occupational hazard of mine. What about a flower? I have to call you something. What about 'Bluebell' for those ribbons?"

"Who are you?" she asked. His speech and dress were at odds, a mix of flash and polish. She had no idea how he fit in the social order.

"I'm the fellow who's going to pull you out of the mud, if you let me."

"Very well then." Cassie gritted her teeth and put her arms around his neck. His cologne was as flashy as his waistcoat.

He closed his hands around her waist with a strong grip and straightened. Cassie felt herself lifted through the air and set on the lower step of the stile. She grimaced at the twinge in her foot from the pull against the mud.

"What?" he asked. "Are you hurt?"

"It's nothing," she said. He was a few inches taller than Cassie, and face-to-face, he regarded her with a frank male interest she had forgotten existed.

"Tell me, Bluebell," he said, "are you off to an assignation with your best beau?"

"You, sir, are impertinent."

He cocked one black brow.

"If you must know, I'm off to put a letter in the post, and I must be on my way."

"You're certain there's no waiting beau. That's a fetching blue ribbon on your hat and you've worn your best frock."

He was quite the flatterer to think she wore her best gown. "You are an authority on female vanity, are you?"

"I have eyes," he said. He offered her a hand and swung a leg over the stile to the other side.

Cassie took his hand and allowed him to help her over the fence. When she stepped down on the other side, she shook off his hold. Her skirts remained hitched up, and she was eager to lower them as soon as the gentleman left her, if he was a gentleman.

A quick glance at her muddy boot reminded her of the cost of modesty. "Thank you for your assistance, Mr. ...?"

"Wait," he said. "Let me get a branch to wipe that boot of yours, or you'll have the devil of a time getting the mud off your skirts." He snapped a dry branch from a bush of common broom.

"Stop," Cassie protested. "You've been quite helpful. You may be on your way."

"Independent, are you, Bluebell?" he asked. "I like that. You're sure you're not an earl's daughter."

"If I were, would you go away?" His objection to earl's daughters was oddly specific.

"I'm afraid I'd have to," he said with a rueful smile. "I promised my friend, Raven, no earl's daughters for me."

"Well, I'm not an earl's daughter," she said, "and I'm not *Bluebell*."

"I've got to call you something." He dropped into a crouch at her feet, and she felt the branch against her boot. "There," he said, straightening and tossing the branch aside.

Cassie dropped her skirts at once. She didn't know whether she was more annoyed or amused. But she had to admit she was curious about a man who apparently had objections to ladies of rank. "Who are you?"

He pulled a card from a pocket and handed it to her with a bow. "Jay Kydd, Miss …?"

The card read KYDD BROTHERS HORSE AND CARRIAGE REPOSITORY, HUDSON SQUARE, LONDON. She had heard the name somewhere recently, and tried to think of the context.

"Bluebell to you," she said. "Thank you again, Mr. Kydd." She offered the card back to him.

"Keep it."

She dropped it in her basket and began to walk toward the village. Naturally, he took no hint from her actions, but fell into step beside her. She really should learn to practice a little of Grandmama's hauteur. Then the context of the name came back to her. Sir Adrian had mentioned a man name Kydd to Grandmama in connection with her stables.

She turned to her companion. "Are you here to ... help Sir Adrian?"

"You know him?" He gave her a sharp glance.

"He's the talk of the village," Cassie said.

"He's my best mate, Raven," Mr. Kydd admitted. "Jay and Raven," he explained. "We were boys together in London and in the country. Before ... well, before he got that *sir* of his at any rate."

Now her curiosity was truly piqued, but she kept her gaze on the path. Sir Adrian was merely her tenant. She had no business being curious about him. He paid his rent and abided by their agreement. That was all that mattered.

"Bluebell?" said the man beside her. "Want to hear the story of Jay and Raven?"

"I want to take this letter to the post."

"Listen to me," he coaxed, "and you'll have the edge on all your village friends when the gossip starts."

At that she laughed. Mr. Kydd plainly thought her a village girl to be teased and flirted with. Why not? For the moment she could be Bluebell, not a dead duke's damaged daughter. As Bluebell she could give in to her curiosity. The name *Raven* intrigued her.

"Very well," she said. "Tell me the story of Raven and Jay."

CHAPTER EIGHT

RAVEN RETURNED TO the Crown after meeting Dawes to go over the plans he'd made for renovating key rooms. He was entirely satisfied with Dawes. The man worked regularly on several estates in the area. Raven wanted the work done quickly, if possible, but he meant to maintain the original character of the hall.

He found Jay at ease in a smoky corner of the taproom with the coachman and a pair of grooms from his grandfather's stables in town. Jay appeared to be in lively spirits, telling some anecdote to the others. He waved Raven over to their table, and had the tapster draw another pint.

"You'll be glad to know," Jay said, handing Raven the pint, "that things are in hand at Verwood for the introduction of your vehicles and horses to their new quarters."

Raven raised his mug. "Thank you. No complaints from Her Grace?"

Jay shook his head. "The spacing is good, and Snell, the head Verwood groomsman, says we can count on Dick Crockett to steady Hermes. Once he's settled, I expect the horses closest to yours will fall in line. I'll spend the week with them in the paddock, making sure, letting them get acquainted."

"That long? I thought you were eager to get back to

town."

Jay grinned. "Turns out," he said, "that the village of Wormley has some unexpected charms."

Raven laughed. "And her name is?"

"Bluebell."

He almost choked on his ale.

Jay whacked him on the back. "Don't worry, she's definitely a two-footed lass, and not an earl's daughter. Independent and spirited."

"Where did you meet this spirited miss?"

Jay shook a finger at him. "Now that's my business."

"And she's agreed to see you again?"

"She's a bit standoffish, but my guess is that she'll be at Sunday services."

"You are smitten if you're thinking of going to church."

Jay flashed another grin. "Likely I'll wait outside and catch her as she leaves."

"And did you solve the mystery of Her Grace closing the stud?"

Jay took a pull on his drink. "I have Mrs. Crockett's theory. Have you heard that one?"

"Yes, that Her Grace's granddaughter had a riding accident." Raven was familiar now with Lady Cassandra's dipping gait.

"My money's still on Hermes as the key to the mystery, but I have to say there's nothing wrong with his formation or movement. I haven't seen any scars or marks indicating an injury. Still, I'll keep my ears open this week. I ordered our landlord's best dinner. You're paying, aren't you?"

A WEEK AFTER Cassie learned that Sir Adrian's friends called him "Raven" *Raven* sent a message with a boy runner that he had something to show her at the big house.

Cassie had not been able to let go of that little bit of information about him. The name was like a pebble in her shoe. She thought she'd shaken it out, but it returned to bother her. For one thing it suited him better than his title with his dark good looks and endless assurance. There was something cheeky about a raven. They did not scatter like lesser birds. A carriage could bear down on a raven in the roadway, and only at the last possible instant would a raven hop out of harm's way, as if it relished a brush with iron wheels. Raven struck Cassie as equally unflinching in the face of danger.

For another, the name came with a history she had not imagined for him. According to Jay Kydd, Raven had taken the name Adrian only to please his grandfather. As boys Jay and Raven had lived apart from their families in a rooftop gang of waifs in London. As Jay told the story their life was one of grand adventure, but to Cassie it sounded cold, uncomfortable, desperate, and dangerous.

She had not seen Jay Kydd again, though she'd heard of him from Grandmama, who, though she might not be susceptible to his charm, was an admirer of his way with horses.

In the drive, several drays waited to be unloaded, their contents covered with canvas, their drivers standing in a group, talking and sending curls of pipe smoke into the morning air. The hall's great door was open and the marble tiles covered in more canvas. She kept to the side for a pair of men carrying a load of planks, their voices and footsteps echoing in the empty hall.

The boy who'd brought her Raven's message earlier, jumped up from a stool just inside the door. "Miss, ye'll find 'im in the great hall. I'll show ye."

Cassie did not stop him or say that she knew the way, that it was her house. It no longer resembled her house. The walls were shrouded in canvas in addition to the floors. Male voices and hammering filled the air. The great hall, the largest room in the house, had been transformed as well. The arm chairs and console tables were gone, the paneling and windows hidden behind canvas, the great chandelier removed, its chain hanging bare from the high plaster ceiling, and underfoot more canvas. She wondered where the Aubusson carpet had gone. Scaffolding had been erected around the room to reach the ceiling. An open door on the north side of the house let in a rectangle of wan light. She stood for a moment, adjusting to the gloom.

Raven stood with Dawes, looking over a long roll of paper on a makeshift table to one side of the door. A lamp on the end of the table illuminated the white of his shirt sleeves. Dawes saw Cassie and cleared his throat. Raven turned, saw her, and said something to Dawes, who nodded and went out the terrace door.

Raven came to Cassie with his usual energetic stride. Without a coat, with his sleeves rolled up and a plain brown waistcoat, he still had that authority of bearing and manner.

"You're wondering what I'm up to, I expect," he said.

"A little," she said. "I did not think this room needed work."

"It's not the room itself. It's the ceiling." He pointed to the geometric pattern of plasterwork over their heads.

"The ceiling?" She looked up.

"I had it inspected. It's sixty years old according to Verwood's records. You might not have noticed any cracks or sagging because of the pattern, but Dawes tells me that it has pulled away from the lath in too many places to be repaired."

"It could collapse?" She looked up again. She had not noticed because they had not used the great hall in years.

"In the worst case, but we're going to take it down, and I want your opinion on a new design by Jackson & Sons. Care to advise?" He gestured toward the makeshift table with its roll of paper.

She nodded. "Do you plan to use the great hall much?" She couldn't help but ask. In her grandmother's youth it had been used for balls, but Raven was a single man with no acquaintance in Wormley. Of course, he could bring friends from London.

"Actually," he said with a smile, "I'm thinking of giving a ball."

"For friends from London?"

"For the neighborhood," he said.

"But you don't know anyone—" That smile of his stopped her. "Do you?"

"I might, but I thought perhaps I could count on your help in that matter."

"My help?" He would not ask for her help if he had any idea of her reputation in the neighborhood.

"I thought I might accompany the Verwood ladies to church."

"Oh, of course," she said. He was right about that. If he appeared in St. Andrew's, everyone in the neighborhood, high and low, would be curious about him and impressed. His good looks, his air of fashion, and his money would have everyone talking. And people were already talking about the work he was doing at Verwood, employing carpenters and masons, painters, and soon, apparently, plasterers.

Cassie looked at the airy design of garlands and fruits and flowers laid out on the makeshift table. There were great ovals, and overflowing baskets and the coat of arms of the Dukes of Verwood.

"How much is all of this costing you?" she asked.

"This bit, not so much, maybe eight hundred pounds. The rest, a great deal."

"Can you really spend so much?"

"Am I good for it? Yes."

"But," she sighed, "you don't own the house. You…"

"I am a temporary tenant? Are you trying to protect me from…"

"Folly and extravagance? I guess so. I have pinched pennies for so long, I can't imagine these grand expenditures of yours."

From somewhere above them came a resounding crash. Cassie started, and Raven reached out a hand to steady her. "Someone has dropped a load of planks."

Cassie drew in a breath. "When do you anticipate giving your ball?"

"At the July full moon. The work will be done by then."

His extraordinary confidence struck her again. And his freedom to spend. How opposite they were. He could decide to give a ball, and then lease a property and refurbish it no matter the cost to fill a room with mere acquaintances. She could not decide to buy a new gown without scheming to scratch together the means.

"You'll come to my ball, won't you?"

She looked up at him, resolved to tell him that her ball-going days were over, but she didn't know how to explain herself. The past was the past. What happened had happened. She had worked out a way of getting through her days, but until he leased Verwood, she had not thought of changing the pattern of her life. Now she was trying to figure out how to do it, waiting for an answer to her letter to her mother's cousins. But she could not dance, that was a step too far.

For once he looked boyish, less commanding, more eager. He could have no way of knowing that what he offered called to mind things lost and gone forever.

"You need not invite your ... landlord..." she began when a sound like the first crack of thunder overhead made her look up.

Raven grabbed her hand and pulled her into his arms, falling back with her against the wall, under the scaffolding as the crack became a rumble, and a great patch of plaster hit the plank above their heads, exploding into fragments. Dust rained down and swirled about them.

"Close your eyes," he ordered. His lips brushed her ear. He pushed her head into his chest, and spun, so that she was pressed against the wall, her body covered with his own.

Cassie huddled against him as the falling plaster became a cascade of broken chunks of lime and powdered gypsum, thumping on the scaffolding over their heads, shaking the framework around them, filling the air with dust and noise. The world contracted to a hollow of linen and wool that smelled of Raven, of bergamot and labdanum, spice and energy. Her cheek pressed against his chest. His heart beat steadily under her ear. His arms held her firmly against his solid warmth, offering protection. Around them the air shook and swirled. She kept her eyes closed and breathed in the scent of him with a little shock of recognition that their bodies fit together easily, and that over the past few weeks she had come to know how he smelled.

The thumping, shaking storm of falling plaster seemed endless until the noise subsided to a few plops of plaster hitting the scaffolding overhead. From beyond the great hall, voices shouted and footsteps pounded. Cassie stirred, pulling back in his hold, but he did not release her at once.

"Wait," he commanded, his body stiff and alert.

There came another loud *crack*, a *swoosh*, and a *smash* that sent dust and debris flying again. After a pause, he released her, stepping back a pace. His dark hair and brows were powdered white with plaster dust. It covered his shoulders and arms.

"You're unharmed?" His voice was low and full of concern.

"Perfectly," she said. It wasn't true. She had been held by him, and now the sheltering hold had been withdrawn. The air tasted of grit.

As she stared up at him, his expression tightened, the

warmth in his eyes quickly turning cold. "Your dress is ruined," he said. "I'll get you another."

She shook her head. "You have other things to attend to."

"Sir Adrian," a man called, and Raven turned to him.

"We're unharmed. Give us a moment." He offered a chalk-covered hand and helped her climb over a pile of debris, the fallen plaster crunching under their feet. She stopped and looked up to the dark lines of exposed lath above them.

"We did mean to take the old ceiling down," he said, his face grim again.

"But not so quickly." She tried to make light of it. "You'll have your project done well in time for that July moon."

"That's the plan. Let me see you back to the dower house."

"No need."

"I insist."

"Very well." She picked her way around and over the piles of rubble. She did not understand him, but she recognized the pattern. He'd gone from warm concern to brusque coldness. His change of manner was just as well. She did not want to mistake the shelter of his arm in an accident for any other sentiment. The warmth he sometimes showed her was not personal. It came from his pleasure in the project and his anticipation of showing off the house in the future, not from any interest in her.

As they passed out of the great hall, more men arrived to stare at the exposed ceiling and piles of broken plaster. Raven stopped to speak to one of them about cleaning up the debris, then Cassie and Raven moved through the marble hall to the outside. On the porch she glanced at him and could not resist a smile.

"What?" He stood, brushing the dust from his shoulders.

"You've become quite the distinguished white-haired gentleman," she said.

"Your suitable tenant?" He laughed and shook his head, raking his hands through his hair, shedding more dust. "You have not fared any better." His face sobered, and he reached out and plucked a bit of plaster from her hair, took her hand, turned it palm up, and dropped a tiny bud of some past garland in her hand. "Seriously," he said, "can your gown be saved?"

"Oh, I think so." She started down the stairs. He would be surprised at how much could be saved if there were no funds for replacements. She glanced over her shoulder. It was the whiteness of his eyebrows that gave him the look of an actor in a play. "Come on," she said. "Walk me home, if you will, and get back to your grand project."

He was familiar with her limp by now, though they never spoke of it, and he adjusted his stride to hers. She wondered if he'd forgotten it when he'd asked her to come to his ball. Probably.

As they passed the edge of the lake, he gave the water a longing glance. "There are no rules against tenants taking a dip, are there?"

She laughed. "Be my guest."

Where the road veered off the main drive to the dower house, she stopped him. "Really, I can manage to get safely home on my own."

"Good," he said. "I'll let you go, but I will hold you to the plan for church on Sunday. And, I'll ask you to look at the new ceiling when it's safe to do so."

He bowed and turned back up the drive toward the big house. Cassie slipped into the woods.

RAVEN REACHED THE edge of the lake in a very few strides. He dropped onto the grass, stripped off his waistcoat, and tugged off his boots, making a neat pile of them in the grass. He was a gentleman. His desires were well-regulated. He could only explain his reaction to unfashionable Cassandra Lavenham as a result of not exercising properly. In the weeks since he'd signed the lease for Verwood, he had had no daily run, no weekly sparring match with one of his friends. His waking hours had been occupied with meeting craftsmen, hiring workers, ordering materials, looking at plans.

Grit stuck to his neck and shoulders. In a flash he saw the white-laced edge of her bodice dusted with plaster. The water stretched out before him, cool and refreshing. He undid his cuffs, pulled his shirt over his head, and rubbed his face and shoulders. The lake, some three hundred yards across, stirred memories of the river at Daventry Hall where he'd learned to swim. He added his shirt to the little pile, stood, and waded out through the reeds. Cold mud oozed between his toes. Then he plunged in. The water closed over his head, cool and bracing. He surfaced and began to stroke for the far side. He made himself think of the old days when

Wenlocke had been Daventry.

In the summer after his marriage, Daventry had insisted that his *boys* learn to swim. Once they'd got the hang of it, they had spent most days in the river. At the end of that summer, Dav, as he was then called, gathered them together up on their roof to ask permission to search for their families. He told them that someone somewhere missed them as his mother and brothers had missed him. He listened as they complained and doubted and got angry. He reminded them of things about themselves that they'd quite forgotten, clues that would help him find their true origins. He told them the decision was theirs. Whatever the search yielded, he would help them establish themselves in the world.

For days they talked of nothing else, lying at the edge of the river, arguing and shivering from hours in the water. Jay had been the first to claim that he remembered his people. They had horses. The others, even Raven, scoffed at him. They knew what they were—the refuse of London, its surplus population, the unwanted, passed from one parish to another, sold for climbing boys, trained to be pickpockets, or sent to the workhouse. Lark and Rook had left the gang to live in London again. All of them knew the pair would end up picking pockets. None of them was like Dav, the kidnapped grandson of the Duke of Wenlocke. The truth about their families would not come with a title and a grand hall. But Jay had been willing to take the risk. In the end they had all chosen to seek their families, all except Robin.

Raven slowed his stroke and lifted his head. The far shore was close now. He rolled to his back and looked at the sky, his heart pounded, his breath came in gusts. He had come a long way from the day he'd agreed to the search for his family. He knew who he was. He had a plan. His goal was hardly farther than the shore of the little lake. Inconvenient feelings for his quirky landlady would not sway him now. The Raven of his London youth had been glad of the things that came his way, damaged or broken, not Sir Adrian Cole. Sir Adrian Cole would give a dazzling ball at Verwood and claim his perfect bride before the end of the summer.

He swam the last few yards of the lake in a flurry of strokes and kicks and stood on the shore, catching his breath, and shaking water from his head, his body plaster-streaked. Lady Amabel Haydon was the woman for him. He would stick to his plan, meet his neighbors, finish his renovations, and invite the world to Verwood.

CHAPTER NINE

Cassie had perhaps underestimated the effect on her neighbors of a fashionable gentleman sitting in the Verwood pew at St. Andrew's. A damp, dismal day had not discouraged church attendance, and St. Andrew's was packed. Though Mr. Montford's sermonizing usually lulled his listeners into a Sunday doze, Cassie did not need to turn round to know that her neighbors were fully awake. She suspected that most pairs of female eyes, and some male ones as well, were directed toward Sir Adrian's tall person. With his appearance in church, he ceased to belong exclusively to the ladies of Verwood. Now their neighbors had claims upon him. A report circulating in the village said he was worth ten thousand pounds per annum. Cassie believed the actual figure was thirty.

With the final triumphant notes of a rousing hymn, a general stir rustled through St. Andrew's. Shuffling and murmurs accompanied the plop of hymnals sliding into holders. Sir Adrian stepped out of the Verwood pew and offered his arm to Grandmama who took it with her usual cool disdain. In Grandmama's mind, it was she who bestowed the favor. Cassie and Honoria followed, past neighbors craning in the pews to catch a glimpse of the gentleman. No one seeing him in his elegant London coat would credit Jay Kydd's story of Sir Adrian's youth as Raven.

Outside, under the dripping eaves of St. Andrew's little porch, Mr. Montford greeted them, and invited them to dinner, an awkward invitation, as Sir Adrian, not his titled landlady, was obviously the true object of Mrs. Montford's warm hospitality. When the press of the crowd behind them became too much to resist, Mr. Montford allowed Sir Adrian to escort Grandmama to her carriage. Once her grandmother had been helped inside, Sir Adrian turned to Cassie, his dark, winged brows as black as a raven's, no plaster dust on him.

"Before you go, a quick word." He offered his arm and led her back to a spot under the trees. "Are there any of your neighbors I should avoid? Those that Her Grace would not welcome at Verwood?"

"Oh, I suspect you can't avoid meeting them all as long as the rain holds off." She grinned at his dilemma, but she did not think Grandmama would actually terminate his lease for inviting any of their more pushing neighbors to Verwood. "You are as coveted as the prize turkey at the fair. Our local hostesses will vie to have you at their tables."

"Prize turkey?" Sir Adrian scanned the crowd as if he sought some familiar face. As she followed his gaze, Cassie saw Jay Kydd leap down from a black curricle standing in the west road beyond the churchyard. She shifted her position slightly to keep Sir Adrian between her and Mr. Kydd. Her encounter with Mr. Kydd now seemed most irregular and a bit mad, certainly out of character. She had avoided any repeat of the occasion. What had she been thinking to enter into conversation with a stranger and let him rattle on telling her his history and Sir Adrian's, believing the whole, and concealing her own identity. She could not think why she'd done it. She supposed that she had been gratified in some way by Mr. Kydd's attentions, and she had to admit that she'd been curious to hear about Raven.

She glanced up at Sir Adrian and realized that she had missed something he'd said. "I beg your pardon."

"Lord Ramsbury and his family don't attend services at St. Andrew's?"

"Lord Ramsbury? No. The family has a private chapel and their own chaplain, a Mr. Bellamy."

"Ah," said Sir Adrian. "I wondered."

"Are you acquainted with the Haydon family?" Cassie asked. He could not know the whole family. He certainly had not recognized Hugh that day at the inn.

"With Lady Amabel I am. We met in London," he said with a smile, a smile that softened and transformed his face. Cassie froze, and an odd tremor shook her. There was no mistaking what that smile meant. Sir Adrian Cole was in love with Lady Amabel Haydon.

Abruptly, Sir Adrian's interest in Verwood made sense. Verwood bordered Ramsbury Park. Proximity to Amabel had been Verwood's chief attraction, not the hall or the grounds. He had come to court Amabel. His determination to improve the hall was for Amabel. She was the object of all his efforts. The realization stirred a sickening knot in Cassie's stomach, a churning mix of alarm and fear, not for herself but for him. The singlemindedness of his admiration for Amabel was too like her own past infatuation with Torrington. She straightened and worked to dispel her agitation. The shock of discovery would wear off. Amabel was not

Torrington. Cassie knew no wrong of Amabel, who had been a lovely child when Cassie had her Season.

"Ah," she said. "It's a short ride to Ramsbury Park from Verwood. You can call on her when the family comes down for the summer." Likely, they would see little of Sir Adrian when the Haydon family arrived. It would be easy for Cassie to check any growing feelings for him. She had been enjoying their exchanges, and had perhaps even been in some danger of finding their tenant likable. Now she would know to keep her distance.

"That is my hope."

In the face of his happy besotted look, Cassie could say no more. She knew what it was to feel that sort of attachment to another. Sir Adrian seemed to suspect no danger, and perhaps there was none. He was strong. For him, love was not broken. He had business in the world. As Raven he had survived hardship. If Amabel failed to return his love, he would not give into melancholy. Cassie had no right to interfere in his affairs. Telling him that Hugh was Amabel's brother would be impertinent, too much like the sort of warning a person in love always ignored. She was hardly the one to instruct another in the conduct of a love affair.

"What?" he said.

"Nothing." Cassie would not interfere. However unpleasant Hugh's disposition, he would see the value of a very rich suitor for his sister. Sir Adrian could handle Hugh.

He gave her an assessing look. "Your face is full of something," he said. "You said you know your neighbors. Perhaps you know Lady Amabel."

"She is six years my junior, so she was not out when I

was in my dancing days."

"Your dancing days?" One of his brows quirked up. "You can't be more than four and twenty. Are you going to tell me that you never dance?"

As soon as he said it, he looked conscious of the awkwardness of the topic. It was the closest he'd come to a mention of her foot. "I beg your pardon," he said. "That was impertinent of me."

She laughed. Let him think her foot was to blame. "Go. Meet your neighbors, but be prepared to dine out for the next fortnight."

He gave her a last questioning glance, made a quick bow, and strode off. At least three hopeful mamas waited with their offspring to meet him. Lady Brock got to him first.

When he stopped to talk with the Brock family, Cassie turned to find her grandmother's carriage gone. Grandmama had not waited. To abandon her granddaughter was an odd start even for Grandmama, but Cassie could not think what she'd done to get into Grandmama's black books this time.

Cassie stood for a moment under a dripping yew. She wasn't far from Verwood. She could easily walk even with her bad foot. In the church yard, families waited for their moment with Sir Adrian. When she turned toward the gate, there was Jay Kydd.

"Bluebell, we meet again," he said. "Where may I take you?"

"I can walk," she said. She could think of nowhere he could take her without exposing her identity.

"In all this mud? What if we simply go for a drive," he offered.

"Very well." She would think of somewhere to have him set her down. And they would have to avoid being seen in the village. "Can we take the Ramsbury road?"

He raised a brow, but handed her up into the carriage and offered her a lap rug. A memory came to mind of driving in the rain with Torrington, but she refused to let it take hold. She was not that girl. She was Bluebell, at least for the next hour. Mr. Kydd sprang up beside her and gave the horses their command. He was a neat driver, and the horses were a perfect pair. Riding with him was nothing like being jolted along in the inn gig.

Where the road forked at the edge of the village, he asked her opinion, and she pointed toward Lord Ramsbury's estate. It was the way most likely to be empty, passing for miles through property that had belonged to Verwood when Cassie was a child. Now those acres were devoted to Lord Ramsbury's game and roamed mainly by Ramsbury's shooting parties when the birds were in season, and by his gamekeepers, who had little to do with the village people.

She imagined Sir Adrian taking the same road soon, full of eagerness, and the knot in her stomach tightened. Cassie wished him no disappointment. She should perhaps have told him that Hugh was Amabel's brother, but she reminded herself that Sir Adrian was a man who didn't let much stand in his way. She raised her chin and let the rain-freshened air rush over her. She was Bluebell at the moment, enjoying a lark.

Before they reached Lord Ramsbury's gates, Mr. Kydd turned them around and slowed his horses. "Feel better?"

"I was not aware of feeling unwell," she said.

"You looked downright blue-deviled when we started."

She laughed. "Do you always say what you're thinking?"

"Mostly," he said. "I looked for you this week, but you gave me the slip."

"Weren't you occupied helping Sir Adrian?"

"For you, Bluebell, I would have made time. Didn't you miss me?"

"I was too busy." In truth she had been thoroughly occupied with helping Honoria arrange the jumbled pages of a draft.

"Who keeps you busy, I wonder? Her Grace?"

Cassie looked away to hide a smile. "No lady so grand as that."

"You know, Bluebell, with a little push I can learn your name. Wormley is a small village."

"Small? Wormley? That's a London man speaking. We have everything a village requires—a green, a shop, a butcher and a grocer, a smith, a vicar, an apothecary. How can you say we are a small village?"

"A vast hub of commerce, eh? But very few families."

"At least four and twenty."

"And where am I to place you in such a company?"

"You needn't place me at all." Mr. Kydd was clever and persistent, like his friend. But Cassie sensed that she was far more intriguing as Bluebell, a little mystery, while as Lady Cassandra Lavenham, she'd be an object of distant civility.

"Afraid of a scold from your employer for letting a flash cove from London take you up?"

"You have no idea."

"But you can't resist me, can you? You may be a bit out

of fashion, but you speak like a lady, so I'm guessing you are governess to some spoiled miss who gives you her cast-off gowns."

She ought to be insulted, especially about the gowns, but for a mad moment Cassie wanted to seize the role he offered. Sense took over. "I would be a poor sort of governess if I deserted my charges after services to go driving with some fine gentleman."

"Fine gentleman? There's an elevation for you. Where's home?"

"A governess makes her home with her employer. But tell me, Mr. Kydd, aren't you off to London soon?"

"Ouch. You're that eager to be rid of me?"

"Just making sure not to be taken in by the charms of a practiced London flirt."

He laughed. "You see through me, do you?"

Maybe that explained her ease with him. He enjoyed teasing her, but his heart was not likely to be engaged. "I'm sure that in London, you'll soon forget your Bluebell."

"You wound me, but I'm off tomorrow. My uncle needs me in town, and Raven's horses have settled in nicely at Verwood. Only Her Grace's bad boy, Hermes, still has his doubts about the newcomers. Raven's bays will toss their heads and ignore him. They know their worth."

Cassie laughed again. Horses might not speak, but Mr. Kydd was right that they could show their feelings plainly and knew their places in the stable hierarchy. Grandmama's very spoiled horses, like the woman herself, looked down on lesser creatures. Mr. Kydd was only wrong that Hermes was a bad boy.

He shook his head, not looking at Cassie, plainly absorbed in thoughts about the horse. "That Hermes is as handsome a devil as I've seen in an age! Fifteen two or three hands. I'm working on Her Grace's man Snell to get his true story. It's a mystery, you see. Snell is tight-lipped, but he admitted that Hermes is out of the Darley Arabian. There might be some Galloway in him as well to give him his size. With that bloodline, he could be the making of the Verwood stud. He's young, no more than five, I'd say. He'd make a remarkable sire. There would be a demand for his get."

"Wouldn't he have to win some purses first? To gain notice?" Cassie asked.

Mr. Kydd gave her an arrested glance, and she was conscious of revealing too much knowledge of the workings of a stud. She had understood his quaint way of speaking of a stallion's *get*, which a village girl should not. She was grateful that Mr. Snell, Grandmama's head groom, was by nature taciturn. Hermes's history was Cassie's history. Once he heard their story, Mr. Kydd would stop flirting with Bluebell.

For a few minutes, a narrow, winding stretch of road required him to attend more to his driving than to her, but she knew he would come back to the mystery, and Cassie had to be careful not to give herself away. Bluebell could go driving with a fast gentleman from London, but Lady Cassandra Lavenham would be the talk of the village for the freedom she was enjoying.

As the road straightened out between open fields, Mr. Kydd returned to Hermes. Cassie smiled. If he gave his heart to anyone, it would be to a horse. "If I had the training of him, I wager he could race in one of the late July meets or by Lammas Day at the latest."

"So soon?" The idea startled her. She closed her hands around a fold of the lap rug. Cassie believed Hermes was past his racing days. The idea that Hermes could race again by the end of summer could not be right. If Hermes could race, then Cassie was to blame for Verwood's latest money woes. It was her accident that had led to Grandmama's decision. If Mr. Kydd was right, it was Cassie who had held them all back, reduced them to leasing Verwood. Surely, his overly optimistic temperament had led him astray. A horse, even one as powerful as Hermes, could not race so soon, not after three years of idleness. She looked up, suddenly conscious that he was watching her.

"Have the blue devils got you again?" he asked.

"Not at all. I think this drive has done me a world of good, thank you. Now, you may set me down." To a stranger there was nothing in the particular bend in the road, but beyond a copse of white hawthorn was a wooded path to Verwood. Cassie pulled the lap rug away and lay it across the back of the seat.

"What? I'm dismissed, am I?" He reined in his pair and looked about. "Here? What did I say?"

"You've said nothing amiss. I must return to my ... people. Keep your horses in hand. I can manage." She climbed down with only a little twinge in her foot as it took her weight.

Mr. Kydd regarded her with a puzzled look. "You know, Bluebell, you are hard on a man's pride."

"But you, Mr. Kydd, have boundless self-assurance, and

won't let one out-of-fashion country maiden flatten you."

He laughed. "You're not so easily rid of me. I have a standing invitation from Raven." He looked around once again. "You're sure of this place?"

She nodded.

He tipped his hat, and drove on.

Cassie waited until his carriage disappeared between the hedgerows, then she crossed the old plank over the ditch at the side of the road and slipped into the copse. She needed to walk. She had some serious thinking to do.

CHAPTER TEN

BY THE TIME she reached Verwood, Cassie's hems were muddied, and her foot throbbed mercilessly, but she went directly to the stables. As she expected, Snell and John Coachman and the stable boys were at their Sunday meal. She closed her eyes a minute to take in the smells of the place and the sounds of horses stirring. She smelled the clover in the hay, the neatsfoot oil on the tack, the whiff of manure, and above all the sweet smell of horseflesh. When she opened her eyes again, she grabbed a handful of oats from the feed room and made her way down the aisle of stalls to Hermes.

Her passage through the stable raised a few nickers from the curious, and when she reached him, Hermes stood in the shadowy stall, ears up, alert, his nostrils aquiver.

"You're not a brute, are you, boy? No matter what people think."

He snorted and swished his tail, but did not come to her.

"We could try again, you and I. I brought you some oats." She held out her hand and opened her palm. It was a pitiful gesture. His trust was worth having and therefore not easily won. She waited, but he remained unmoving.

"The accident was not your fault." She watched his ears catch her voice. "The fault was mine. Snell warned me that you were too young to know your limits."

She pulled back her hand and spread the oats along the top of the stall door crosspiece. "I'll come again," she told him.

She was almost to the end of the aisle when she heard the distinctive low rumble of his nicker, a sound that came from deep in his belly.

CASSIE'S ATTEMPT TO enter the house unnoticed failed. Cook, catching sight of her as she crept through the kitchen, muddy shoes in hand, offered a quick scold, but set water warming and told Cassie a bath would be ready in no time.

Cassie had a long soak and time to reflect on her situation in the glaring light cast on it by the remarks of Sir Adrian and Mr. Kydd. Neither gentleman had the least suspicion of saying anything to shake her, but that had been the result.

After her bath she dressed in one of the old gowns she had been content to wear forever, but now she heard Mr. Kydd's teasing voice describing her clothes as castoffs. She had made no push to change her situation until the numbers in the Verwood ledgers had gone so against her. A tenant had seemed the perfect way to make Verwood pay for itself, and Sir Adrian seemed, if not the perfect tenant, the richest. Now she saw that his staying at Verwood very much depended on the affections of Lord Ramsbury's daughter. Cassie had been idle too long.

As she pulled a stocking over her misshapen foot, she resolved to speak to her grandmother no matter how unbending Grandmama could be. The silk snagged as it always did, and she gently pulled it past the scar. Over the years, she had invented a dozen ways of describing the lump on the top of her foot. Doctor Ormond had put names to her broken bones. The *cuneiforms* and the *metatarsals*, he called them. Whatever their names, what Cassie saw was a mound, like the dirt pushed up by a mad vole as it tunneled through the garden. The low ridge of fused bone angled across her foot, and the shortened foot cocked inward.

It wasn't pretty, but the point was that the bones had healed. Neither she nor Hermes needed to be perfect to carry on. She slipped her foot into one of the loose slippers she wore at home and descended for evening tea.

Her grandmama's sharp stare met her as she entered the sitting room, freshly painted in deep gold, a reminder of their dependence on Sir Adrian's rent.

"And where did you get to, my headstrong girl?" Grandmama sat stiffly upright in a slightly thread-worn, crimson velvet armchair, a relic from the big house.

"I walked home." Cassie crossed to the tea table and took her seat. The fire in the limestone fireplace gave a glow to the deep gold walls. A hint of fading light in the sky caught the silver of the teapot. A glance from Honoria warned Cassie that her grandmother was in a mood. She could no more rush a conversation about Hermes than she could hurry the tea. She lifted the lid on the pot. Nearly ready. Thankfully, Cook had prepared Grandmama's favorite orange-water rout cakes.

"Sir Adrian didn't take you up?" Grandmama began.

"He did not."

"But you and he were speaking when we pulled away." Cassie heard the aggrieved tone, but didn't understand the reason for it, except that Grandmama apparently wanted to provoke a quarrel.

"Only briefly. His new neighbors claimed him."

"He should have made his excuses and taken you up."

"Did you ask him to bring me home, Grandmama?" Cassie frowned. Her grandmother had as much as admitted that she had left Cassie behind deliberately.

"I should not have to ask." Her grandmother looked away. "Sir Adrian should know what is fitting, what is due to me as his landlady."

"I should think that civility to his neighbors was fitting behavior for the tenant of Verwood," Cassie said.

"Hah," said her grandmother. "He may be civil to 'em, but trust me, a man like that will not marry one of their daughters, no matter how many courses and removes those hopeful mama's put before him. He's got ambitions."

Cassie concealed a smile. Her grandmama, who gave the impression of finding ordinary mortals quite beneath her notice, rarely missed anything. Grandmama was right that Sir Adrian's ambitious marriage plans did not include their neighbors' daughters, but she did not guess that he desired to marry Lady Amabel Haydon. Nor would Grandmama imagine that Sir Adrian felt the besotted sort of love that could get one's heart broken. That was the worry. If he did get his heart broken, Cassie was sure he would leave Verwood without a backward glance. That unsettling possibility had occupied her thoughts throughout her bath. Without the income from his rent, they would once again have to rely on Grandmama's jointure and the allowance from Cassie's trust. They would be strapped, wearing old gowns, and making no trips to London. If Hermes could run, maybe they would not need a tenant who had given his heart away.

Cassie poured a cup of tea and took it to her grandmother.

"What else is his leasing of Verwood?" her grandmother asked. "It's his grand scheme to rise in the world. What does his family make? Mustard?"

"That's the *Colman* family, Lottie," Honoria commented. "Sir Adrian is a *Cole*. They make fire engines and plate glass."

"Colman, Cole, neither name has an ounce of distinction. He depends upon being a tenant of Verwood to make his mark in society."

Cassie raised a brow. The sharpness of her grandmother's displeasure surprised her. "The Lavenham's once had undistinguished name, until our ancestors found royal favor."

Honoria gave a gleeful chortle and drew a glare from Grandmama.

"I'm sorry Sir Adrian disappointed you, Grandmama," Cassie said, trying to head off a full blown quarrel. "I'm sure he had no idea that he was expected to offer me a place in his carriage. I didn't think to ask him. You know how I like my walks."

Cassie passed a cup of tea to Honoria and rose to hand round the plate of Cook's fragrant rout cakes. It was true that her grandmother's favoring Sir Adrian did him no harm in their neighbors' eyes, but it was unlike Grandmama to insist on Cassie's accepting a ride from him. The affront to Grandmama's pride at Sir Adrian for not offering the ride seemed at odds with her usual condemnation of his presumption. Clearly, Sir Adrian could not win.

For a few minutes the ladies enjoyed their tea and cakes. Cassie imagined that in other households Sir Adrian's would-be hostesses were planning their menus and their guest lists, thinking up ways to distinguish their offerings from those of their rivals. Mrs. Montford, the vicar's wife, who was to take the lead was probably wondering whether Sir Adrian was fond of an oyster-stuffed roast leg of mutton, or whether he would prefer braised turkey. Cassie smiled at the challenge of it, how to please Sir Adrian and still remain memorable after all the other ladies had their turn at entertaining their new wealthy neighbor.

"May we speak of something else?" Cassie asked.

"Oh yes, let's," Honoria pleaded.

"Very well," said Grandmama. "What would you speak of?"

Cassie set down her cup. There was no easy way to begin. "Hermes."

Grandmama frowned. Honoria froze, her hands caught in the fringe of her shawl. Silence prevailed while the last daylight faded from the sky, and shadows bloomed in the corners of the room. The teacup in Cassie's hand cooled.

"Well, have your say, girl," her grandmother said at last.

Cassie took a steadying breath. "Hasn't Hermes been punished enough for an accident that was not his fault?"

"Punished? Is that what you think? He lives very well, mind you. It's all green pastures and freedom for him."

"But he was born to run, wasn't he? He's young yet. If you began training him, Grandmama, he could run again."

"Foolish girl. What do you know about preparing a horse to run?"

"I know Hermes was meant to win races. Meant to establish the Verwood stud."

"You've not been speaking to that Crockett woman, have you? Or Snell? He knows my thinking. He would never go against my wishes."

"I don't need Snell to tell me that if Hermes won a few purses, gentlemen would bring their mares to Verwood, hoping to breed a champion, and the stud could pay for itself again."

For a moment her grandmother said nothing. Cassie held her breath.

Her grandmother stood, and let her gaze sweep the small sitting room. "Leasing Verwood was your idea, Cassandra. Do not blame me or my horses for finding yourself confined to these narrow walls."

"I don't, Grandmama. I blame only myself. The accident was my fault, not the fault of Hermes. And I have let my situation hold us all back far too long."

"Oh Cassie, no." Honoria twisted the ends of her shawl. "You mustn't say so. You mustn't go back to that dark time."

Cassie turned to Honoria. "Don't worry, Aunt. I see clearly now what happened that night."

"You do?" Honoria asked.

Cassie nodded. She had no recollection of hitting her head that night, but she knew perfectly how her foot had come to be broken. "What happened then matters less than what we do now." She turned back to meet her grandmother's fierce gaze. "Neither Hermes, nor I, are what we once were. If he proves manageable enough for me to ride, will you train him, Grandmama? I know you would like to see him run again."

Honoria gasped.

Grandmama gave Honoria a withering glance, and turned toward the door. Her hand on the knob, she paused and glanced back at Cassie. "You are dreaming, girl. I forbid you to endanger yourself on that horse again."

CHAPTER ELEVEN

Raven stood at the top of Verwood's south steps looking down the sweep of the carriage drive. He was now officially in residence. His small army of masons, carpenters, plasterers, and painters had left Verwood to work on other estates. His grandfather's haulers had delivered those of his possessions he wanted at present, and his lady landlords had disappeared into the dower house. Verwood was his, or as much his as a very tight lease covenant could make it.

This morning Raven meant to walk the two-mile circuit of the inner grounds with an eye to what would most delight Lady Amabel when she visited. He could not decide which fantasy pleased him more, showing it to her in all its newness, or establishing the old public day customs of Verwood mentioned by his neighbors. Of one thing, he was sure. He would give a ball.

As he came down the wide entry steps, gardeners with scythes were at work on the vast lawn. He followed the carriage drive, and paused at the lane leading to the dower house. To his left the little lake sparkled in the morning light. He had had no further temptation to swim in it. His exchanges with Lady Cassandra had become straightforward. One of his boy messengers would find her with a request, and she would send a quick reply. Without fail and with no further visits to the hall, she had approved his choices of paint and paper. He suspected her of avoiding him, and laughed at himself for feeling slighted. Nothing in the lease covenant said that they should like each other. It was right that landlord-tenant intercourse remain purely official.

Past the lane to the dower house, he turned along the outer track that encircled the property. The layout of the grounds ensured that the ladies could come and go from the dower house to the stables unobserved from the hall. He need not think about them at all. Though he shared a pew with them in St. Andrew's on a Sunday, he had no other occasion to encounter the owners of Verwood. Still, he had looked for them at the dinners given by his neighbors, until one of his hostesses, Lady Brock, explained how presumptuous it would be on her part to invite the duchess. She hinted that sorrows plagued Verwood and made its occupants unfit for gaiety.

A double row of elm trees screened the stables from his view as he passed, but he could hear the stirrings of men and *clip clop* of hooves and the imperious voice of the duchess. At seventy-nine she rode daily, and saw to the care of a full stable of horses who lived like equine kings with mountains of fresh straw each morning, buckets of oats, acres of pasture, and a small army of men to keep them sleek and groomed. Not to mention the services of Dick Crockett.

Raven stopped where the path crossed a long avenue through the formal garden of box hedges and plantings. From where he stood, the stones of Verwood's north face glowed honey gold. This was the place to ask for Lady

Amabel's hand. At night under a full moon with lanterns to illuminate the garden paths, and music spilling out of the great hall, he would lead her to a stone bench in the garden to make his proposal. A patch of grass on which to kneel would exactly suit his needs. If he knelt just so, Verwood would stand behind him. It filled him with a great deal of satisfaction that everything was in hand and moving forward.

As he looked from the bench to the hall, the crunch of gravel came from the outer path, and he recognized Lady Cassandra's uneven gait. He retraced his steps to meet her. Except for the gravel, she could have passed him without his notice, the plain brown of her pelisse and the pale green of her gown like the colors of the landscape itself. Only a basket over her arm filled with stalks of some vivid pink blossoms set her apart from the background. She gave him a cool nod as if she would pass by.

On impulse, he stepped into her path. "You've been avoiding me."

She checked her stride and responded to his challenge with a tilt of her head and a flash of her eyes under those strong brows that gave her face character.

"Have I? I'm sure you've been occupied with the work of renovating the hall. Are you pleased with how it's turned out?"

"I am. You should have warned me, you know."

Her gaze turned puzzled. "Warned you?"

There was something in that gaze that he hadn't seen among his neighbors. His new neighbors had showered him with such universal admiration that he would not have minded a bit of Her Grace's aloofness or a challenge from

Lady Cassandra. "About the relentless hospitality of our neighbors."

She laughed at that, a warm, unaffected laugh that transformed her face, lighting up her serious gray eyes.

"Don't laugh," he chided her. "I have performed heroic feats of eating, and had my toes trodden repeatedly by eager dance partners. All without any sharp looks from you."

"Ah," she said. "Too much treacle-soaked sponge cake and oyster-stuffed mutton?"

"Oyster-stuffed mutton?" he groaned. "At least I've been spared that."

"Oh right," she said. "The mutton is Mrs. Montford's special dish, and she postponed her dinner, didn't she?"

He nodded. "But now there's to be a picnic outing to some ruins. You can't escape that one, can you?"

Her eyes brimmed with teasing lights. "You must think me a very poor neighbor, but in truth, the vicar is the only person who is quite up to inviting us Verwood ladies, feeling as he does, that in the eyes of God there are no distinctions of rank."

"So, you'll come to the picnic." The prospect of the event instantly became more appealing with the thought of her company.

"It's a remarkable site, an abandoned Roman city, *Castellum de Castanea*, and the road to it leads through lovely country with excellent prospects all along the way."

"You've seen it?"

"As a girl. The place was discovered in the summer after Waterloo, by a farmer when his plow turned up an ancient pot. He called upon the experts, and they've since uncovered mosaic floors and ancient walls."

"You like that sort of thing, do you?" He had no idea whether she was keen on anything. Were women keen on things? The girls who swarmed around him in London had been interested in the whirl of parties, in dancing, and in his account of the great fire.

"I suppose what surprises me is seeing how cleverly the Romans lived. It encourages one's humility."

"Do you need to be encouraged in humility?"

"Is my grandmother a duchess?" She grinned at him.

"What's in the basket?" he asked.

"Willow herb. Do you mind my foraging in your woods?"

"Your grandmother's woods?"

"But you don't want to be tripping over me ... us on every path."

"Actually, you've made yourself invisible of late, and I wonder, what did I do to offend you?"

"Nothing." She studied the path, as if it held deep secrets, and he wanted her to look at him again with her usual frank openness.

"But you've kept your distance."

She gave a quick shrug. "You had everything in hand. You didn't need me looking over your shoulder."

"Still," he said, "there were times I could have used your opinion. I may have misjudged in the morning room, I think. The green-striped damask on the walls there might be a bit overpowering."

She spun to look at him, and he tried to maintain his gravity at the expression of horror on her face. It was too much and he burst out laughing.

"Oh, you are having me on." Her face changed again, and he almost caught his breath at the sudden prettiness of her, the smoothness of her cheek, the clear gray of her eyes, the perfect point of her heart-shaped chin.

"Am I?" he asked. "You won't know unless you come to the hall."

"What? Now? I interrupted. You were on your way ... somewhere."

"To make a circuit of the grounds. Will you walk with me? You could point out the beauties of Verwood. I want to know what to show my ... guests."

"Have you invited some guests?"

"I'm making a list."

She straightened and resettled the basket over her arm, and he sensed that he'd kept her as long as he could. "You should take them to the ice house. It's in the loveliest part of the woods and not far."

"You won't take a peek at the new ceiling in the great hall."

"No."

"But you promise to come to my ball. I won't take no for an answer."

She gave him a sad smile. "I think you must. Good day, Sir Adrian."

CHAPTER TWELVE

THE DAY OF Mrs. Montford's expedition to the nearby Roman ruins promised to be warm, and Raven was glad of an early start. The party made something of a parade with the ladies in carriages and the gentlemen riding. The dowager duchess, Miss Thornhill, Lady Cassandra, and a widow, Mrs. Duncan, rode in Her Grace's elegant yellow barouche. Mrs. Duncan and her son, a solicitor of forty-five, widowed like his mother, were the Montford's neighbors. In the Montford carriage were Mrs. Montford, her daughter Miranda, eighteen, and her sons, Henry, eleven, and Charles, nine. Behind the carriages came a wagon of picnic hampers and servants. Seven miles of pleasant road were accomplished in little over two hours so that they arrived at the Ruggles farm before the heat became oppressive. Mr. Ruggles, the farmer met them at his gate and showed them a shaded spot where the carriages and horses could be kept. There was an oak-studded hill to ascend to an overlook of the old Roman town.

Raven dismounted, and while he assisted the duchess and her party, the Montford boys leapt from their mother's carriage and charged up the hill, oblivious of their mother's cry to wait. Their father directed a stern admonition to the boys' backs not to descend to the ruins without the whole party. Raven had a brief word with Lady Cassandra and a touch of her hand in his before the party fell into three groups, two of picnickers and one of the servants with their burdens. Raven had only an instant to wonder how Lady Cassandra would manage with her foot before he was claimed by his hosts and their daughter.

From the top of the hill, Farmer Ruggles pointed out remains of the old Roman town that lay at the edge of his fields. It had once had four gates, a grid of streets, and beyond the town the round grass-covered mound of an old amphitheater. The antiquarians had uncovered the crumbled outlines in brick and cement of the walls of several buildings. The tallest of the old walls, more than thirty feet high, jutted straight out from the hillside with a series of arched niches. In the southeast corner of the site, a barnlike structure had been erected, which, Ruggles explained, covered a mosaic floor, and housed finds of Roman artifacts.

While Mr. Montford asked about the dates of the town and its likely connection to other Roman settlements, the two boys chased each other around the hilltop, waving sticks like swords. When the servants arrived with the picnic, Mrs. Montford turned her attention to directing their efforts, and Ruggles invited them all to descend. The duchess waved them on, and Miss Thornhill and widowed Mrs. Duncan stayed behind to assist. The boys raced straight down the hill and into the grid of streets, while their elders wound their way down a twisting path.

Raven found himself paired with Miss Montford. Ahead of him on the path, Lady Cassandra made her way unassisted down the hill.

"I hope my father didn't bore you," Miss Montford said. "He can prose on about his antiquities."

"Not at all." Raven offered his hand to help her over a rocky patch.

"I'm sure you'd prefer to be in London." She paused to look out over the ruined town, its ancient roads now grassy paths, and its former buildings, low mounds of rock-studded cement. Sticks and stakes protruded from the old walls and the ground, marking the work of the antiquarians. Overhead the sky was blue and the sun warm.

"What makes you think I'd rather be in London?" Raven asked.

"London is never dull, is it? And it's quite grand, I suppose, the balls, I mean."

They reached the bottom of the hill and began to stroll along a grassy lane. "I take it," Raven said, "that you'd like to go to London."

"I do wish I could, but Mama says the expense is not to be thought of, and that I must be content with our Wormley assemblies. I'm sure they can't compare with what you've seen."

"Is there never a grand ball in the neighborhood of Wormley? At one of the manor houses?"

"Not in forever. You mustn't think I'm fishing for you to give a ball, though."

He laughed.

"Would you give a ball? Verwood would be a lovely place for one." She peeped up at him from under the brim of her straw bonnet. "You must invite everyone young and no one dull and old."

"Are there many old dull people in Wormley?"

"Scores of them," she said with sudden vehemence. "Mama and Papa know them all. I daresay, you are the youngest gentleman ever to come to one of Mama's parties. Feebleness is a positive plague in the country."

Miss Montford's two brothers stood peering over Lady Cassandra's shoulder where she knelt to look at something, her blue skirts against the grass. "Your brothers hardly seem old or dull," he commented.

Miss Montford's gaze followed his. "But look what happens to people in the country," she said. "I'm sure Lady Cassandra was young once, but now she gets put in the carriage with the old people. And Mama invites Mr. Duncan for her. Lord, I never want to be *that* old."

"Do you regard four and twenty as past all hope then?" Raven kept his voice light. His companion's view of early onset decrepitude was amusing, but he didn't like Lady Cassandra being paired with Mr. Duncan. He supposed a man of forty-five could be drawn to a woman half his age, but Raven couldn't see Duncan as a fit suitor for Lady Cassandra in age or rank. The duchess wouldn't allow it.

In the center of the old town the sun beat down quite mercilessly. Miss Montford fumbled with her parasol, and Raven offered assistance.

Ahead of them on the grassy path, Henry, the older boy, straightened and held something aloft. "Look what we found," he shouted. The other members of the party, alerted by his cry, converged on the place where Lady Cassandra knelt. Mr. Montford reached the boys first and held up their find, a small light-colored blue-green bottle, rectangular in shape with a broken handle. Left to herself, Lady Cassandra came to her feet with some effort.

"Is it really old?" Henry asked.

"First or second century," Ruggles said. "We have found a good bit of glass, but mainly in fragments."

Henry took the bottle from his father and held it to his nose. "What was in it do you think?" he asked.

"I'm told," said Ruggles, "that the square shape likely means it was used for shipping, and this"—he gestured to the broad grassy path where they stood—"was likely their *Oxford Street* if you will, where the Romans did their shopping. So, I'd say, olive oil or fish sauce."

Henry jerked the bottle away from his nose, and they all laughed.

"Why the blue green?" asked Mr. Duncan.

"Iron oxide in the silica," Raven said. No one appeared to hear him except Lady Cassandra.

"Can we keep it?" Henry asked.

Mr. Ruggles shook his head. "But I'll show you how we mark our finds, and you shall be named as a finder."

Henry hung his head and mumbled something.

"Speak up, my boy," his father encouraged him.

"Can't say I found it. It was her." He pointed to Lady Cassandra.

"Ah," she said, smiling at Henry. "I saw the hint of blue in the soil, but you and Charlie dug it out with your sticks. You must have the credit."

"First," said Mr. Ruggles, "we put a numbered stake in the ground to mark the spot. Then, if you come along, boys, we'll add your names to our roll of finders."

"No thank you," said Henry. "May we keep looking? Charlie and I want to find something we can keep."

Mr. Ruggles laughed. "There's a raven's nest. Can you find that? The birds keep stealing our markers."

The boys' faces lit up. "May we, Papa?" Henry asked.

"One hour." Mr. Montford wiped his brow. "Don't miss your mother's picnic. Now Ruggles, take us to those mosaics."

The boys dashed off, and the rest of the party moved at a languid pace toward the area covered by a tall shed. Raven looked for an opportunity to walk with Lady Cassandra, but Mr. Duncan offered her his arm, and though she declined, she fell into step beside the widower.

Raven was used by now to her dipping walk and her refusal to accept help. One could not call her gait graceful, but her back was straight, her head high, and her movement had a character he could only call strength of will. She was far from decrepit.

Beside him, Miss Montford put her arm through Raven's, her parasol angled to shade her face. "I must say I have a poor idea of these Romans, if their Oxford Street was a narrow lane of fish sauce vendors."

"You think these Romans were a dull lot, here in the country."

"Their town did die," she said.

"Point taken," he agreed. He smiled at her. He had been marked to be her partner. If his plan for the day was a bust, the gentlemanly thing to do was to play the part he'd been handed with good grace. But he would do nothing to raise maidenly or maternal hopes. His interest lay elsewhere.

Miranda Montford was a pretty girl, fair-haired and rosy-cheeked with round blue eyes. He wondered that he didn't find her frankness engaging. It was not her fault that she lacked Amabel's unusual beauty or Lady Cassandra's wit.

Though the barnlike shed erected to protect the mosaic floor offered shade, it was quite warm inside the structure. A raised wooden walkway surrounded the old Roman floor with its outer border of blue and white tiles in interlocking loops and its central figure of a man on a raft in a stormy sea. When Mr. Montford identified the figure on the raft as Ulysses of the ancient epic and began to explain the story to Lady Cassandra and Mr. Duncan, Miss Montford tugged on Raven's arm and gave him a pleading look.

"It's too warm for Miss Montford," Raven said. "Let me get her into the air under the trees."

THEY WERE NOT long in the shade of the oaks at the top of the hill, before the rest of the party joined them. Raven was glad to see that Lady Cassandra did not appear fatigued.

Cloth-covered platters filled two tables. The older ladies of the party sat in folding chairs, and rugs spread on the ground invited the rest of the party. A welcome puff of breeze stirred the air. There was a bit of bustle and milling about with Mrs. Montford advising them all of the menu and directing her guests to places on the rugs. Once again, the arrangement separated Raven from Lady Cassandra. He saw Miss Montford settled on a patch of rug and went to procure her some lemonade. As a maid poured, he looked over a platter of sandwiches.

Lady Cassandra appeared at his side. "What do think?" she asked. "The soused lamb, or the cold chicken?"

He glanced at her flushed cheeks and bright eyes. The lace at her bodice clung to her warm skin. "Where is your suitor?" he asked. The question, which had unexpectedly popped into his mind, sounded cross even in his own ears.

Her brows went up. "Mr. Duncan, who is *not* my suitor, is very properly seeing to his mother's comfort. And, if you don't wish to offend our hostess, go for the soused lamb. It's her specialty."

She turned away, leaving Raven staring at the sandwiches and cursing his own clumsiness in shutting down the only conversational opening she'd offered him all day. He chose the soused lamb for himself and the cold chicken for Miss Montford. With any luck the heat would soon put an end to the picnic.

CASSIE SIPPED HER lemonade and picked at her sandwich, breaking it into bites. No one paid any attention to her. The Romans had not disappointed, but it was lovely to sit in the shade and feel the breeze. A few gray-bellied clouds sailed past overhead, fluffy harbingers of rain.

Cassie was only slightly vexed with Sir Adrian. She could not blame him for thinking of Mr. Duncan as her suitor. Plainly, Mrs. Montford had included him in the party so that Miranda could have Sir Adrian to herself. Cassie hoped his attention to the girl had raised no expectations. She supposed he was waiting for Lady Amabel's arrival in the country to reveal where his heart lay.

A little cry from Mrs. Montford interrupted her thoughts. "My strawberry tarts!" She held a checked cloth above an empty plate.

Her husband came to her side. "What is it, my dear?"

"My tarts are gone."

"All of them?"

Mrs. Montford glanced around. "Where are the boys?"

"They've gone in search of a raven's nest."

Mrs. Duncan shuddered. "Nasty, ill-omened creatures with their great beaks."

Sir Adrian stiffened but said nothing. Cassie rose to her feet. "Clever and cheeky more like," she said, looking at him.

She had spotted the nest earlier as they'd come up the hill from the ruins. It sat in a hollow where the old masonry had crumbled at the end of the standing wall that protruded from the hillside. She doubted the boys could reach the nest, but they could easily eat all the tarts. She turned to the Montford's. "I know where the nest is."

"Can you show us?" Mr. Montford asked.

Cassie led the way, and Mr. Montford, Mr. Duncan, and Sir Adrian followed. As they approached the spot where the narrow wall jutted out from the hill, a series of frantic guttural cries rent the air. Cassie halted, her heart in her throat, at the sight of the boys. Henry sat midway along the top of the crumbling wall, his legs dangling on either side, an airy gap and a steep drop in front of him. Below Henry, Charlie clung to the jutting stones of the wall's face, his feet on a narrow ledge. A huge raven made a diving pass at

Henry, and he ducked, flattening himself against the top of the wall.

Cassie pointed to a large, basket-like mound of twigs in a hollow above the last arch at least thirty feet from the ground. "There must be fledglings in the nest."

Mr. Montford halted a few paces ahead of Cassie, where the curve of the hill turned sharply down to meet the wall. "Henry," he shouted, "come back at once!"

"I can't," cried the boy. The raven dove again, skimming over the top of the clinging child.

"Papa," Charlie wailed from his niche. "I'm stuck, too."

Sir Adrian turned to Cassie with a mute appeal and offered his hand. Whatever he had in mind, she took his hand. They scrambled down the hill where the slope was gentler, using tufts of grass like stepping stones, Mr. Duncan following behind them. At the bottom, Sir Adrian studied the wall as he stripped off his coat and boots, and rolled up his shirt sleeves. "Talk to Charlie. Keep him calm. I must get to Henry first."

"Cole," Mr. Duncan protested, "You can't mean to climb that thing. Sheer madness!" "Unless you have a ladder handy, Duncan, I see nothing for it but to climb."

Cassie positioned herself under the younger boy's perch. High as he was, maybe two body lengths above her, Charlie must have had an easy climb until he reached the niche, a rough patch of irregular cobble-like stones stuck in crumbling cement. With each hand he clutched one of the protruding stones, his feet on a narrow ledge.

"Charlie," she called. "I'm standing below you. Hang on!"

"I can't. I can't. The bird will get me." The rising breeze ruffled the boy's shirt.

"Charlie, were you trying to help Henry?" Cassie tried to distract him.

"I was. Then the birds got angry."

"They have babies in their nest. They want to keep you away."

"The bird will peck me," he cried.

"He won't if you put your face to the stones."

Cassie looked over her shoulder for Sir Adrian. He climbed with nimble assurance, finding hand and toeholds in the brick work at the lower end of the wall. The latent strength she had sensed in him from their first meeting was now plain in the easy play of his arms and back as he climbed. Where the lintel of an ancient door made a ledge, he pulled himself up into the open arch below the nest. His nearness drew the bird, and the raven swooped at him, screeching and clawing the air above his head. He reached around a narrow pillar, and took hold of a jutting brick. It broke away, and a portion of the wall showered down. Charlie wailed again.

"I can't hold on anymore," he cried.

"Yes, you can, Charlie." Cassie stepped up to the wall, and put her good foot on a row of stones at the base. Above and to her right, Sir Adrian changed direction.

Taking hold of a narrow pillar, Cassie pulled herself up. She grasped the pillar and pressed her face to the warm stones, finding her balance. There was no way she could reach the boy.

"Charlie," she called. "Look up. Watch Sir Adrian."

"Lady Cassandra, come down," Mr. Duncan ordered.

"I'm staying with Charlie."

"Charlie," Sir Adrian shouted. "Get ready. I'm going to take your arm and hand you down to Mr. Duncan."

Stones rolled and bounced down the side of the old wall. Then Sir Adrian cried, "Got you." Charlie yelped, and Cassie saw him hanging in the air beside her.

In an instant, Duncan came forward to grab the boy. Cassie slid her hand down the pillar at her side and lowered her good foot toward the ground. Another shower of stones rained down, and her foot slipped. Her knee banged hard against the stones.

Then Mr. Duncan took her arm, pulled her from the wall. Her bad foot landed hard, as he spun her to face him. "Lady Cassandra, one hardly knows what to say to a woman of your years. There was no occasion for you to endanger yourself. You have been foolish beyond permission."

Cassie gently disengaged herself from his hold. "Have I? Your concern is no doubt kindly meant, Mr. Duncan, but a woman of *my years* decides for herself what the occasion requires."

Charlie scrambled up the hill to his father, and Cassie turned back to Sir Adrian. He'd reached the broken level of the wall directly below Henry, so that the flattened boy and the man were face-to-face. The angry raven still dove at them, but Sir Adrian spoke quietly to the boy, keeping Henry's focus on him. The wind snatched away their words, but at last Henry sat up, his hands on the top of the wall. Then, at a nod from Sir Adrian, the boy began to inch his bottom along the wall toward the hill. When there was room, Sir Adrian hoisted himself up. And together they worked their way toward the hillside. The raven wheeled up into the air and descended above the nest, still protesting with raucous cries. Mr. Montford sent Charlie running for the others.

It went against the grain, but Cassie allowed Mr. Duncan to help her up the hill. The breeze grew stronger, and the clouds came thicker as they climbed.

By the time Sir Adrian and Henry reached the place where the wall met the steep slope, Charlie had returned with the two coachmen. The duchess's man lay flat in the grass and stretched his arms down the slope, while the other men grasped his ankles. Sir Adrian helped Henry turn to face the hill and stand, and finally to reach up until the coachman grabbed the boy's hands. The men at the top began to pull the coachman back from the edge, and Henry got his feet under him against the hill. In the blink of an eye, the boy was over the top and safely in his father's arms, sobbing his relief.

As the first raindrops fell, Sir Adrian stood outlined against sky and cloud, tall and straight, like some performer in Astley's circus. Cassie could not look away. He might be Sir Adrian Cole to the world, but in her mind, he must be Raven. Mr. Kydd's account of their boyhood adventures which she had taken as fantasy must be true. Raven moved swiftly along the top of the wall and where it fell away to the lower level, he crouched and dropped lightly down into the broken arch. He lowered himself over the edge and worked his way down the face of the wall. Only when he reached the ground and took up his coat and boots, could she turn away.

The party at the top of the hill moved quickly to their picnic spot under the oaks, the two coachmen in advance. As they went, Mr. Montford scolded, and the boys, scratched and sun burned, bore their father's anger. Charlie stopped once to cast up what appeared to be the remains of strawberry tart. The picnic area was empty when they reached it except for Mrs. Montford's serving girl, who explained that the carriages awaited them. The two coachmen hurried on down the hill.

Cassie reluctantly accepted Mr. Duncan's arm. At least he was still cross with her, so no conversation was required. For once she had no reason to regret her faltering walk, but Raven did not catch up before they reached her grandmama's carriage. She had no chance to tell him of her meeting with Jay Kydd. In the rain, no further delay was possible. The carriage top had been put up, and Mr. Duncan handed Cassie in beside his mother. The ladies exclaimed at once about the stain on her gown from her bloodied knee.

CHAPTER THIRTEEN

ON ENTERING LADY Huntingdon's ball, Raven was obliged to stop and exchange pleasantries with a number of guests, including his friend Ned Farrington. It was the first moment since his arrival in London that he'd stood still. Even in his dreams he'd been running and then crawling, scrambling down a narrow, dark passage. He hadn't had that dream in years, and he could only suppose that it returned because he'd climbed that Roman wall. At the time the incident brought back memories of Wenlocke and the others, but since Raven's return to the city, he'd remembered the earlier time on his own before the gang had taken him in.

Or maybe it was London itself that had brought on the dream. He'd grown used to the quiet of the country and the freshness of its air. London didn't sleep. By day, the whole vast city labored. By night, the rich partied under brilliant lights, while others plied unsavory trades in the dark, and the weary slept uneasily.

Lady Huntingdon's ballroom was warm and brilliant with light. The babble of talk and music was loud. The competing scents of perfume and persons made a mix that even the pots of white blooms around the perimeter of the room could not disguise with their powerful fragrance.

Judging from the crowd, Lady Huntingdon could call her ball a crush. He and Ned stepped away from the reception line to stand just above the ballroom.

"Did you find a place in the country to suit you?" Ned asked.

"Verwood, do you know it?" Raven let his gaze scan the room. It was easily eighty feet in length. A dance was in progress, and the center of the room looked like a swirling sea of pale silks and black evening wear with feathers bobbing on the surface. He could not see Amabel.

"Verwood's not the duke's seat, is it? I thought he had a place in Kent."

"He does. The hall is a small property he deeded to his mother, the dowager, when he succeeded to the title."

"Right." Ned nodded. "I know the name. There's some old scandal attached to it."

"Anything I should know?"

"I doubt it. Just a bit of old tittle tattle. Where is the lovely Amabel?"

"I'm looking." Amabel would be dancing, not languishing about waiting for him. If he did not spot her at once, it was not that he'd forgotten her, only that one bobbing, feathered female head looked very much like another.

"I leave you to it, then." Ned clapped him on the shoulder. "I'm off for the card room."

The set ended, and as the floor cleared, Raven spotted Amabel. She wore the white silk of a debutante, her gown low across her shoulders and fitted to her waist. Peach silk ribbons threaded through the lace of her bodice gave a glow to her complexion. Her golden curls were caught up in more peach ribbons on either side of her face. Silk dancing slippers peeped from beneath her ankle-length skirts. She came straight to him, and he released a breath he'd been holding. He had been right after all to return to London. She was everything he wanted, fair and lively, with dancing blue eyes in a heart-shaped face, and a quick, lightness of motion that brought her to his side in a flash.

Across the room, the companions she'd left behind simply gaped after her.

"Where have you been?" she tapped his arm with her fan. "I thought you were coming to the Drummond party."

"I meant to be there," he said. "There was a fire…" It had been another test of the new Cole engines. This time the fire had spread from a cloth warehouse to a street of crowded lodgings.

"A fire? Oh well, I suppose that will do for an excuse." She linked her arm in his, and they began to walk. "It has been so dull here without you." Her mouth contracted into a little moue.

"I doubt that you've been dull. Not you. You never could be dull."

"But aren't you afraid to be away from me?"

"Should I be?" He shook off a fleeting recollection of gray eyes under dark brows in another face.

"I have had offers, you know." She peeped up at him.

"Have you?" He looked down into her perfect face with its smooth cheeks and smoky lashes under the elaborate coiffure, which she could never manage on her own.

She tapped his arm with her fan again. "You knew I would. How could I not? It is only what is expected in a girl's first Season. It's a feather in a girl's cap to bag a viscount or an earl. But no one like you."

"Are you telling me there's a queue?"

"Only Alcock and Somerton. I thought you were never coming back. And now we've only a fortnight left in London, and then when will I see you again?"

"I could take a house near you for the summer." He wanted to keep Verwood a surprise.

"Would you? Even if London were to burn to the ground?"

"Let it burn." It was a reckless declaration. He was quite busy with new orders for their engines and discussions with Braidwood about how to better organize London's resources against fire. He and Grandfather Cole were having their perpetual argument about employing boys and girls in the ironworks. Grandfather said they were cheap, their small fingers were essential for some of the more intricate parts of the machines, and their families needed the earnings. Raven argued that they could earn more for their families if they got an education first. He did not remind Grandfather Cole that he, Raven, had crawled under spinning mules for bits of cotton until a boy not much bigger than himself had helped him run away.

Again, Amabel's little moue appeared, an attractive pursing of her full lower lip that made a man want to kiss away her troubles. "But there are no suitable houses near us."

"What none?" He supposed she didn't think of Verwood because the family had hardly advertised the place.

"I'll ask Mother. She'll know."

"Where is your mother? I should pay my respects."

"She's in the card room, so we can dance all we like."

"Living dangerously, are you?"

"There's so little time, and we must make the most of it. Lady Huntingdon's orchestra is not very good, but I suppose that with the right partner I won't care."

Raven hadn't noticed any flaw in the music, but he hadn't a trained ear. Amabel was adept at the harp, a difficult instrument. "By all means, let us dance then."

Couples began to take to the floor for a waltz, and Raven led Amabel to a place in the circle of dancers. One of her gloved hands settled in his, and the other touched lightly on his shoulder. He put a hand to her waist, secure in its fortress of whalebone and buckram, and the lilting waltz began. It was like moving in a dream, floating, effortlessly, borne up by the music.

He grinned down at her. Her forehead creased in a tiny frown.

"What am I to call you?" she asked. "*Sir Adrian* sounds stiff and formal, and Mr. Cole sounds so … plain."

"Would a title please you?"

Her eyes brightened. "I don't depend on your having a title, of course. It is only that your wife will be plain…"

"…Lady Cole. You don't want to be Lady Cole."

"It's a small thing. It hardly matters to me, you know. I will always be an earl's daughter, but it would be nice for children, if there are children someday. You could get a title, you know, a real title. It would have to be a new patent, like the ones from three years ago, but you have such achievements, you deserve one."

"You know I make things go my way. If Lady Amabel

wants me to have a title, I'll find a way. My friend Wenlocke might help."

"Wenlocke?"

He nodded.

"You didn't tell me you knew Wenlocke. I thought Ned Farrington was your only titled friend."

"I've known Wenlocke since we were boys."

She smiled at him again with her breathtaking smile. "But what am I to call you then?"

He cocked his head, pretending to consider the problem, and whirled her deeper into the dance. It was on the tip of his tongue to tell her to call him *Raven*. But Amabel belonged to his new life, not the old.

"*Cole* is too plain. What about Colin, Cornelius, Augustus, or Fitzwilliam?"

CHAPTER FOURTEEN

IN THE TWO days of rain that followed the Montford picnic, Cassie had no opportunity to walk, no chance to see Sir Adrian. She helped Honoria shelve her books and tried not to worry overmuch about any delay in telling their tenant of her encounter with Mr. Kydd. She felt that once she told Sir Adrian, her odd freak of pretending to be Bluebell would appear in its proper light, not as a deception, but as a lark of sorts, and not as an attempt to ferret out truths about his past as a boy called Raven.

On the third day, the sun came out, and Grandmama returned from the stables before nine to insist that Cassie come at once to help with Sir Adrian's messenger boys.

"He's gone and left them to get up to every sort of mischief."

"Gone?" Cassie looked up from a stack of books on the floor.

"Off to London, of course. Now those boys are idle and up to no good."

"Oh," Honoria said, "he's not *gone*." She gave Cassie a questioning look. "He's *away*."

Cassie pulled herself together. The brief alarm passed. She was annoyed at herself for being susceptible to it. Of course, Sir Adrian wasn't gone. He had plans. He was to give a summer ball. His messenger boys were still here.

Grandmama flashed an impatient glare at Honoria. "Don't quibble about words, Honoria. Cassie, you know those boys. Get them sorted. They can't remain idle and underfoot, and I can't have them wandering about either. They'll spook the horses."

Cassie turned to Honoria, standing in front of her writing table. "I'll return as soon as I can, Aunt."

"You go, love. We've made great progress." Honoria gestured at the piles of books on the floor. "We're sorted. We just need to shelve."

Grandmama sniffed and turned on her heel. Cassie gave her aunt a quick hug.

SHE ARRIVED AT the stables with a basket of sandwiches from Cook, expecting from Grandmama's report to find mayhem. But the stables had an air of quiet busyness that made her think that her grandmother had exaggerated the boys' antics. Then she found them.

Over the past weeks, she'd come to know their names. Joe, Ben, and Tim were roughly the same age, which Cassie guessed to be eight. They were skinny and ruddy-cheeked with almost identical mops of brown hair and thick London accents that often required her to ask for repetition. Sir Adrian had outfitted them in gray wool breeches and caps, blue shirts, and sturdy shoes. Now they sat, unmoving, gazing into Hermes's open stall.

As Cassie approached, Hermes sensed her, and tossed his

head. The boys looked up and Joe, who seemed to be their leader, put a finger to his lips. Cassie glanced into the stall and met Dick Crockett's gaze. Dick smiled and gave her his greeting sign. Cassie nodded in reply.

"Please, Lady C," Joe whispered. "Don't make us leave. Dick lets us watch 'im."

"I won't," Cassie whispered back. She wondered how Dick had made their acquaintance and even more how he had got them to sit quietly.

"'e's softening the 'orse," said Joe.

Cassie nodded. She was familiar with the ritual with which Dick always began his work. He wanted a horse to stand and let him hold its hooves, but first he wanted to know that the horse had no injuries or lingering pain that would make the animal uneasy. Perhaps because Dick's primary language was a language of gesture, he used his hands to talk to horses.

She began to lower herself to the floor beside the boys when Joe held up a hand. "Wait Lady C." He dashed off down the main aisle of stalls and returned with a stool for her to sit on.

Meanwhile, Dick, in his leather apron with his sleeves rolled up, stood on Hermes's near side, his left hand below Hermes's shoulder, his right moving gently up from Hermes's left eye, over the poll, and along a line just below the ridge of the neck and withers. As Hermes grew easy under the gentle touch, Cassie marveled again at the youth's way with animals.

The boys, to her surprise, sat unmoving, and she wondered what they'd been up to that had prompted her grandmother's complaint. And how Dick had managed to cast a spell over them. When Hermes's head drooped and his eyes began to close in drowsy contentment, Dick grinned at Cassie and the boys. He examined each of Hermes's hooves in turn, applying a hoof pick when needed, and then stepped away from the horse and out of the stall, closing the door behind him.

He signaled with a finger to his lips for the boys to remain silent. Then he led them out of the stables. Outside in the sun, the boys immediately fell into a shoving match. Until Cassie cried, "Stop."

"Lady C," began Joe. "Do you speak Dick's sign language?"

"A very little," she said.

"I'm learning," said Ben.

"A fat lot you know," said Tim.

"Wot we want to know, Lady C," said Joe, "is, can that 'orse run? Can 'ermes run? Is 'e fast? 'e looks fast."

"We think," said Ben, "that Dick knows."

Cassie turned to Dick, and made the sign that she knew meant *question*. She both spoke the question, and pantomimed with her fingers the motion of running.

Dick appeared to comprehend instantly, and nodded vigorously. He signed for the boys, and let them mimic his gestures. From the pocket of his leather apron, he drew a pad and a pencil. He wrote, *Snell runs Hermes in his pasture. No saddle. No rider.*

Cassie borrowed Dick's pad and pencil and wrote. "*Does my grandmother know?*"

Dick nodded.

Cassie shook her head. She wondered at the concealment. Here was Grandmama forbidding Cassie to go near the horse, but secretly allowing Hermes to run. It made no sense, but her grandmother answered to no one. She could do what she liked with her horses. Still Cassie resolved to speak to her grandmother. To the boys, Cassie said, "Hermes can run, and if you get on Mr. Snell's good side, you can probably watch him."

"Mr. Snell doesn't like us," said Joe.

"'e sez we cause trouble," added Ben. "But we only come on account of Mr. K."

Joe and Tim turned on Ben and offered him a flurry of whacks with their caps.

After the blows and Ben's yelps subsided Cassie asked, "Mr. K?"

His companions glared at Ben.

"It's only the stable boys that don't like us, Lady C," said Tim. "They sez we want to take their jobs and we have no place 'ere. It's war between us and 'em." He punched the air with his fist.

"Oh dear," said Cassie. "A stable is no place for a war. I think you need to tell me what Mr. K has to do with it."

The boys' expressions turned sheepish.

Cassie held up her basket. "I have sandwiches. Mr. K is Mr. Kydd?"

"'e is, Lady C," Joe admitted. "Gave us each a bob to spy for 'im."

"Spy?"

"'e wants us to find out if 'ermes can run. Mr. K said 'e'd give us more when 'e comes back if we see the 'orse run."

"Ah," said Cassie. "And do you know when he will return?"

The boys looked at each other, and shrugged.

Cassie refused to be uneasy about Mr. Kydd's return. She would simply tell Sir Adrian and Mr. Kydd about Bluebell and be done with it. Another thought occurred. Maybe the boys could spy for her and warn her when the two gentlemen returned. In the meantime she would see for herself how Hermes was doing and tell her grandmother that she, Cassie, was ready to ride again.

She squared her shoulders. "Shall we go eat and talk about how to end this war and how you can earn that bob?"

ON THE MORNING after his return from London, common courtesy required that Raven call upon the ladies of the dower house. His young messengers were hanging about to see Jay Kydd, so Raven sent Joe to ask when the ladies might be available to receive him. Joe returned promptly with the reply that Lady C was on her way to pay him a call. Raven left the boys waiting for Kydd to finish a hearty country breakfast, and set out to meet his landlady in the lane.

Verwood was lovelier than he remembered. The trees in leaf overhead changed the quality of light, and scents he couldn't name filled the air. When he reached the lane that branched off the carriage drive, he saw Lady Cassandra coming toward him with her characteristic lurching stride. He had counted on his stay in London to obscure the strong impression she'd made on his senses, but seeing her brought back the press of her hand in his and her steadiness when the Montford boys were in trouble. She was altered, too. A deep blue riding habit clung to her light figure.

Coming up to him, she halted. "How was your trip?"

"I didn't know you rode." He spoke the thing that was on his mind.

One of her dark brows quirked quizzically upward. "I've just returned to it after … some time. You must have heard someone speak of the *accident*."

"Only that there was an accident. Were you thrown?"

"No, though perhaps I deserved to be for riding a young horse so hard and so far."

"I cannot imagine you careless of a horse."

"It is good of you to think well of me, but in this case, I don't deserve your admiration." Her frank gaze didn't falter. "Will you walk with me? I am headed for the stables, and wanted a private word with you."

"A private word?" he said. "Intriguing, but first, will you tell me about the accident?"

"I think I must," she said.

"Only if you want to. I would rather hear of it from you than from your neighbors."

She sent him a wry glance. "Yes. I think it is better to hear things directly from those involved rather than secondhand, don't you?"

He nodded.

"Very well, then. It was dark and late, and Hermes and I were tired from a long, cross-country run. He was a bit lame, and I was leading him along the road. We were nearly home when a carriage came around a corner fast. Its lanterns flashed in Hermes's eyes. He reared and came down hard on my foot. When I reached for his lead, his head hit mine, and I was knocked into the ditch. I must have fainted. He stayed with me until Snell found me in the morning." She gave a dismissive little shrug. "Old history."

It was his turn to offer a wry smile. "I'm guessing that your physician's attention was directed at the head injury."

"It was. My foot had swollen in the boot, and when they cut away the leather to examine the break, it was decided to wait for the swelling to subside. Then the bones fused."

It did not surprise him that she spoke in her usual matter-of-fact way. He was curious about the foot whether anything had been tried to repair it, but he sensed that her revelations were at an end. They walked on toward the stable courtyard where he was used to waiting for the dowager's permission to enter.

He had first learned to recognize steadiness under fire as a boy in Wenlocke's gang, and he'd come to value it more as he worked with firefighting crews in London. Lady Cassandra's steadiness had impressed him from the beginning of their acquaintance. Seeing the Montford boys on the crumbling wall, he had reached for her hand instinctively, sensing that she would be of more assistance than the distraught father or the scolding neighbor.

They reached the stable courtyard and halted. "Thank you for telling me."

She nodded. "You've got me off track. I came to meet you in the lane to tell you something quite different."

"I'm listening."

"I have a confession to make." For once, she did not

meet his gaze.

"You? A confession?" It was the last thing he expected from her.

"Yes. Before you left for London, before ... the ceiling fell, I met your friend Mr. Kydd."

Raven stiffened and hardly knew why. Jay had not mentioned meeting Lady Cassandra, but why should he? Raven was conscious of an instant surge of male jealousy, to which he was not entitled. He had no claim on her. She was merely his landlady, one of them, at any rate. He could not claim to have *discovered* her, this unusual woman hidden away on an obscure estate who fit her surroundings so perfectly.

"There's more," she said. "I didn't give him my name. I let him call me Bluebell and encouraged him to think I was a girl from the village."

She was Jay's village girl. The one Jay enjoyed flirting with. "You met him more than once?"

"Twice," she said. "I meant to tell you on the day of the picnic, but we were occupied with other concerns."

"Was there something between you and Kydd that you felt you needed to *confess*?" He used her word.

"Not at all. Your friend is a flirt and a tease, but I doubt his heart can be won by any two-legged creature, least of all one like me. Of course, I owe him an apology for the deception. I believed he would change his manner to me if he knew my true name, or perhaps he wouldn't talk to me at all."

Raven thought she had an odd opinion of herself not to recognize the nature of Jay Kydd's attentions to her. "He didn't offer you any insult, did he?"

"Never. But I must tell you—"

"What?" He spoke too quickly, too sharply.

She gave him a puzzled look. "He told me that you were, are, *Raven*. And," she said, "I confess, I think the name suits you. Is that impertinent of me?"

She stunned him. Whatever name he'd had as a boy before Wenlocke called him *Raven* was lost along with the memories of that dark time that only haunted him in dreams. *Raven* was the name that had given him courage and friends. Yet his grandfather never used the name, and Raven himself had not told it to Amabel. The name was a part of his old self that he put aside in his new life as a gentleman until Lady Cassandra spoke it and brought it into the present. She had some quality that his grandfather and Amabel lacked. Raven could not name it, but it was there in her defense of Dick Crockett and in her defense of ravens at the picnic. She had called them clever, cheeky birds. She saw in the name the courage it was meant to inspire.

The clop of hooves and the sound of boys' voices brought him back to the present. "So, you knew. That day you knew?"

"Yes, I hope there will be no awkwardness between us."

"That's why you told me about the accident, isn't it?"

"I admit that I was inclined to think Mr. Kydd's tales of your youthful exploits on the rooftops of London were fanciful, until I saw you climb that ruin."

"You still think I am an acceptable tenant for Verwood?" He had seen nothing in her manner to indicate that his old name had changed her opinion of him, but he had to ask.

"Oh," she said with a grin, "a most acceptable tenant.

You pay the rent."

He laughed. She was not a woman to inflate a man's sense of himself, but there was something in her calm acceptance of imperfections that he liked.

"Anyway," she said. "I will disabuse Mr. Kydd of the notion that I am Bluebell. So you need not fear that he will make further disclosures of your misspent youth. Did you know that he employed your messengers to spy on Hermes while you were away?"

"That does not surprise me. Jay has been horse-mad as long as I've known him."

"I hope you won't mind if I encourage him to nudge Grandmama to train Hermes."

"Ah," he said. "You *do* mean to be rid of me as a tenant."

She gave him a questioning look. "What makes you think that?"

"If Hermes wins prizes and your grandmother reopens her stud, you won't need to lease the hall."

"First," she said. "Hermes has to be willing to accept a rider. He's had a long stretch of freedom."

"Wait," he said. "Is that why you've donned a habit? You're not seriously considering riding him, are you?"

Her expression changed to one of gentle sorrow. "I'm not the rider for Hermes, but I will sit on his back today and show him that he's not to blame for any ... of this, of the changes here. He is young and strong, and perhaps Mr. Kydd will know someone to ride him as he deserves to be ridden."

"Of course," he said. It made sense that she would turn to Jay Kydd for advice about a horse. Jay would be helpful and knowing. Raven just wished his friend were not so charming.

"Bluebell!"

At the cry, Cassie turned. Jay Kydd strode toward them, his face darkened by a frown.

"What's this, Raven? You've turned poacher on me. I thought the only rule was to stay away from *earls'* daughters." Kydd turned his glare on Cassie.

"Mr. Kydd, I beg your pardon," Cassie said. "I owe you an explanation."

"Who are you then?" Kydd demanded.

"Jay, may I present Lady Cassandra Lavenham," said Raven.

"You're Her Grace's granddaughter?" Kydd stiffened, and his expression changed from wrath to chagrin. He gave Cassie a brief, formal bow. "Well, my lady, I guess the joke is on me."

"Mr. Kydd," said Cassie, extending her hand. "I apologize for the deception. You were never meant to be the object of a joke. I thought only that you might not speak to me if you believed I was a person of … rank."

"Like your grandmother?" He cocked a brow at her. His gaze took in her blue riding habit, which, she had to admit, was just what Grandmama would wear.

"Yes, but you will forgive me." He still hadn't taken her hand, but she refused to bend.

"Will I?"

"Yes. Because I'm going to take you to see Hermes run and help you talk Grandmama round to letting him race."

The play of expressions on Kydd's face was comical, offended male pride warring with his mad love of horses.

At last, he shook her hand, and his grin broke through. "You do know how to get around a man. What am I to call you then?"

The three messenger boys surrounded Kydd, tugging at his coat. "We calls 'er Lady C," announced Joe. "And you owe us a bob each."

"Lady C it is, then," said Kydd. He dug in his pocket and produced a jingle of coins, dropping one in each of the boys' outstretched hands. "Let's see that horse."

DELAYED BY THE conversation with Raven and Jay Kydd, Cassie and the little crowd she'd gathered moved into the stable. Days earlier, Cassie had told her grandmother her intention to ride. Things had to change even if Cassie must endure the perpetual frost of Grandmama's displeasure. This morning Cassie meant to make a beginning. She hadn't counted on a full escort. Only Raven would miss the event. With his characteristic change from warmth to cool distance, he had bowed and taken himself off. It was Dick Crockett who opened the stall and went to stand at Hermes's head. The boys settled on the stable floor, and Cassie stood next to Dick, talking to the horse, watching his ears and tail. Jay Kydd offered Hermes a sniff of Cassie's old tack, letting the horse catch the scent of her on the old bridle and saddle.

Then, with quick, light hands, he put them on the horse.

"You'll take me for a ride won't you, boy?" she asked the horse. Hermes, she thought, must wonder at the crowd he'd drawn to his stall, but he seemed to take their attention in stride. The plan was for Cassie to take a short ride around Grandmama's largest paddock. It was laughable really to make such a production of the thing. Before her accident, Cassie would have slipped away on her own without even a groom and ridden across miles of open countryside. Today, after Hermes's jaunt around the paddock, he would be free to run in his usual pasture.

At a nod from Kydd, Cassie and Dick stepped away, and Kydd led Hermes from his stall.

Their small party trooped out to the stable courtyard, where, as luck would have it, they met the dowager returning from her morning ride on Arabella, her favorite bay mare. Mr. Snell was with her on Mercury, a chestnut gelding, another of her grandmother's favorites. The horses whinnied and danced, and two other grooms rushed forward to help settle the animals. The dowager dismounted without assistance, and faced Cassie and Mr. Kydd. She gave Dick Crockett a quick sharp glance that questioned his loyalty.

"What's this?" she demanded. "An invasion?"

"Grandmama, I believe you've met Mr. Kydd and know Kydd Brothers, his family's firm in London."

"Your grace." Kydd bowed.

"Don't *your grace* me, young man. I won't have you telling me how to run my stables no matter how many horses your uncle sells in London."

"Never ma'am," said Mr. Kydd.

"So, what are you about then?" The dowager fixed her sternest glare on him.

"I hear, ma'am, that there's a July meeting at Chichester."

"Grandmama," Cassie intervened, "I'm going to ride Hermes around his paddock. No galloping, no jumping. I merely want him to know that he is not to blame for the past." She lifted her chin. She should be afraid, but she wasn't. "It is time to put the accident behind us for me and for Hermes."

"And you need this scurvy lot around you for courage, do you?"

"These are Hermes's staunchest admirers, who only want to see him run, as he was meant to run. He has been running, hasn't he, Grandmama, in secret, under Mr. Snell's watchful eye?"

Mr. Snell looked away.

"Mere exercise to keep him sound and strong. No horse of mine will grow fat and lazy."

Cassie wanted to tell Grandmama what a fraud she was. "And if Hermes has kept sound and strong, will you let him race?"

"Hah! You have no idea of the work required to bring a horse to the field. By July? You're dreaming, girl." Her grandmother glared at her.

"It's work you know well, Grandmama, and you have those who are willing to help, and if we start now…"

"That horse hasn't carried a rider in three years."

"But he will today." Cassie refused to bend.

"Very well. See that you don't break another limb." Her

grandmother turned away and strode into the stable. Snell followed with the two grooms leading the other horses.

Cassie drew a deep breath.

"Still game?" Kydd asked her.

"Still game," she replied, and turned toward the paddock. The boys dashed ahead and scrambled up onto the fence. Dick Crockett opened the gate. Kydd led Hermes inside. He stepped high and tossed his head, but under Kydd's influence, he stood at the mounting block.

"How do you want to do this?" Kydd asked.

"I don't know," she said with a laugh, suddenly conscious that when she put her damaged foot in Kydd's linked hands, the uncooperative foot was likely to crumple.

Kydd stepped back and studied the situation for a moment. He signaled to Dick Crockett, who stepped up to hold Hermes's head and keep him calm.

"Here's what we'll do. Take hold of the high pommel, and keep one hand on my right shoulder. Ready?"

Cassie did as he suggested, putting her foot in his hands, taking hold of the sidesaddle's pommel. Kydd's shoulder was solid and steady under her other hand. He lifted his linked palms, while she pushed against his shoulder, and then she was in the saddle on Hermes's back, her knees around the two pommels, her back straight, her body centered on the horse. Hermes took a few dancing steps to the right and then settled, alert, waiting for her command. She stroked his neck. The boys whistled and hooted.

For a moment she simply enjoyed the familiar symmetry of being aligned with a horse and the sense of Hermes's power and sure-footedness under her. She gave him the command to walk on, and he began to circle the paddock. She and Hermes moved as one. Her body stayed straight in the saddle without the listing jolt of her walk, and hot tears stung her eyes. It was daft to feel so happy. She dashed away the stupid tears, and patted Hermes's neck. He was as perfectly behaved as she'd thought he'd be. When they reached the far end of the paddock and turned back toward the little crowd watching them, Cassie thought she saw the blue of her grandmother's habit disappear into the stable. Cassie shortened the reins, leaned forward, and gave Hermes the command to trot. He moved smoothly into the jaunty, faster gait that lifted her in the saddle. Once again they made a circuit of the paddock, showing off a little, rider and horse in unison, until she brought Hermes to a halt before his admirers. Dick was the first to touch the horse and let him know he'd done well.

Jay Kydd grinned up at her. "I forgive you everything, Bluebell," he said.

CHAPTER FIFTEEN

WHEN THE BRASS clock on the mantel in his study struck nine, Raven stopped trying to make sense of a plan sent to him by Braidwood for a metropolitan firefighting force. The idea was something like what Peel had accomplished for the police, and Raven thought it was an idea whose time had come. He pushed back from his desk and went to pour himself a brandy. For perhaps the dozenth time, he wondered where Jay Kydd had got to.

Everything about the study at Verwood proclaimed Raven a gentleman of means, Sir Adrian Cole. The walls were richly paneled, the bookcases filled with leather-bound volumes on a wide range of subjects, the carpet thick underfoot, and the brandy, aged in oak barrels, smooth as silk. He had only to glance around at the furnishings and paintings, however, to be reminded that Verwood was on loan to him. The old man in the large portrait over the hearth was not Raven's grandfather, but a former duke. The fair-haired boy, painted with his dog under a pair of trees, was not one of Raven's mates but Lady Cassandra's dead brother, who, if he had survived his time in the army, would now be the duke. Lady Cassandra appeared in a small sketch, as a young version of herself astride a pony. Raven raised his glass to the figures in the portraits. It did not matter that they once occupied the house. He was the one here now, and he meant to stay.

Brandy in hand, he turned to the window. From the southwest corner of the house the study looked down the long sweep of the drive, and he had not tired of the view. The June sky was pale blue above the chestnut trees. Dark forms of birds and insects, not yet settled for the night, flitted from branch to branch. Frogs and crickets made a loud chorus from the lake. Now that he was familiar with the landscape, he could see the gap in the trees where the lane led to the dower house.

All day he had kept his mind busy with his plans for the summer and kept at bay thoughts of Lady Cassandra. Their conversation had ended too soon. He wanted to know what she thought about his being Raven. She was the first person outside the circle of his closest friends to know something of his other life, though not the whole. He was the son of an officer with whom his mother had a liaison sometime during the early years of the great war with Napoleon. Letters his grandfather possessed showed that there had been an intention to marry, but the officer had died in Portugal. Raven's grandfather admitted that he had been enraged over his daughter's pregnancy, and that his anger had driven her from her home. It had been Wenlocke's research that had uncovered where she had given birth to Raven and the Foundling Hospital to which she'd given him when she could no longer care for him. He had escaped both the hospital and a mill before he'd met Wenlocke.

Lady Cassandra had offered her account of the accident as an equal exchange for what she'd learned about Raven's past. But her story concealed as much as it revealed. He wondered what had sent her out on an overlong solitary ride with no groom in attendance, and why now she had determined to ride the horse again. He told himself that all such speculation was fruitless and inappropriate. Lady Cassandra was his landlady, a person with whom his only tie was a lease covenant. It should not bother him that Jay would be there to watch her ride Hermes for the first time in three years, but the idea had lodged in his mind like a bubble only he could see in an otherwise perfect sheet of glass.

If Jay managed to charm the dowager and train the horse and the horse had a win, Raven would still have Verwood. His mind should remain centered on the surprise he planned for Lady Amabel and ball he planned to give. He took another swallow of the brandy. In a week Amabel would be at her father's estate, and all the distraction of Lady Cassandra and her horse would come to an end.

A quick jaunty rap sounded on the study door, and Jay strolled in. "What's this? Your library?" he asked.

"Study," Raven said. "Where have you been? I missed you at dinner."

"Drinking your health at the inn. You're quite the hero there. Hiring people. Spending money. Routing the local bully." Jay went straight for the brandy decanter, lifting it and taking a sniff. "Putting on airs, aren't you? Brandy, servants, and all this?" He waved a hand at the paneled walls and bookshelves.

"Join me," Raven lifted his glass.

"Don't mind if I do." Jay poured himself a glass and settled in one of the room's green leather armchairs. "So, what did you get up to today? Because, I tell you, you missed seeing a fine horse."

"Did you talk the dowager into running Hermes?"

"Only a matter of time. I'm sure the old girl's keen to run him. But she turned stiff as a poker when your lady friend wanted to ride."

"The old girl? That's the dowager to you. And my lady *friend?*"

"Bluebell," said Jay with a grin. "I'm keeping my name for her. It suits her. She's not your London fashion plate. The girl's a Trojan. Faced right up to the old ... dowager."

"I think she's had some practice," Raven said drily.

"Whatever that horse did to her, she rode him today like a trooper. A perfect seat, and great hands. You'd never guess she has a bum foot. Do you know what happened?"

"It was an accident caused by someone driving fast. She was leading Hermes when he reared and came down on her foot. Apparently, the doctors let the bones fuse wrong."

"Well, it's a shame. She was made to gallop." Jay swirled the brandy in his glass. "Though odds are that it's the bum foot that keeps her here. Otherwise, she'd have been married to some toff with a title by now."

Unaccountably, Raven found himself wanting to change the subject. Jay's easy assumption of a connection with Lady Cassandra was irksome. "You think the horse can win some prize money?"

"I'm sure he can, but it will take work. And Crockett. Those hands of his are magic. I'll be up early tomorrow."

Raven wanted to ask how long Jay meant to stay, but he held his tongue. In another week Amabel would be here. He found Jay watching him.

"That is, if you don't mind. I won't stay long, for I should be off to London to look for a rider for Hermes and find out who has horses running this season. It helps to know the field."

The sky outside began to darken. Jay gave a prodigious yawn, put aside his brandy class and pushed himself up out of the chair. "Sorry, Raven, I didn't ask you about your lady, your earl's daughter. She's coming here?"

"Not to Verwood, but to her father's house, about five miles away."

"When?"

"Next week."

"Does she know you've taken Verwood?"

"No. I mean it to be a surprise."

"When you call on her, you should ride Achilles. He's your best mount."

RAVEN HAD WRITTEN to Lady Ramsbury asking if he might call upon her daughter, and a cordial reply invited him to visit. By the road the distance was an easy five miles. Another mile through the estate's woods and fields led to the house, built, Raven guessed, sometime before 1700. It was fiercely symmetrical with ornate diamond brickwork, a striking number of windows in old multiple-paned style, and paired columns framing a tall, narrow entrance. A cupola with a golden ball glinted in the sunlight atop the roof.

A stately butler greeted Raven. A liveried footman saw to

his horse, and he was announced at the entrance to a long white-and-gold room with a high ceiling and a dark-blue carpet underfoot. Amabel and her mother sat over needlework at one end of the room, and Amabel's golden harp stood in a sunny corner.

Amabel saw him and flung aside her sewing, coming to his side and drawing him to her mother. "Mama, doesn't Sir Adrian look perfect for the country?"

Lady Ramsbury offered her hand, and Raven bowed over it. "Do not let my daughter embarrass you, Sir Adrian." She returned her attention to her needle and the bright threads of a piece she was working.

"But, I'm right, Mama. He must know our country ways. Have you been spying on us, sir?" she asked.

"Merely growing accustomed." Raven was not sure he had judged rightly after all. Both ladies were elaborately coiffed and gowned in pale green silk. The sameness of their dress rather than of feature marked the pair as mother and daughter. Raven remembered a stray comment of Jay's that Lady Cassandra was not a fashion plate. Perhaps Raven had been misled by her and by his neighbors in Wormley as to the degree of dress expected in a noble household even in summer in the country.

"And where are you staying, Sir Adrian?" asked the countess. "Did we have notice of your coming our way?"

"Oh, you knew he was coming, Mama, for I told you." Amabel gave Raven a mischievous look that made him rethink the letter he'd received.

"I've taken a place near Wormley, ma'am," he said.

At that the countess looked up briefly. "Have you? A

hunting box? Do you hunt?"

"I have in the past."

"Ah, before your trade in London consumed you, I imagine."

"Exactly, ma'am."

"You may join Ramsbury's hunt. If you wish." Lady Ramsbury spoke to her needlework.

"Won't I have something to say about that?" Amabel asked. "After all, he's come to visit me, not Papa. And I'd like to show him the grounds, if I may."

"Of course, dear. You seem to have arranged things to your satisfaction."

Once again, the suspicion crossed Raven's mind that Amabel herself had answered his letter.

Amabel gave her mother a kiss, and took Raven by the hand. "Let's walk round the lake," she said. She pulled Raven to the door, and when it closed behind them, she smiled up at him with a gleam of mischief in her eyes and a hint of dimples in her cheeks. "You have saved me. My cousins are due to arrive within the hour. They are two of the dullest girls you will ever meet, and my aunt is a champion complainer."

"Won't your mother feel abandoned if you leave her to entertain the tedious cousins?" he asked.

"Mama can depress anyone's pretensions," she said. "And you mustn't mind her. She might want me to marry a title, as if I cared a scrap about that. But really, she knows that I must have a handsome, darling man who adores me. And, besides, we've already decided that you will have a title one day."

"Lady Amabel wills it so," he said. "By the way, did you send me that letter approving my visit?"

She flashed a triumphant smile at him. "Let me get a parasol."

For a few minutes Raven admired the soaring staircase in the entry hall with its elaborately carved white balustrade, trying to reconcile his pleasure in seeing Amabel, with a mild unease at the cunning with which she had secured approval for his visit. His misgivings vanished when she returned in a fetching straw bonnet, tied under her chin with a peach-colored ribbon, and with a dainty parasol over one shoulder.

She led him to the rear of the house where a wide expanse of grass sloped down to a lake considerably larger than the lake at Verwood with what looked to be a small Grecian temple on the hill opposite.

"You know…" She peeped up at him from under the parasol, her golden lashes catching the light. "We could row across to the folly if you'd like?"

He grinned at that. "You mean, *Sir Adrian would you care to row me across the lake?*"

A musical peal of laughter was her reply. She tripped lightly down the grass. At the lake edge, he helped her into a skiff tied to a short dock. He shed his coat and hat, climbed in to man the oars, and cast off. A breeze on the water ruffled the fringe of her parasol. This was what he'd come for, to exert himself under her admiring gaze. He had only the most fleeting thought that she wanted him to be someone he wasn't.

On the other side, the skiff slid up the gravel shore. He hopped out, helped her to alight, and secured the boat.

Again, she took his hand, and led him up the hill to the folly. The interior was cool and shadowy, and they sat on the steps overlooking the lake and the house.

"Don't you wish," she said, "that you had a device that could capture a scene exactly, just as it is in the moment? It is so tedious to draw or paint. One looks back and forth between the thing and one's drawing, and nothing stays quite still while one does it."

"And what would you capture with your device?" he asked.

"Oh, so many things. Ramsbury Park, my family. Then we wouldn't have sit, cross and disagreeable for hours, to have our portrait made." She struck a stiff formal pose, lifting her chin high, and glancing sideways at him.

"Do you find your family disagreeable?"

"No. Just sitting, silly," she laughed. "What would you capture?"

A shockingly disloyal thought popped into his head. He dismissed it. He was with Amabel not Lady Cassandra. "Perhaps I'd capture my grandfather. He's a bit like your family, unwilling to sit for his portrait."

"He's very important to you, isn't he? You're his heir," she said with sudden earnestness.

"I am."

"Will he like me, do you suppose?"

"He will find you adorable."

"Good. Now where did you say you were staying?"

"I didn't. I wanted to surprise you."

"Well then, surprise me." Amabel plucked at her skirts arranging their fall over her knees.

"Verwood. I've taken the place on a lease."

Her expression was not quite what he expected. Her lips pursed in the familiar little pout, that someday he thought he might kiss. "You're not pleased?"

She squeezed his hand. "I am. It's like taking a house at Brighton for the summer. I never thought of that. Only isn't Verwood terribly run down and neglected?"

"Not at all. One of these days I'll show you. It may not be as grand as this place, but it has its ... beauty."

A shadow of vexation altered her expression. "But what's happened to the ladies of Verwood? The dour dowager and the dithery aunt?"

"They are quite comfortable in the dower house." Raven liked his landladies, but he could not fault Amabel for her words. He had had a similar impression of the ladies at first.

She cast him a sly glance. "Even Lady Cassandra? I suppose she's quite the invalid these days."

"What makes you think that?" He was conscious of a stiffening of his posture.

"Don't be angry, Sir Adrian. It's just that people have a name for her."

"And what is that?" He tried to keep his voice level and bland, as if the matter were one of mere curiosity.

"It's not kind," she said with an imploring look.

"Can you tell me anyway?" he asked.

"As long as you promise not to be angry. I did not invent the phrase. I know it's dreadful what happened to her."

He nodded, nerving himself, keeping his gaze on the view. Across the lake a liveried servant emerged from the house and started down the grassy hill.

"She's called *the dead duke's damaged daughter.*"

If a man had spoken the words, Raven would have knocked him down. The cruel name said everything about Cassandra's circumstances and nothing about her. There was no doubt in his mind that Cassandra had heard those words. Her wounded foot was nothing to them.

The liveried servant reached the little dock and waved at them. Raven stood with careful easiness and offered his hand to Amabel. "It looks as if your escape is over. Shall I row you back?"

She turned a contrite, worried face up to his. "You'll come again, won't you?"

"Every day if you'll let me."

He was rewarded with a radiant smile.

CHAPTER SIXTEEN

RAVEN'S DAILY RIDE to Ramsbury Park quickly became a habit until one morning dark clouds threatened. At his window, he contemplated asking for his carriage. The dowager's rule that Raven advise her grooms of his intention to use a horse or carriage was particularly irksome in such moments. He put aside his irritation to work on the guest list for the ball.

By midmorning when no rain appeared, he decided to risk making the journey on horseback and sent for a boy to inform the stable to saddle his usual mount. No boy appeared. A quick search of the house by his staff did not turn up Joe, Ben, or Tim. Raven sent a footman to the stable, who returned with the news that the boys were not there, either.

Vexed with them and with himself, Raven left the hall by the front entrance. Preoccupied with his plans for the ball, he had been lax, letting them spend hours watching Hermes's training. And he had been teaching them to swim. Now, he was repaid for allowing them so much freedom. He could think of a dozen places where they could get into trouble, starting with the lake. He strode down the drive and scanned the gray, choppy waters, relieved not to find them, and angry at the same time for the worry they caused him. With his temper rising, he headed for the stable.

On the north side of the house where the outer walk met the path through the formal garden, he heard shouts and the clash of metal as if some mortal combat were underway. He halted and listened more closely. The sound of distinctly boyish voices came from the other side of the hedge, from the very spot where he meant to propose to Amabel. He strode toward the sound and burst through the yew hedge and stopped cold. Joe, Ben, and Tim, with fierce frowning faces and swords drawn, stood looking at the fallen figure of Honoria Thornhill. She lay insensible on the grass, one hand clasped to her bosom, faded brown skirts oddly hiked around her knees, her stockings grass-stained. The boys saw him, and their expressions turned shame-faced. Raven hurried to the fallen woman's side and dropped to a knee to see what could be done for her.

He saw no wound, no blood, and thought perhaps she'd hit her head. He turned over her limp hand to find a pulse and stared at ink-stained fingers.

"Sir A," said Joe. "Miss T is teaching us sword fighting."

"And dying," added Ben.

Raven lifted the edge of her lace cap, looking for a head wound, and Miss Thornhill opened one eye. "Oh dear," she said. "Sir Adrian. What must you think!" She tried to push up on one elbow. "I can explain."

"First, are you hurt?" Raven asked. She shook her head, and the lace cap slid farther down over one ear. He offered a hand and helped her to her feet. Her skirts were tangled in some sort of knot, and she tugged at them in her flustered way. Amabel's words about the *dithery aunt* came instantly to mind. Raven turned aside to let Honoria rearrange her skirts.

He leveled a quelling gaze on the boys, who, he noted, wore colorful odds and ends of scarves and jackets over their blue shirts and gray trousers. "Explain," he said.

"We're acting a scene in one of Miss T's stories." Tim pointed to a notebook lying open on the stone bench next to a pencil case and a lady's straw bonnet.

Joe, with what Raven recognized as Miss Thornhill's usual shawl hanging from his shoulders like a cape, and a scrap of red cloth tied around his sword arm, announced, "I am Don Adeo, the Admirable. What country am I from, miss?"

"Portugal, dear," said Miss Thornhill.

"I'm a Portuguese colonel fighting for my country against ... who are we against, miss?"

"Joe, you blockhead. We're against the Frogs, old Boney's men at Busaco," said Ben.

"Are you the enemy, Tim?" Raven asked.

"Not me, I'm Richard Crawley, British Rifleman. You see I've got this green uniform to wear." He tugged at the lapels of a lady's spencer jacket.

"We take turns being the French commander—'Yew the 'Orrible." Ben held a black mustache up to his lips. "We could show you how we do it."

A suspicion was dawning on Raven about what he was seeing, and a stricken look from Honoria rather confirmed his thinking. "Show me," he told the boys.

Ben stuck his mustache on, and he and Joe took positions opposite each other on the strip of grass in front of the very bench where Raven imagined himself proposing to

Amabel. They raised their swords, hands on hips, knees bent.

"Miss," called Joe, "read the part about 'Yew the 'Orrible."

Raven looked to Honoria Thornhill. She did not meet his gaze, but took up the notebook from the stone bench and flipped through its pages.

"She writes the action down as we fights," confided Ben.

"Ready?" Honoria's voice wavered. "We'll just do a small part for Sir Adrian. We've interrupted his day." She cleared her throat and began to read.

> *At midday as the battle raged, Rifleman Crawley came upon his friend Don Adeo holding off a fierce French officer with a bristling mustache. Blood flowed from Don Adeo's sword arm. The noble Portuguese officer stood before his fallen steed.*
>
> *"You must pay me sixty gold coins," the Frenchman cried, "or I will slay your horse."*
>
> *"Never," cried Don Adeo. He staggered and fell to one knee barely able to parry his enemy's blows.*
>
> *Rifleman Crawley, seeing his friend's distress, leapt into the fray, driving the French officer back from the fallen Don Adeo. The Frenchman retreated under the fury of Crawley's blows, leaping up upon a tall boulder, and shouting down, "Hugh the Horrible will have his revenge!"*

Tim jumped up on the bench, struck a pose, then dropped down on the other side, and disappeared into the hedge. The boys looked to Raven, while he stood rigid with comprehension. He realized that it was his part to applaud.

He clapped, even as his mind, stuck on the name of the French officer and the sum of sixty gold pieces.

"Thank you, lads," Honoria said. "You've played your parts quite well. Now, I'm sure, Sir Adrian has need of you. Let me have those costumes, and I'll leave you to get on with your work, or journey, or whatever you have planned." She collected her bonnet and pencil case.

The boys squirmed out of their borrowed clothes without a word, looking from her to Raven. Raven motioned them to sit upon the bench and took up the pile of clothes. "Don't move until I return. I'm walking Miss Thornhill to the dower house."

He offered his arm. She hesitated, giving him a beseeching look, but he didn't budge. At last, she took his arm. They began to walk. "I do apologize," she said. "I should have asked your permission to involve them. Sometimes they get quite in the way of the work going forward with Hermes."

"I imagine they do," said Raven mildly, as they turned into the path that led to the dower house. He meant to keep his temper in check until he understood what he'd seen.

"Cassie asked me if I could keep them occupied this morning, and they do like to be active."

Cassie. The name distracted him for a moment. She wasn't Lady Cassandra or Bluebell. She was Cassie.

Honoria Thornhill looked up at him, and he went back to his questioning. "So, you write stories."

Her hand on his arm twitched. "Fictions," she said firmly.

"But they aren't entirely fiction, are they?" he persisted.

"Well, writers do take inspiration from the ... scenes

around them, but then imagination takes over. A local bully becomes a French officer."

"You don't fear that the local bully might recognize himself in your work?"

"Never," she said. "No one connects my stories with ... me or with this place."

"You publish anonymously then?" he asked. They had come within sight of the dower house.

Honoria released his arm, and faced him squarely, her notebook clutched to her chest with her ink-stained hands. "Only Cassie knows about my ... work. Lottie would never approve, so, you see, I must remain an unknown author."

"Won't the story of *Hugh the Horrible* threaten that? Am I right in thinking that I've met the man who inspired your French officer?"

Honoria blushed. "You needn't worry. Horrible Hugh is no reader, and he'd never open a novel. He's a member of the sporting set, follows the races, hunts, rather like his father Lord Ramsbury."

"Horrible Hugh is Hugh Haydon, Lord Ramsbury's son?" The knowledge rocked him. One minute he had his balance, the next the ground shifted under his feet. All his carefully laid plans meant nothing. The scene in the inn yard came back to him in vivid detail. How many times had the story been told carelessly since by friends of Dick Crockett? Raven had figured as the hero, defending the vulnerable, but now he saw himself as the fool, the man who unknowingly offended the brother of the woman he loved. Hugh would not forget the slight.

Worse, Raven had compounded his offense with his daily

visits to Ramsbury Park. He had accepted the hospitality of a family that would likely turn him out on his ear when they knew what he'd done. He had risked all his hopes and plans without knowing the danger he courted. But one person had known the risk and had not offered a word of warning.

For a week Raven had seen nothing of his landladies, which he had thought for the best. For a week he had congratulated himself on the wisdom of avoiding Lady Cassandra. *Cassie.* He feared that meeting her, he would betray his awareness of the cruelty she'd endured. He was under no obligation to tell her what he'd heard, or from whom he'd heard it, but he didn't like the idea of concealing the thing from her. He knew London society loved to mock its own. If Wellington or Melbourne or King William himself could be caricatured in the print shop windows, then no one was safe from society's barbs. For a week he had been full of sympathy for a woman who had let him make a fool of himself.

At the door of the dower house, he stopped and faced Honoria.

"Miss Thornhill, where's your niece?" he asked. He handed her the boys' costumes.

Honoria offered him a pleading glance. He merely raised one brow.

Honoria's shoulders slumped. "Cassie walked to the village this morning."

Raven bowed and strode off. He knew a thing or two about heat and how to judge the temperature of a flame from its color. His anger was white hot. His sympathy for Cassandra Lavenham was ash.

CASSIE GLANCED AT the sullen gray sky and adjusted the basket on her arm. The day had grown dark, and the clouds would open any minute. She took hold of her skirts and climbed the last stile between the village and Verwood. She did not want to be caught in a downpour, but she could not pass the stile without pausing to think of her first meeting with Jay Kydd. Since that day so much had changed. Verwood, which had seemed a dead place, was now alive again.

It was all owing to Raven. Gaining him as a tenant had had unexpected benefits. The ladies of Verwood had enlarged their little family, which now included Jay and the three boys, who were great favorites with Dick Crockett and Honoria. Grandmama might appear to be keeping aloof, but Cassie was not fooled. The stable was a happier place. Jay and Snell claimed that Hermes was making great progress and planned to put a jockey on him in the next week. Jay was quickly learning Dick Crockett's hand language, and the boys, when not with the horses, had evidently made friends in both kitchens. Even Raven, who was seldom at Verwood, was fond of the boys. In the mornings, he was teaching them to swim. Cassie had some concern that their confidence might outstrip their actual ability. She should talk with Raven about it, but she had not seen him since he'd begun his daily visits to Ramsbury Park. It was sad, she thought, that he had brought Verwood to life, and no longer wished to be there, but she understood.

His courting must be going well. Cassie would not have guessed that pretty Amabel would suit him. His character seemed made of sterner stuff, but she admitted that he did like perfection, and Amabel was that. The work he had done on the hall and the gardens showed his care with detail. Cassie had forgotten how truly lovely Verwood's gardens could be. Now if she could get home before the rain, she could sip her tea and enjoy her overflowing cup of happiness.

Thunder rumbled in the distance, and she started for the dower house, but stopped at once. From Verwood, Raven bore down on her with rapid, angry strides, dressed for riding, but hatless and plainly in a mad hurry. Instinctively, she braced herself. "Oh, I did not expect to see you. Are you not going to Ramsbury Park today?"

He stopped directly in her path, and regarded her coldly. "My plans have changed."

"I'm sorry." She was at a loss meeting him in this out of the way spot. "I suppose the weather…"

"The change has nothing to do with the weather, and everything to do with you."

"Me?"

"I trusted you," he bit out the words, closing the distance between them.

"And now you don't?" It was a shocking thing to suggest.

"Your deceit—"

"My what? I beg your pardon. How have I been deceitful?" She tried to control her temper. His glare was withering, his mouth set in a harsh line. He was angry with her, and she could not think why. An intemperate reply from her could not help the conversation.

"You knew Hugh, *Horrible Hugh*, as your aunt calls him, was Lord Ramsbury's son, Lady Amabel's brother, and you didn't tell me."

Cassie did not know how to defend herself. It was true. "Has Hugh returned to Ramsbury Park? I should warn the Crocketts?"

"Warn the Crocketts?" The words burst from him. "Help them, but not me! I told *you* my plans. *You.* No one else. By all means help Dick Crockett, save him, but let me ride off day after day blissfully unaware of my offense against Lady Amabel's family, an offense which could sink me in their estimation and ruin everything I've worked for. I deserved better from you."

Cassie was confused. If Hugh had not returned, how had Raven's hopes been dashed? "How did you discover Hugh's connection to Amabel?"

Contempt curled his fine mouth, as if he were about to say something utterly distasteful. "Your aunt," he said, "is making Hugh the Horrible the villain of her next novel. Did you know that, too?"

Cassie shook her head. Her heart sank. Somehow Raven had discovered that Honoria wrote novels. "Has she put Hugh in her Portugal story? How do *you* know that?"

"So you did know."

"I did not." The first drops of rain hit her shoulders, heavy and cold. The storm, like his anger, was going to break over them. She wore a short summer cloak and a straw bonnet. He stood bare-headed. With a sudden rush, the rain came down, a thick, leaden river of wet. It ran down Raven's face, flattened his hair against his head, and caught in his lashes. In seconds it drenched him. The mingled scents of warm, damp earth and grass rose around them. He stood immobile as stone.

"Honoria's got Joe, Ben, and Tim playing characters from the book, waving swords about on the lawn." His voice rose over the hiss and splatter of the rain. "I recognized the scene at once. Hugh is a particularly nasty French officer who demands *sixty* gold pieces from the hero. Honoria assured me that the real Hugh would never see himself in her literary efforts because he was not a reader, but a sporting man, like his father, Lord Ramsbury."

Cassie winced. It was an awkward way for Raven to learn the truth, but surely learning it from Honoria was not the disaster he seemed to think. "Oh dear. I am sorry. I will speak to her."

"By all means. Dissuade Honoria from her folly. Give her the chance to avoid what—ridicule, humiliation, a lawsuit? And leave me open to the loss of all my hopes."

Rain dripped from the brim of Cassie's bonnet. The icy, contemptuous voice stirred her own anger, the heat of it blocking out the chill of her wet cloak. She tried to compose herself. "You surprised me that day with your plan to court Amabel. It was an unexpected confidence, and it would have been presumptuous of me to advise you in any way."

"You are not dull-witted or dithery like your aunt. The moment I told you Amabel was my object, you knew Hugh would be a problem for me."

"Dithery?" Cassie stiffened at the insult. "Go. We are done now. You've said quite enough. I understand you."

He blocked her path. The rain washed over his person in blowing curtains of water. His burning gaze settled on her mouth. He seemed on the verge of speaking, yet said nothing. Cassie's thin cloak grew heavy. Her soggy bonnet no longer protected her. If he would only move, she could get home before the pain took over.

At last, he spoke. "I can't leave you in this rain." He tore off his coat and draped it over her shoulders.

"Of course, you can. I am quite capable of making my way home on my own." She tried to shrug his coat off.

He gripped her shoulders, looking down into her face, the rain molding the thin lawn of his shirt to his arms. "Yes, the *dead duke's damaged daughter* needs no one's help."

She gasped. She couldn't help it. The old taunt hit her like a blow. Instantly, he looked appalled at what he'd said, but it was too late. She wrenched herself out of his grasp.

"Cassie!" His voice was an anguished cry. "I didn't mean—"

"You know what your problem is," she told him. She was shouting now over the rain, and over the plea in his voice, which she refused to hear. "You don't want to apologize to Hugh. You know he's undeserving of your apology. Being Amabel's brother does not make him less of a coward or a bully."

"What can I say to *her*?"

"You could tell her the truth. You could say, *Dearest, loveliest Amabel, your brother Hugh is an offensive worm, but I'm willing to overlook his vile behavior for your sake.*"

He exhaled a sharp, bitter laugh. "You are outrageous."

"Am I?" She was beyond caring what he thought. She had been mistaken to regard him as different from any of them who had mocked her.

Rain ran in shining rivulets down his face. His coal-dark

eyes turned bleak, teasing lights extinguished. "You know I can't say that."

"Will you grovel then? Pretend you don't know what he is. Tell Hugh that you acted hastily, that you didn't stop to see things his way, that you hope you and he can start again? Will you admire his horses, his latest curricle, his best guns? I promise you, you won't like yourself if you do."

"You're full of helpful ideas. And Amabel? How am I to make her understand?"

Cassie felt her anger dissolve in the rain. He stood impossibly close, in torment, his pain-filled gaze fixed on her. She knew that sort of pain, but his could end. Amabel might be angry, but she would forgive him if he let her.

She lifted his coat from her shoulders and handed it to him. He took the dripping wool.

"Tell her your plans for the July ball. Tell her that you just learned that you met her brother. You can tell her what happened, at least, a version of what happened, leaving out Hugh's nastiness. Tell her you would have behaved quite differently had you understood who Hugh was. Ask for her help to start over with Hugh. If she loves you, she will forgive you."

She turned to go. He reached out a hand, but she shook her head. He let his hand drop. With a few steps she moved beyond his gaze, letting the rain cut her off from him.

CHAPTER SEVENTEEN

CASSIE MOVED BLINDLY through the rain. Her sole object was to distance herself from Raven. The path ahead became a narrow tunnel of green gloom. Rain shut out the world except for the few feet in front of her. It beat against her with the ceaseless insistence of her angry thoughts. Raven accused her of deceit, but she was the one who had been duped. In their first meeting, his kindness and his willingness to defend Dick Crockett against Hugh had marked Raven as a man of principle. Now, she understood him better. His defense of Dick had been out of character. His value for rank and position drove him.

At last, she saw the glimmer of lights from the dower house kitchen. She cut across the rabbit field, indifferent to the uneven ground, her skirts collecting mud and grass as she moved. Outside the kitchen door, she paused to catch her breath. With luck, Cook would help her shed her wet cloak and bonnet and get up to her room alone. A bath and something warm to drink would prepare her to face Honoria and Grandmama. She must appear as if nothing had happened to overset her. A laugh, a single dry spasm of amusement, burst from her aching throat, to think that an hour earlier she had imagined drinking a cup of happiness.

She opened the door, and met the stare of five pairs of

eyes. Grandmama, in one of her deep blue riding habits, sat at the head of the kitchen's scarred old work table. Honoria sat on one side, and the boys on the other, wrapped in blankets and huddled over steaming mugs. Instead of the usual mixing bowls and spoons and sieves and mallets, the table was strewn with a wet array of jackets, toy swords, and one of Honoria's notebooks. A clothesline had been strung between the brick fireplace and the cabinets, hung with three shirts and three pairs of trousers.

"Lady C," cried Joe. "Ye've been in Noah's flood like us!"

Joe received a quelling glance from Grandmama.

Cassie tried for a smile, but was not sure she managed it. She stepped into the kitchen, set her basket down on the slates, and closed the door. The heat of the room hit her and the smell of marmalade on warm bread.

"Did Sir Adrian find you, love?" asked Honoria, twisting the ends of her shawl as always. Cassie recognized the warning in the question.

"He did." Cassie removed her sodden bonnet. Her bad foot suddenly made its complaint known, and she grabbed the tall back of the closest chair for balance. With a little cry, Cook hurried to Cassie's side.

"Get that cloak off and get near the fire, child," Grandmama snapped.

Cassie reached for the strings of her cloak with stiff, cold hands, trying to understand Honoria's warning. It seemed as if the boys' playacting Honoria's story had not only been discovered by Raven, but also by her grandmother. Cook took Cassie by the shoulders and turned her to remove the sopping garment, keeping up a low murmur of concern, handing Hannah, her scullery maid, the dripping cloak. In a minute Cassie sat with her back to the fire and a cup of hot tea before her. She steadied her shaking hands and lifted the cup to her mouth under Grandmama's watchful gaze. The boys kept their heads down. Honoria huddled in her chair. Outside, the rain drummed on the flagstones of the kitchen courtyard. Inside, spits turned and pots boiled. A reckoning was coming, and Cassie would have to face it before she could think about Raven's cruel words.

She looked up and met her grandmother's stern gaze.

"What is this novel-writing nonsense you and Honoria have been carrying on behind my back?"

Cassie winced at the *behind my back* phrase. It was too close to Raven's accusation that she had deliberately kept the truth about Hugh from him. She pushed the thought away, and looked to Honoria, who cast her a pleading glance. "It's not nonsense, Grandmama. Aunt Honoria is a born storyteller. It is sad that she remains anonymous when she could have recognition in her own right."

"What sort of recognition is it for a lady to be known as a scribbler? And where has her storytelling gotten her? She has seriously offended Sir Adrian if this lot is to be believed." Grandmama's gaze swept the boys. "And to persist and offend Ramsbury and his absurd son is out of the question."

"Is Sir Adrian very angry?" Honoria asked.

"Not with you, Aunt, and besides he will calm down. You must change the name of your villain, of course."

Honoria nodded. "Done. My villain shall be Valmont the Vengeful."

"Stop!" Grandmama thumped the table with her fist.

The boys jumped in their seats. "You can't mean to continue this writing business under my roof."

Cassie set down her teacup. However much she might regret her mistaken estimation of Raven, one good thing remained of his being their tenant. Rent. Because he paid rent, Cassie was free to use her own funds however she wished. "Honoria and I can go to London, Grandmama, if she and her writing are no longer welcome at Verwood."

"Insolent girl. You will do no such thing. Do you know that your Mr. Kydd has found a rider for Hermes? You want Hermes to run, do you not?"

Cassie looked from her grandmother to Honoria, a little lost at the turn the conversation had taken. "I do want Hermes to run, but what has that to do with Honoria's writing?"

"You began this horse race scheme, miss, and you will see it through. I expect you to remain at Verwood until Hermes is ready for his first race."

"But that will not be until late July!" Cassie cried. It was intolerable to contemplate lingering at Verwood while Raven prepared for his grand ball. Worse to imagine being there while the people who had mocked her danced, and she hobbled on.

Grandmama was watching, her gaze shrewd and knowing, and Cassie pulled herself together. She must not allow anything of the blow Raven had dealt her to show.

"Yes, July, after Sir Adrian's ball."

Cassie started. She had thought her grandmother too absorbed in her horses to know what Raven planned.

"Of course, I know about his ball, miss, and if you want

me to run that horse at Chichester, then you will show your face at that ball."

"You can't mean it, Grandmama. What possible reason could I have for attending a ball?"

"You will go for Verwood. We will all go. Verwood does not bow to Ramsbury Park. Then you can run off to London."

Her grandmother turned to Honoria. "And you, Honoria, will write no more of your drivel about our neighbor. Only a complete ninny offends Ramsbury. I won't lose another acre of this estate to that man, certainly not on account of his despicable son."

Her grandmother stood. The boys popped to their feet. Cook and Hannah stopped their work. Cassie started to push up out of her chair.

"Sit girl," Grandmama ordered. "Have the sense to get warm and dry. I won't have you catching your death now." She turned her glare on Honoria. "You led these three into folly. See that they are fed, and send them back to Sir Adrian when the rain stops."

RAVEN DID NOT know how long he stood in the rain before any thought intruded other than the sting of her indifference. He had mistaken her civility for friendship. Her solicitude for Dick Crockett had wounded his pride, and he had lashed out at her with that cruel phrase. Rain dripped from his chin. His clothes clung to him, and his skin burned with an icy chill. He could not remember being so angry.

His claim to be a gentleman was swallowed up in the mortification of behaving in such an ungentlemanly manner. He had seen at once from the boys' playacting how his treatment of Hugh would look to Amabel. He should have gone directly to her. Instead, he had sought out Cassie to quarrel. He turned his face up in the rain.

It made no sense to go to Ramsbury Park now. He would go in the morning. He slogged back to the garden to find the boys. They were not to blame for Honoria's folly or his. When he didn't find them on the bench, he broke the dowager's rule and went to the stable to look for them. They were not there either, and Raven was met by stares that plainly declared he was a bedlamite. He arranged, as calmly as he could, for his carriage to take a message to Ramsbury Park with his apology for being unable to call.

He trudged back to the hall. In the entry, servants met him with a brief flurry of solicitude, scurrying to bring him towels and mop up the floor after him.

Jay appeared from the study. "You look like a drowned rat. What happened?"

"Did the boys come back?" Raven toweled his dripping head.

Jay frowned. "The dowager found them in the garden. She sent a note round. They are drying out in her kitchen. You told them to sit on a bench in the rain?"

"May I dry off before you grill me?"

Jay raised his hands and backed away. Raven trudged up the stairs.

In Raven's dressing room, his man, Hackwood, treated Raven's ruined clothes with calm efficiency, peeling away wet layers of wool and linen and offering towels. Ruined coats were nothing new. Raven had lost more than one coat fighting fires. A bath was prepared for him, and a hot cordial to drink. His first thought on sinking into the tub was to wonder if someone had prepared a bath for Cassie. He gritted his teeth. The idea of Cassie in her bath roused the most ungentlemanly of thoughts.

He tipped his head back against the lip of the tub and closed his eyes against an image of a white arm resting along the rim of a copper bath. Maybe he did not understand women. Since he'd left Cambridge, he had devoted himself to making a success of the glass business and then to the design of new fire engines for his grandfather to build. He had had no thought of a wife. He knew some wives. They were fine women, but he had not imagined wanting one. From time to time at the duke's dinners for their old gang, he saw Wenlocke's duchess, who had been their grinder at Daventry Hall when they were boys, and the wives of Wenlocke's brothers, Sir Xander and Sir William. He supposed they were beautiful women, but around them he had always been perfectly at ease, usually laughing, and neither dazzled nor disturbed.

Only Amabel had dazzled him. She had danced with him in the fashionable world that had largely ignored him before the fire. From the moment the newspaper accounts of the blaze had named him and his Cole engines, West End hostesses had sought him for their gatherings. To dozens of silk-clad young ladies fanning their rosy faces, he had described the flames, the heat, the roar of the fire, the collapsing beams and swirling embers. The others could not compare to Amabel with her golden curls and sparkling eyes. When she took his hand and led him into a waltz, she confirmed what he had believed all along, that he was meant to rise in the world, to break the barrier of rank.

For months he had thought only of Amabel, acted only to win her. He had hired Trimley to find a house near her father's estate to show her that he could offer her the life of a lady of rank. Everything he had done at Verwood had been to make the place worthy of her, as perfect as she, herself, was. Now when he was ready to unveil Verwood to her, he discovered that in a moment of arrogance, he had jeopardized her good opinion. He had believed he understood the little scene in the inn yard, that Hugh was a villain and that Dick Crockett was the injured party. He had rushed in, a mistake as fatal as aiming a fire hose at the flames, not the fuel.

As the bath grew cold, a different truth intruded. He had not thought only of Amabel. He supposed that was the most maddening thing about his situation. He had wanted his renovations to please Cassie. He had needed her approval to abide by the dowager's rules, but he had wanted that approval as well. Not because she was beautiful. Next to Amabel, Cassie's muted appearance was unremarkable. Her intelligent gray eyes, her strong brow, her wide mouth, and dark hair were signs of strength and directness, not soft beauty. But he had believed he could count on her. He thought of her as a sort of friend, someone he could trust. That must explain his anger. He had trusted her, and she had kept the truth from him. She had let him continue in ignorance of Hugh's connection to Amabel, as if his happiness were a matter of no concern to her.

He pushed up out of the tub and toweled off. He would put the ugly scene behind him. He had learned his lesson. Confiding in Cassie had been a blunder. Still, he did not like the ungenerous part he'd played in their argument. Now that his anger had cooled, only the cruel taunt remained. He had wanted to hurt her, and that made no sense. He would apologize as soon as the rain stopped. He would walk over to the dower house and ask for a moment of her time, no more. Even as he imagined knocking on her door, he knew she would not see him.

He reached for the clothes Hackwood had set out for him. He would *write* her an apology. Writing that apology would be his first task. Once he had apologized, he could put the incident and Cassie behind him. There was nothing else to do. He had lost her good opinion, and deservedly so. From now on he would think only of Amabel. He would ask for Amabel's help with the ball. He would explain his missteps in meeting her brother, and he would let go of his repugnance for Hugh. The man was going to be his brother-in-law.

He tied the sash of a silk banyan around his waist and strode to the desk in his bedroom. A curtain billowed in a gust of wind, and he closed the window behind his desk. He found pen, ink, and paper, and settled down. And immediately encountered a problem. He did not know how to address her. *Dear Cassie.* He had just learned her name, but he could not use it. He settled for formality—*Dear Madam*—and began.

He was sanding the page when Jay knocked and entered.

"Where did you get to? Not to Ramsbury Park, I take it. Did you think the rain would not fall on *Sir* Adrian?" Jay strolled in and took his favorite armchair.

Raven put his letter aside and moved to stand by the hearth with his back to the fire. "Do you know Hugh Haydon?"

Jay's lip curled. "Viscount Farnley? He's the sort of fellow one tries to avoid."

"Why?"

Jay ticked off the reasons on his fingers. "He doesn't win well. He never loses well. And he always thinks he's picked a winner. What made you think of him? Has he come back? Has he been snooping around Hermes? He's been known to mess with other people's horses before a race."

An expletive came to Raven's mind. He hadn't been wrong about Hugh. But it didn't matter. For Amabel's sake, Raven was going to accept Hugh. "As far as I know, Hugh is off following the horses."

"Good. Because Hermes will do better for us, if he enters the race as an unknown. He's really coming along, and Bluebell has got Dick Crockett working on making lighter shoes for him."

"Don't call her *Bluebell*," Raven snapped. He turned to the fire. He could feel Jay's stare, as he prodded the coals to life.

"Excuse me. If she has no objection to the name, what objection can you have?"

"She's Lady Cassandra to you, I should think." Raven was being peevish, and he knew it. Jay's easy familiarity with Cassie suddenly rankled.

"What's set you off? You're on your high ropes. You have no idea how we get on together in the stables."

"I merely expect you to treat my landlady with respect."

Jay glared at him. "*Your* landlady, is she? I have a higher regard for her than that. She's not *your* anything." Jay paused. "You've changed, you know. Not with your grandfather's money, but with this courtship thing."

"You think I shouldn't court a lady of rank? We grew up in a duke's household, didn't we?" Raven watched the coals begin to glow.

"So we know better than to be drawn in by a title. What's a title next to ... the real man or woman?"

"I am not courting Lady Amabel for her title."

Jay snorted. "You're trying to rival Wenlocke is what you're doing. This grand house, that woman. It's not enough for you to find your doting grandfather and have him be rich as ten aldermen, you have to be better than the rest of us. Remember who we were before Wenlocke found us. We were boys no one wanted, only good enough to be sent up chimneys or down into cesspools or to scramble under the looms for lint until our fingers got caught in the machines."

"London was wrong to rate us as nothing."

"If you say so, but"—Jay pushed up out of the chair—"you're so sure you're right about everything. What if you're wrong about this?" Jay waved a hand in a great circle at the room. "All those West End ladies flocked to you and flattered you because you put out that blaze, but what do they know or care about you? Your head is swollen as big as one of Green's balloons, and I've had enough of your toplofty hospitality."

"You're free to lodge elsewhere."

"Fine, I will." Jay strode for the door. "The Crocketts will be glad to have me."

The door slammed.

Raven turned back to his letter. He was not toplofty. He had not sought Amabel for her rank. He loved her. He would just take his apology to the dower house.

ALONE IN HER room after a bath, Cassie sat at her dressing table and tried to face, as squarely as she could, her decision to conceal from Raven the fact that Hugh was Amabel's brother. In that moment, she supposed, her vanity had been wounded by his evident admiration for another woman. Not that she had expected him to show an interest in her, but that he so evidently saw her as *out of the running* as Jay Kydd would say. Maybe the flattery of Jay Kydd's attentions had turned her head, made her think she could still catch a gentleman's eye, and Raven had dashed those hopes.

Honoria's soft knock sounded on her door as Cassie dried her hair.

"Come in," Cassie called, straightening, composing herself to face Honoria's concern.

Honoria came forward into the light, and her gaze met Cassie's. "Oh love, you look done in. Sir A must have been very angry."

"He was." Cassie lowered her brush to her lap, suddenly without energy.

Honoria took the brush from Cassie's limp hand, and

Cassie submitted to the familiar ritual of her girlhood, as Honoria began to run the brush through Cassie's hair.

"I am so sorry. I never meant ... I never thought ... I cannot see why he should be angry with you. You don't write drivel or put people you know into books. He should be angry with me, not you."

"No, Aunt, he did have reason to be angry with me. You see, he told me that he wanted to marry Amabel Haydon." Cassie met her aunt's gaze in the mirror above her dressing table.

Honoria stopped moving the brush. "Does he love her? How very odd!"

"Nothing is less odd. Amabel is lovely, and she comes from a family of—"

Honoria began to brush again. "—rank. Does Sir A wish to rise in the world by marrying? I had thought him more sensible than that, more conscious of his own value. Those Ramsburys may have all the position in the world, but they are hardly noted for setting the Thames on fire."

"We only know Hugh's faults, Aunt," Cassie said gently. "And Hugh is the real cause of Sir A's anger with me. I did not tell him that Hugh was Amabel's brother. So, when he learned of the connection from you and the boys, he was quite ... distressed."

"Is that what it is then?" Honoria put aside the brush and twisted Cassie's hair into a knot at her nape. "I saw him just now, and the man looked chastened or no, maybe the right word is *bereft*, he looks absolutely *bereft*."

To be so bereft, he must love Amabel, Cassie thought. "He came here?"

"Yes. I answered the door. I confess I was hiding from Lottie. I tried to stand up to her, really, I did, but she makes me feel so small, so useless. What have I ever brought to Verwood? I depend entirely on her good will. And now I have nothing to offer." Honoria sank onto the bench at the foot of Cassie's bed.

Cassie twisted to look at her. "Aunt, you have a great deal to offer, but Sir A came here?"

"He brought you a letter." Honoria reached into her pocket and withdrew a folded sheet, closed with a waxed seal. Cassie could not imagine what more there could be to say between them.

Cassie took the letter. Just holding it brought back the pain. She had not thought it possible for the old taunt to hurt her again, but coming from Raven, the words had a special sting. She had no doubt where he had heard the phrase. They had traded places. She had turned away from the fashionable world, while he had entered it.

She looked up to find Honoria watching her. "I thought…" she began. "Shall I leave you with your letter?" Honoria stood and pulled her shawl close about her.

"Yes, I think that's best. But, Aunt, Grandmama will not remain angry long, and you and I will find a way to get to London and to keep you writing." Cassie offered her aunt a smile.

Honoria nodded and turned to the door. There she stopped and looked back over her shoulder at the letter in Cassie's lap. "You know, dear, I think writing has unsettled my brain. I thought Sir A was in love with you."

Cassie shook her head. The door closed. She held the

letter in her lap as the last light of the day faded. Then she broke the seal.

Dear Madam,

I write to apologize for my appalling behavior in speaking to you as I did this afternoon. To do so was unforgivable. You may wonder how I came to behave in such an ungentlemanly manner, and we must inevitably disagree on what, in the moment, I considered sufficient provocation for such anger.

Whether I am able to realize my hopes of an attachment to Lady Amabel Haydon, I have been glad of my time at Verwood. I thank you for your generous help in the work of restoring the hall. Now that the work is complete, there is little occasion for our paths to cross. It is my hope that the pain my offense has caused will lessen when I am not immediately before you. Only excepting the Verwood ball in July, at which politeness dictates that you make an appearance.

With every wish for your happiness and for the future success of Hermes, which Jay Kydd tells me is likely, I remain,

Raven

It was a letter that agitated more than it soothed. She was grateful for his acknowledgment of the wrong he had done. She could not agree more heartily that their paths need not cross. But she did not understand why he had signed the letter as he had.

She had no intention of appearing at his ball. From now on she would haunt the stables. By Grandmama's rules,

Raven was not permitted there. She had only to figure out a way around Grandmama's decision that Cassie attend the ball. Then she and Honoria could escape to London.

CHAPTER EIGHTEEN

WHEN RAVEN NEXT rode to Ramsbury Park, he discovered that new guests had arrived in his absence, the Countess of Embledon, accompanied by her daughter Lady Hyacinthe and her son, Viscount Tyne. The party of young people had spent most of the previous long, wet day playing cards, and were now keen for outdoor amusement. At Tyne's suggestion, they settled on tennis, and the viscount gave lessons to each of the ladies in turn, taking on the rest, and showing his prowess.

Raven entered in with as much spirit as he could summon, trying to control his impatience to speak with Amabel. Every once in a while, she gave him a quick glance, as if to say, she, too, wished they could be alone together for a talk. He tried to hold onto his patience. At last, as they strolled back to the house from the tennis, she drew enough apart from the group for them to have a private exchange.

"We missed you yesterday, and you've been out of sorts today. Something's wrong, isn't it?" The tennis had brightened her cheeks and eyes.

"There's something I need to tell you," he said.

"So serious," she said. "We'll find a time before you leave. You can't expect me to ignore my guests. Tyne is a particular friend of my brother Hugh."

The reference to Hugh stopped Raven in his tracks, but Amabel gave his arm a tug, and he offered her a brief smile.

Amabel's duty to her guests included a long afternoon of lying about listening to Tyne tell stories. They occupied the high-ceilinged white-and-gold drawing room, the ladies sitting in admiring postures around Tyne. As Raven saw it, Tyne was enjoying the same admiration he, Raven, had once enjoyed for his story of the fire. But Tyne's stories were different, and his humor had an acid edge. He told a long story about a fat friend of his who had fallen into a dispute with his tailor over the cost of coat. The tailor insisted on a higher charge because more cloth was required for the garment than usual. The fat gentleman insisted that his coats should cost no more than those of his friends and stood over the tailor as he measured a bolt of cloth. As the story progressed, it was difficult to tell which of the two men was the ultimate butt of the viscount's joke, but everyone laughed heartily when the tailor sent the fat gentleman a coat with no sleeves.

Restlessness consumed Raven. He didn't want to talk about fat men and coats. With difficulty he managed the required laughter and maintained the languid posture of the group. It occurred to him that he was seeing Amabel's world from the inside, with the curtains pulled back. Amabel did not seem as rapt in the stories as the others, but she accepted the tone of Tyne's humor. As hostess, she sat at Tyne's right, and paid attention to his need for lemonade or cake. When she caught Raven frowning, she sent him a chiding look. At last, the party broke up with the cousins pleading a need to refresh themselves. Raven strolled out through the wide

French doors onto the terrace.

On the terrace, he rehearsed in his head the explanation of his encounter with Hugh. His discomfort must be due to his lack of openness with Amabel. Once he had a chance to tell her about his meeting with Hugh and to see whether she could forgive him, then he wouldn't be so impatient with Tyne. He turned at the sound of her light quick steps on the flags of the terrace, and she stepped to his side and slipped her arm in his. "They are all settled. Now you can tell me what's on your mind."

Relief flooded him. She had not been ignoring him. She had been attending to her guests. "First," he said, "I'm going to give a ball. Will you help?"

She tilted her head, looking up at him as if he'd made no sense. "A ball? How will you manage that? Do gentlemen know anything about giving balls?"

"Why do you think I'm telling you my plan? Will you help?"

"When?" Her expression was doubtful.

"At the July full moon."

"So soon!"

"I want your opinion about everything—music, food, flowers."

"But where can you give a ball? There are no assembly rooms in Wormley, and Basingstoke is too distant." She was resisting the plan, and he feared that if he could not get her support, he would never be able to speak about Hugh. He took her hands in his.

"At Verwood, of course. There's a large hall that opens onto a terrace and garden."

"And you say it's not shabby."

Instinct warned him not to mention the work he'd done. He had a momentary recollection of Cassie covered in plaster dust. "Not at all, but I will want your help with the decoration."

"There's very little time. You must send your invitations at once. And you must include our guests. If the countess and Tyne come, you will be sure of a success."

He didn't like hearing that Tyne must be included, but at least she was no longer doubting that there could be a ball. "Then you will help?"

"Of course." She smiled up at him, that ravishing smile. He reached out to touch one of the shining golden curls, pulling on it lightly, uncoiling it.

"Shall we return? I can't be away too long, Mama will notice."

"There is something else," he said. "I have a confession to make. I've met your brother."

She gave him a puzzled look. "You met Hugh, where and how? I didn't think you were part of the sporting set."

"I'm not. I met him here in Wormley, and not under the best of circumstances. We—"

"Quarreled?" she asked, her dimples plain. "Hugh does have a temper."

"I stepped in where perhaps I should not have."

"Oh dear. Did you scold him? Like Papa?"

"Hugh was involved in an accident with a young man driving a cart, and Hugh's curricle was damaged. The young man couldn't pay for the damage, so I gave your brother the money."

"Oh, that! You mean the deaf boy with the donkey. I dare say you thought Hugh was unkind to the boy, though his cart is something of a hazard."

For a moment Raven lost the thread of his confession. Her dismissal of the incident as trivial should put his fears to rest, but in the phrase *the deaf boy with the donkey* he heard the echo of that other cruel phrase.

Amabel nudged him with her elbow. "You gave Hugh money for his vehicle, and…"

Raven had come to the most difficult part of his confession. "It made your brother quite angry."

"He does have a temper. But I can handle Hugh."

He stopped her, and turned her gently to face him. "Are you angry with me?"

She shook her head. Her golden curls bounced with the movement. "No, but I think you've been a clunch. My brother gave a bill for that curricle to Papa and he paid, too. Hugh does know how to get his way." She laughed that same merry peal.

Raven supposed he should find the story funny, but he could not. It was too much like the stories he'd heard all afternoon of someone being duped or taken advantage of by another.

"Don't look so serious. Let's plan that ball of yours and forget my brother."

CHAPTER NINETEEN

THE DRY SPELL that set in after Raven's quarrel with Cassie continued as the ball approached. Raven filled his days with a thousand and one details, more even, he thought than the renovation of the hall required. When things were well in hand, musicians and menu, flowers and candles, lanterns for the formal garden, extra help to assist with the carriages, he took a brief trip to London for a ring.

Late in the afternoon of the day before the ball, Wenlocke and his duchess arrived at Verwood. While preparations kept the servants busy in the hall, Raven took his guests around the property, and enjoyed their compliments on the beauty of the place and the renovations he'd made. A simple supper on the terrace followed. It had been impossible not to invite Jay to join them. Raven's grandfather was there, as well.

Around the table in the long, lingering day, Grandfather Cole was willing to admit that Raven had done good work renovating the hall, but he continued to wonder why Raven wanted to spend more time in the country, no matter how pretty his neighbor was.

"Nothing to do in the country," Grandfather complained. He did not himself ride, shoot, or fish.

"Can't agree with you, there, Mr. Cole," Jay chimed in.

Wenlocke lifted a brow, and Jay took the cue. "There's plenty of work for me. I'm training a horse for the dowager."

The duchess, a lover of ponies, looked at Raven. "We didn't see your stables, did we, Raven?"

Raven caught a questioning glance from Jay. "No, ma'am. My agreement with the dowager does not include her stables, so I don't generally go there. But Jay can tell you how the training goes."

Wenlocke and the duchess exchanged a glance before she turned to Jay again. "Do tell us about this horse, Jay."

"He's a bit of a secret, ma'am." Jay smiled.

"A secret? How so?" she asked, her vivid blue eyes alight. She had always been one to get them talking even as boys when they'd felt particularly awkward. Wenlocke sat back, wine in hand, to watch his wife in action.

"He's not run for three years, and we hope to surprise his rivals when we bring him on."

"And when will that be?" the duchess asked.

"The dowager will decide, but I'm pushing for the end of July at the Duke of Richmond's for some flat racing. At five, Hermes has the stamina for the six-furlong. If he can place, the dowager would be pleased."

As the questioning progressed, Raven attended to the food on his plate. He knew that Hermes's training continued, but since Jay moved to the Crocketts, Raven had heard nothing. Instantly, he wondered whether Cassie would go to the race with her grandmother. He had avoided seeing her, or she had avoided him, but he had felt that she was nearby. Now, perhaps, she would leave Verwood.

The duchess asked questions about training methods,

and, finally, how Jay meant to get the horse to Chichester, some fifty miles away.

"Moving a horse that distance is always a difficulty, but the dowager has a plan. She's had some experience getting a horse there." Jay turned to Raven. "Maybe, Raven, when you finish designing fire engines, you could design a traveling horse box. It will be a slog getting Hermes to the course. We'll start directly after your ball, I should think."

Raven looked up, and realized that Wenlocke, ever the keen observer of people, had been watching him. When they were boys in London, it had been Wenlocke's power of reading others that had kept them out of the clutches of those apparently amiable persons who sold boys into all forms of bondage. And Wenlocke had always known when one of his companions was troubled. Wherever they slept, Wenlocke made sure that the nightmares were kept at bay.

"And who will be your jockey?" the duchess continued.

"An unknown named Lester Oakley. He'll make his name on Hermes, I suspect. But the real secret of our success is the dowager's farrier, Dick Crockett. He's got magic hands for calming a horse. We will take him with us, a sort of secret weapon."

"So, the dowager is thinking of re-opening the Verwood stud?" Wenlocke spoke casually, but the tone did not fool Raven. It was like Wenlocke to investigate a situation before entering.

Jay nodded. "Hermes is five. Most of the purses are for two- and three-year-olds. If Hermes has some good outings this summer and fall, there might be interest in Verwood again."

"I understand that her grace is famously set in her views of proper training. Did you win her over to the Jay Kydd method?" Wenlocke asked.

Jay laughed. "It helped that I happened to agree with her about the harm of sweating and stoving. And then I had Bluebell, the dowager's granddaughter on my side. Have you met her?" He glanced at Raven.

"Bluebell?" The duchess looked curious.

"My name for Lady Cassandra. She encouraged her grandmother to take up where they'd left off Hermes's training years ago."

Raven worked at appearing indifferent. He had spent days, now weeks, trying to forget Cassie, and yet the mere mention of her name brought her rain-soaked image sharply to mind. Again, he felt Wenlocke's gaze on him. He roused himself to turn the conversation to other topics, asking about the Wenlocke children.

When the sky at last began to darken, they stood to say their good nights. Jay strode off briskly for the stables. Grandfather called for his man to assist him. The duchess offered Raven a kiss on the cheek and her best wishes for his ball. She planned to call upon the dowager in the morning.

Wenlocke took his wife's hand. "May we borrow your moonlit garden for a while, Raven?"

Raven nodded and turned away.

BY NINE ON the evening of Raven's ball, an excited young footman reported that carriages lined the drive. Servants stood outside to manage the traffic, and in the entry hall, to help the guests with coats and hats. Raven met his guests inside the great hall now transformed for the ball. The dowager stood on his right, and on his left, Grandfather Cole, and Honoria. One by one the neighboring families entered, making their bows, and staring wide-eyed at the transformation he had wrought in the old room. Tall brass tripods topped with a dozen glowing candles, chandeliers, and large white urns overflowing with summer blooms concealed the dark paneled walls and brightened the old place. Above was the new plaster ceiling. The orchestra, on its dais, played lively airs.

Amabel was to arrive a little before ten, and Raven hoped he could take her directly to the bench in the garden to make her his before the duties of hosting claimed him. The important thing was to secure Amabel's hand. Among those duties, the most worrisome was dancing the opening set with Cassie. If she came. The dowager seemed to have no doubt about the matter, but Raven could not be sure. He had not seen Cassie since the rain in June. The past weeks had been warm and dry as if rain had been banished from England.

Standing beside him, the dowager and Grandfather Cole had little to say to one another. Grandfather's insistence that steam-engines would soon replace the horse had not pleased the dowager. Now only Honoria made an effort to engage Grandfather in conversation. Raven caught snatches of his grandfather's booming voice rising above the babble in the room.

"Don't know why the boy wants to bury himself in the country like this," was Grandfather's comment.

"You can see, Mr. Cole, that he's quite well-liked here," Honoria suggested.

"He wants me to meet this chit he's taken a fancy to. I don't hold much with all this title nonsense, but if the dowry's right, the connection could be good for business. God knows, the boy's not done any business while he planned this frippery ball, a colossal waste of a man's blunt."

"But your business prospers, does it not?"

"It does. We've got orders for the Cole engine coming from five cities in America and three more in England."

"How gratifying to know your engine designs are so highly regarded."

Here the conversation was interrupted by the entrance of the Duke and Duchess of Wenlocke. The duke with his cool authority and the delicate duchess with her springy golden hair and easy grace drew all eyes. The duchess offered Raven her hands and a warm smile. Wenlocke clapped Raven on the shoulder, and nodded approval.

People turned to stare, as the duchess, once the Princess Giovanna Saville of Malfada, called "the fairy princess" by the papers, greeted the dowager, who unbent slightly to smile. Grandfather Cole simply wrapped her in a great hug, from which she emerged with a twinkling grin. Her husband straightened her silk headdress, dislodged by the old man's hug.

Raven grew more impatient as the room filled. There was no sign of Amabel. He wanted her to make an entrance, to draw the eye of every guest as the Duchess of Wenlocke had done. The ball was for her. The ring was in his pocket. Whatever misgivings nagged him in the last month, he was ready to put them aside. He had stuck to his plan of not seeing Cassie. And he believed it had helped, still thoughts of her had a way of intruding at odd moments of the day. He would see the boys go down to the lane to the dower house and know that they were going to see her. He would see the dowager's carriage leave for Sunday services and know that Cassie was inside. He would see Jay Kydd in Dick Crockett's wagon heading to the Crocketts after a day of training and know that Jay had likely spoken with her. He would hear of her from the craftsmen and merchants who had supplied the ball, invariably congratulating him on bringing Verwood back to life like the old days when Lady Cassandra was the beauty of the town.

At last, the word came that a pair of carriages had arrived from Ramsbury Park. Viscount Tyne escorted his sister and mother, glittering in silk and jewels, and looking above their company. Amabel's two young cousins appeared more excited for the ball. Then the earl and countess came in with Amabel herself. Her parents hung back a little, letting Amabel make her entrance. She did not disappoint in a rose-colored gown with a sparkling tiara on her golden curls and her vivid eyes bright. She curtsied prettily to the dowager, and gave her hand to Raven's grandfather with becoming modesty.

"Now, aren't you every bit as pretty as my grandson said you would be," his grandfather said.

Raven greeted her parents and then took her arm. There was no warmth in their greeting, but they seemed to approve the hall. Just as he'd hoped, Amabel drew the notice of the room, and an admiring hush followed them, as he led her to meet Wenlocke and his duchess.

"My goodness," she said. "What a crush! I had no idea you had so many acquaintances in the country."

"It is a neighborhood ball," he said.

"How very democratic of you!"

"Do you like the hall?"

She made a show of giving the room a careful scrutiny. "I do. You did all this for me, I think. I'm glad you took my advice about the flowers. And I like the idea of the little tables."

"I have reserved a pair of them for the Ramsbury party, but first I want you to meet my oldest friend, Wenlocke, that is my long-standing friend."

Raven did not know what either of the parties felt about the meeting. Polite greetings were exchanged, but his friends did not immediately see Amabel's perfection.

As they turned away, Amabel said, "I didn't know you counted a duke as a friend."

"Since we were boys," he said, tugging her toward the terrace and the garden beyond.

"Where are you taking me?" she asked, her lips in their familiar pout.

"You've not seen the garden yet."

She checked her step and looked up at him. "Must you really dance the first set with Lady Cassandra?"

"I must."

"Then I shall have to make do with Tyne." She tossed her head. "He doesn't have your ear for the beat, you know. Maybe we should get lost in the garden."

He gave her a warm smile. "We can try." He led her out

onto the terrace. The moon was bright overhead, and dozens of lanterns dotted the paths.

She gave a little gasp of delight, and he squeezed her hand. "I'm glad you like it."

"I do," she said. "But…"

"But?"

"I would like it so much more if it were truly yours. Do you see them often … your landladies?"

"Hardly at all. The dowager has forbidden me to enter the stables."

"Does Lady Cassandra ride? I thought after her accident that she gave up riding."

"Actually, she walks a great deal, but her rambles don't take her near me." That was the truth. Cassie was quite good at avoiding him. It threw him off his stride to be speaking of Cassie with Amabel. He reached in his pocket to check for the ring box.

They descended the terrace stairs and strolled along a grass path through the center of the garden, their way lighted by colored lanterns. The air was cooler than the ballroom, but warm enough to inspire the male crickets to sing their song. A few other guests stood on the terrace or wandered about the paths.

Raven led Amabel to the bench he had chosen. All summer he had thought of it as an enchanted place. Now, moonlight bathed, the stone looked cold. He spread his coat over the bench, and Amabel sat and folded her hands in her lap. Her dress glimmered like a shining river of silk.

He stood before her. "You must know that I have been looking forward to this moment for some time."

She nodded, her posture expectant, her eyes bright, the tiara on her curls glittering.

He had practiced different ways to tell her he loved her. None seemed right. The words wouldn't come. He decided there would be time to declare his love later. He still felt off his stride, and he settled for being accurate about his pursuit of her. "From the moment we met, your smile, your laughter inspired in me a regard I had not felt before, and which I hoped one day you could return." He dropped down on one knee, and took her hands in his. "If you can return that regard, would you do me the honor of becoming my wife?"

Music drifted out from the hall. A woman laughed gaily from the terrace. The crickets chirped on. Amabel tilted her head to study him, and he could not be sure if what she saw in his face made her hesitate to answer, or if she regretted those other suitors she'd turned down. He did not dare draw a breath. There was a chance she would refuse him. The grass was wet under his knee.

At last, she smiled. "Yes, I will marry you."

He raised her left hand to his lips and placed a kiss there. Later, he would worry about kissing her lips. He rose and joined her on the bench. "I have something for you." He took her hand again and unbuttoned her glove, sliding it down her arm, and tugging her hand free of the satin. Then he pulled the little Rundell, Bridge & Co. box from his pocket, and opened it.

Amabel squealed with delight, and clapped her hands to her lips. "It's beautiful," she said.

"It's fitting then," he said.

She held out her hand for him to slip the ring onto her

finger. In the moonlight, the diamonds glittered coldly. "We must go back inside. I must see it in the light."

He helped her up, and she tucked one arm in his, still holding out her other hand in the moonlight. When they reached the terrace, she stopped and turned to him. "We will have a brilliant wedding, and you will go higher. I know it."

As they reentered the ball, Raven caught the eye of the orchestra leader. The musicians had played for over an hour, and their leader was clearly ready to begin the dancing. A quick look around the ballroom did not reveal Cassie to Raven. Perhaps she had decided not to come after all. The plan was for Amabel to tell her news to her parents first, and then for she and Raven, standing with her parents and his grandfather, to announce their engagement to all the guests. And everything was going according to plan.

He looked for his grandfather and found the dowager first, her keen eye focused on a knot of gentlemen at the door. Among them, Grandfather Cole stood out, unmistakable for his height and head of black hair. Wenlocke was in the group with his easy authority, along with a red-faced Earl of Ramsbury, a furious, white-faced Jay Kydd, and a sneering Hugh Haydon. Raven led Amabel to her mother, and excused himself as Amabel showed the ring to the other ladies. The cousins squealed as much as Amabel had done.

Raven cut through the dancers to reach the gentlemen at the door. His gaze met Hugh's, and Hugh started. "You."

"Farnley," said Wenlocke evenly, "may I present Sir

Adrian Cole. I believe he's just become engaged to your sister."

The others turned to look across the ballroom where Amabel held out her be-ringed hand for her mother's admiration.

Hugh's mocking gaze didn't falter. Lord Ramsbury looked grim.

"It's true, sir," Raven said to his future father-in-law. "Lady Amabel and I were coming to tell you."

"She's accepted you then, has she?"

"She has."

Ramsbury nodded, but offered no congratulations.

Raven turned back to Hugh. "Welcome to Verwood, Farnley. You're in time for the dancing." Raven meant to swallow his distaste for the man, even if Hugh's resentment would not be easily overcome.

There followed a frozen moment in which the parties measured one another. Raven tried to avoid Jay's eye, but it was no good. His old friend was plainly furious at the welcome Hugh received and could not be contained.

"Hah, Farnley's as welcome in a stable as a case of the strangles!" Jay burst out. "I found him nosing about the dowager's horses."

It was an ugly accusation. Wenlocke shifted slightly to stand at Jay's side.

Hugh looked bored. "I arrived late and drove my rig straight there. I looked for a groom, but no one seemed to be about."

It was the sort of speech Raven had grown accustomed to among Amabel's friends, a convenient version of events.

Raven knew how such talk worked now. "You must not have seen the grooms waiting to assist our guests."

"Just so, I missed them in the dark."

"Missed them!" Jay broke in again. "Slithered past them like a snake in the grass."

Wenlocke put a hand on Jay's shoulder. "Come, Jay, let's rally Sir Adrian's servants to make sure they don't miss any other late-arriving guests."

Jay looked as if he might shrug off the friendly hand, in favor of planting a facer on Hugh, but it was Wenlocke's hand, and one didn't dismiss Wenlocke. Jay and Raven were the duke's men. Loyalty to him was a permanent part of who they were.

"Gentlemen." Wenlocke turned away. Jay gave Hugh one last savage glance and followed Wenlocke.

Hugh looked over the ballroom. "Interesting company you keep, Cole. I suppose it's mixing in trade that makes a man less nice in his taste."

"I don't know," Raven replied. "I've been mixing at Ramsbury Park. Will you join your family as Amabel and I make our announcement?"

Hugh spun to face Raven. "My father may have approved this unequal alliance, he's always short of the ready, but don't think that your thousands of pounds can make you one of us." Hugh gave the great hall a sneering glance. "This may dazzle Amabel for a time, but you are like a toy she'll tire of and cast aside."

"Your sister picked me. I don't expect to be one of you." Raven knew, as he said it, how true that was. "I will be Amabel's husband and will endeavor to promote her happiness."

Hugh snorted. "Then you will have your work cut out for you. I doubt she wants a husband at all. She doesn't like being ruled, you know."

Raven walked away. Whatever the truth of Amabel's character, whether she was vain or shallow, Raven doubted that Hugh had the least interest in her happiness. He made his way across the room to claim his fiancée at the tables reserved for the Ramsbury party.

With a little milling about, they arranged themselves in front of the orchestra dais.

CASSIE HAD ENTERED the ballroom as Jay Kydd stormed out, unseeing, with a handsome golden-haired man who had to be the Duke of Wenlocke. Then she saw Raven and Amabel, surrounded by her family and his grandfather in front of the dais. The Earl of Ramsbury proposed a toast. Amabel beamed. Hugh sneered. Raven stood with a smile frozen on his face. She didn't think he saw her. She had learned the hard lesson of presenting a strong face to the world even as everything inside her screamed in pain. Now she stood as Raven sealed his fate. Momentarily, when she had seen Hugh's angry face, she had thought maybe he had come to break up Raven's plan. But she supposed that was not in Hugh's power. He might dislike his sister's marrying Raven, but he had neither the sense of principle nor concern for others that might lead him to action.

Honoria came to Cassie's side, and gave her hand a quick

squeeze, which almost was her undoing. A hollow ache in her chest now threatened to spread to all her limbs. She did not know how she could dance the opening set with him.

"He's confused," Honoria said. "He will realize he's chosen wrong."

"But he has chosen," Cassie said.

"Well, he can't be happy about it. He can't have asked that girl to marry him, knowing he loves you."

Cassie gave her aunt a sympathetic glance. Honoria loved her happy endings. "He doesn't know he loves me."

"But how can he get out of the thing now?" Honoria cried.

Cassie returned the squeeze of her aunt's hand. "He can't." Only Amabel could release him now. "Aunt, we can't help him. Instead let's think of London. Will you go to Hatchard's or Lackington's first?"

At the end of the earl's remarks, everyone did as they were expected to do, raising their glasses, and cheering on cue. Several young ladies slumped, visibly disappointed in Raven's choice, as if they had wearied of the ball before it began.

RAVEN STEPPED OUT of the circle of Amabel's family and friends. It was time to open the ball, and he had not yet seen Cassie. When the room suddenly hushed again, he became aware of his guests turning to the entrance. He turned to follow the crowd's interest.

There stood Cassie, a Cassie he had never seen, but still

Cassie. She wore an utterly fashionable pale blue gown of some fabric that seemed spun of air. It nipped her waist and bared her shoulders. Dark curls cascaded down her neck from a simple arrangement on her head. Silver threads of pearls in the dark strands caught the light. She passed into the room, warmly and easily acknowledging greetings from her neighbors, and like that, everyone forgot Amabel, forgot the engagement. His neighbors had come for her. The crowd opened a path for Cassie to the orchestra where she and Raven would lead the first dance. For a moment, she hesitated. Raven knew she had not wanted to make so public an appearance. Then she began to walk, her head held high, with that unmistakable dipping step of hers that could be so awkward. In this moment her walk caught the lilting rhythm of the music.

Amabel tugged his arm. "That's not Lady Cassandra, is it?" she asked.

"It is," said Raven, grimly. Once again, he felt duped. For him, Cassie had worn old straw bonnets, and faded, out-of-fashion gowns. She'd never done anything to her hair except to twist it in a knot at her nape. He had never seen the hollows at the base of her throat, or the sweet smooth flesh of her arms. *You could have warned me*, he thought.

And he knew that he had been blind. She had been before him all the time, but he had been thinking that Amabel was what he wanted, that winning her would undo the world's judgment of him. But the world's judgment didn't matter. It could wound a person deeply, but it could not change who you were or alter the essence of one's character. Cassie knew that. Her walk with all eyes upon her showed that she knew that.

CASSIE REACHED THE place where she must begin the dance with Raven. Her neighbors' welcome had made the long walk possible. Without them, she never would have made it with so many eyes upon her. She was conscious of Amabel and her party in the crowd. They knew the full story of Cassie's folly and humiliation. They had spread the hurtful phrase. But she could not be shattered again. The room was full of friends. Grandmama and Honoria were there. Cassie turned to face the crowd, standing as tall and as straight as she could.

Raven strode forward to stand at her side. He looked magnificent in the black-and-white of his evening wear that could not entirely disguise his muscularity. It was shocking how, seeing him, instantly undid all the efforts of a month of forgetting. She would have to begin again once this night was over. And she must get to London. She must replace the images in her head with other impressions. He was frowning at her.

"I've offended you again," she said.

"Not, at all." He took her hand. "So, you decided you could dance with me."

Other couples began to take the floor.

"Grandmama was most persuasive. I will try not to let the side down."

Lady Amabel and her partner, a young man Cassie did not know, took their places as the lines formed.

"Amabel forgave you, I take it," she said.

"She did." He was tight-lipped and unsmiling.

"Then everything has gone according to your plan. The room looks beautiful, and it is wonderful to see it full of people. A house like Verwood is meant to be connected to its neighbors. Thank you."

The musicians ceased their tuning. Cassie faced Raven. He looked somber and grim. He should be radiating joy. She smiled at him. Then the orchestra struck up, a rather stately tune of an earlier time. They bowed to each other, and prompted by the music, took light steps to meet in the middle.

"It's a dance," she reminded him in passing. "You are stuck with me for mere minutes."

On the opposite side, she turned to face him again. She should heed her own words. It was only a dance, but the dancing would undo all the work she had done to forget him. She might be unhappy, but she could not see why he should be so. All his efforts had brought Amabel to the lovely evening that he had made for her.

When the dance brought them together again as they moved down the line, he said, "We ended our brief friendship badly. I am sorry for that."

"Then you have forgiven me for not telling you about Hugh?" It was some comfort that he regretted their terrible quarrel in the rain. For that she was grateful. They would not part as enemies. A turn took her away from him for a moment, and they came together again and joined hands to advance down the line.

"Have you forgiven me?" he asked.

"Yes," she said. She had forgiven him, too easily, too completely. He wanted to be part of the world she'd left behind, a world she had taken for granted. Before the disaster of her Season and her accident, she had assumed that she would always have a place in that world. She knew better now.

The stately dance required them to join hands over head and behind their backs. Each time he seemed reluctant to let her fingers go. His gaze never left hers. The music made a space where they danced alone. The advance and retreat of the dance mimicked their friendship.

They reached the end of the line. The last moments of the dance required one more bow, one more coming toward each other and taking hands. The music ended with their hands still joined and his eyes gazing into hers. In a heart-stopping moment, she realized that he knew, knew that she loved him. It should be mortifying, but it was instead a release of pent-up feelings that had had no expression since they had begun. And then his face changed, matched her own, pain written plain on his features. He knew that he loved her, too. His eyes admitted it. But he would marry Amabel. She feared she would start shaking and not be able to stop.

There was a burst of clapping around them, and he tucked her arm into his and walked her to her grandmother and his grandfather. She caught the looks on their faces, Grandmama knowing, Mr. Cole confused. She turned her gaze to Raven's evening shoes as he bowed his farewell. He would go to Amabel now.

When the supper interval began, Cassie slipped away.

She had nearly fulfilled her bargain with Grandmama. London beckoned.

RAVEN DANCED WITH Amabel and with a half dozen of his neighbors' daughters before the waltz he had saved for his betrothed. He made every effort to avoid looking for Cassie in the crowd. He was aware of having betrayed himself in the last moment of their dance.

Now that he knew his heart, the evening seemed interminable. His vision was extraordinarily clear. He could see each step of the way that led him to this moment. He could see the blue flame at the heart of each candle and the individual petals on the pink dog roses trailing from the tall urns. He had created a triumph for Amabel, and he owed her his allegiance even if that allegiance was compromised because his heart did not belong to her. She was lovely still, though her loveliness was a surface thing, a matter of paint and gilding rather than the grain of her being. But he could choose to make her happy. It was no small thing in life to care about another's happiness. They might live more in London than in the country. Her sphere would be with her friends and his might shift back to his business.

CHAPTER TWENTY

Cassie and Honoria were to spend a fortnight in London with her mother's cousin, Marianne Howarth. Then they would travel to Chichester to meet Grandmama for Hermes's first outing in the flat races.

The Howarth town house in Brunswick Square proved to be a good place for Cassie's project of forgetting Raven. Marianne, who had at first written to say that of course they could come, but that she might be occupied with other duties, was now keen to show them her favorite parts of London, and to share her expertise about shops and spots of historical importance. She was a tireless promoter of the benefits of living in Brunswick Square.

Cassie and Honoria had a room on the third story facing the square itself. In the first week of their visit, Marianne took them to Hatchard's and Lackington's for books and to the shops on Oxford Street, including the Pantheon Bazaar. She led them through her own neighborhood to the Reading Room of the British Museum where Honoria was able to procure a reader's pass. With so much activity and with the conversation of the household centered around Marianne's grown children and their prospects, Cassie never thought of Raven above three or four times an hour.

Like others before her, Marianne believed Brunswick

Square with its modest modern town houses, airy open space, and conveniences which attracted a class of professional men, to be an ideal place to live in London. The square had a village atmosphere with neighbors greeting one another, stretches of grass dotted with plane trees, and at one end open fields and a view up to Hampstead. Cassie found the walking excellent.

It felt very different from the London she remembered from her unhappy Season. It might be possible, she thought, to take a house in the neighborhood. Honoria could write, and Cassie could find something to do, she was sure. As well as being home to prosperous professional men and their families, the neighborhood was home to waifs of every sort. A quaint old church ministered to the climbing boys with a splendid Christmas dinner each year. Cassie suspected that more could be done.

The greatest neighborhood institution was the Foundling Hospital, which had taken in London's unwanted infants for nearly a hundred years, educated them, and sent them off in the world to be apprenticed or to enter service. The hospital had associations with musicians and painters, and its chapel was famous as the place where the great composer Handel himself had performed. As Cassie entered for Sunday services, she congratulated herself on the progress she'd made in a mere week. She was learning to live in a world in which Raven would soon be married to Amabel.

The chapel impressed with its soaring ceiling and great windows letting in light. At the east end, the children, girls in their white caps, boys in their uniforms, sat on the upper level, ranged in tiers with the pipes of a great organ reaching up behind them. As Cassie climbed the stairs to the second level boxes, a bright yellow plaque on the wall caught her gaze. It named Mr. Jedidiah Cole as a benefactor who had provided a fund for clothing and blankets for the children. Instantly, her progress in forgetting Raven came to an end. Cassie tugged Marianne's sleeve and pointed to the plaque.

"Marianne, do you know the story behind this philanthropy?"

"Of course. Mr. Cole's grandson was a foundling here. It's one of those stories the governors like to tell the public. Sadly, few of the foundlings are ever reunited with their original families, though I imagine the mothers must hope."

Marianne continued up the steps while Cassie remained standing transfixed by a sudden rush of thoughts, unable to take a step. Raven's past could hardly matter to her any longer. The smart thing was to let thoughts of him go. But she could not. Of course, the mothers must hope, but what did the children think? What hopes did they have of finding their families? Raven had lived here. He had been a boy in this place, separated from his family, anonymous in his uniform. She took a deep breath and concentrated on climbing. Marianne, with her usual expertise, found them seats in the very front of the upper box, with an excellent view of the crowd below and of the foundlings themselves in their neat rows. All Cassie could think was that Raven had been one of them. And that he had never accepted the place in society marked out for him by the institution.

Marianne exchanged words with Honoria. When she turned back to Cassie, she said, "Honoria tells me you've met Mr. Cole. No wonder you noticed the plaque. Shall I tell you the story?"

Cassie pressed her hands together in her lap. It was not in her power to say 'no.'

"Mr. Cole is a fairly recent patron of the hospital. It turns out that his daughter bore a son to a young officer bound for the Peninsula War, who died there. She presented herself and the infant to the hospital without confessing her true identity, though she did name the father's regiment. As is their practice, the governors of the hospital particularly want to accept the orphaned offspring of military men."

"What became of the mother then?"

"No one knows. In theory a mother can reclaim her child if she leaves a token, half of which is affixed to the child's papers. She keeps the other half. Many write notes, or leave a bit of cloth, or half a coin. In practice, so little is done for these mothers that their circumstances rarely improve."

Below them the chapel was filling up. "Mr. Cole's daughter did not go back to her family then?"

"Not that I have ever heard. The hospital actually lost the child when he was quite young."

"Lost him? How?"

"Once a year they take the boys to Primrose Hill for an outing. On one occasion, several boys disappeared. The hospital covered up the scandal, and it isn't clear whether the boys left on their own, or whether they were lured away by the sort of unscrupulous persons who want to sell small boys to the sweeps or the mills."

"So how did Mr. Cole ever reconnect with his grandson?" Cassie knew very well that the old man had connected with Raven and had made Raven his heir.

"Ah, well, I don't suppose you've heard of the Duke of Wenlocke, have you?"

"I have." She could not say that she had met him, but the duchess had called at the dower house and Cassie remembered the handsome duke from Raven's ball. Jay Kydd had told her that Wenlocke had once been a lost boy himself. The other boys had looked up to him as a sort of shepherd, keeping them safe in London.

"It was Wenlocke who reunited them," Marianne said. "He has quite an interest in the children of London. When he shows up at a school or a hospital, I suspect that the governors, whoever they are, start scraping and bowing at the thought of the money he might bestow on them."

Cassie had more questions, but the service was about to begin. The children rose to their feet. The congregation followed. The organist began the first hymn, written by the poet Cowper. The famous chaplain led them in prayer and preached and the children sang and the hour passed. It was a powerful service, but one in which Cassie felt a bit lost, not a part of the community as she was in St. Andrew's at home with Mr. Montford putting them all into a Sunday snooze. And she had to admit to herself that she had not been her most attentive, consumed as she was with thoughts of Raven again.

It was only when they were walking home that Marianne again took up the subject of Wenlocke.

"Oh, we've met him and his duchess," Honoria announced cheerfully. "They were guests of our tenant, Sir Adrian Cole, just this month."

Marianne looked both surprised and annoyed at being

unable to astonish them with her superior knowledge. It was her story, and here they were, mere country guests, appearing to know more of the matter than she, a true Londoner, did.

Cassie smoothed her cousin's ruffled feathers, explaining that their meeting had been of the briefest sort at a crowded ball and not an occasion for them to learn what they really wanted to know about the handsome duke. They really were dependent on Marianne if she could enlighten them.

"Very well," she said. "I have it on good authority from my friend Eloise, who is a patroness at a school in Bread Street, where one of Wenlocke's sisters-in-law is the headmistress, that Wenlocke, who was kidnapped himself as a boy, has made it his mission to investigate the parentage of the boys who were with him when he was … on his own."

"On his own? In London? A boy?" Honoria shuddered.

"His family searched for him for years, I believe, before he was found and reunited with them and came into his title. Now, you see why he finds the families of the other boys."

"And Sir Adrian was one of them?" Honoria asked.

"Yes. It turned out that Mr. Jedediah Cole advertised for his daughter when she disappeared. He had no suspicion of the child, you see. He merely thought she had eloped. He did not think of the Foundling Hospital, but Wenlocke, well, he knew that young women of good character could find themselves of necessity turning to the hospital."

"And the hospital had Sir Adrian's records?" Cassie asked.

"They keep excellent records," Marianne insisted.

"How remarkable!" Honoria marveled. "Sir Adrian has such an air of confidence and determination. One would never think he had been like these wretched waifs one sees in your neighborhood, Marianne."

Cassie could think it. Raven was tough under his polished exterior. She had seen him stand up for Dick Crockett. He knew bullies. She had seen him climb a wall to rescue the Montford boys. He knew the dangers boys could get into. She had borne his anger at her over Hugh. He knew that things could be snatched away from one in spite of care and effort. He had distanced himself from the boy he had been. He knew how London rated its ragged, barefoot boys, only fit for the lowliest work, easily discarded. And he had defied that rating.

When they reached Marianne's town house, a courier had left a message from Grandmama. YOUR HORSE NEEDS YOU. COME AT ONCE. I HAVE TAKEN A HOUSE IN ST. MARTIN'S SQUARE, CHICHESTER, FOR THE LAST FORTNIGHT OF JULY.

A WEEK AFTER the ball, the young people at Ramsbury Park exhausted the local entertainments. On a warm afternoon, they had retreated to the white-and-gold drawing room for ices when the idea of an outing to Chichester to see the races occurred to Hugh. Amabel immediately took up the idea and turned to Raven laughing, excited. "Oh, do say you will go."

Raven frowned. He planned to return to London, and he distrusted Hugh's motive for wanting to attend the race. According to Jay, Hugh had been on the point of opening Hermes's stall when Jay had come across him the night of the ball. The dowager, Kydd, Snell, and Dick Crockett had left for Chichester with the horse two days after the ball. Raven did not expect Cassie to attend the race, but he was not ready to see her if she did.

Hugh lay sprawled on another couch, but sat up and fixed his gaze on Raven. "Such a prodigious frown, Cole, from the man who wants to make my sister happy."

Raven bit back a retort. Whatever the truth of Amabel's character, whether she was vain or shallow, Raven doubted that Hugh had the least interest in her happiness. Hugh was a bitter medicine best taken in small doses, but, Raven admitted, a corrective one. In the first week of his engagement to Amabel, his idea of their marriage had changed rapidly like the projected scenes in a theater. He had thought that he would bring Amabel to Verwood, that she would find a place in his life. Now he saw that Verwood would never please her. She needed a great deal of gaiety and excitement. Even Ramsbury Park was not enough for her, and she could not be pried out of her own circle, which he had been permitted to enter as a suitor. He already suspected that Hugh was right on one point, that Amabel would not like Raven half so well as a husband.

It was one of the ideas that had only occurred to him in the week since the ball. He *liked* Cassie. Perhaps that was why he had been blind to her as a woman to love. He had not understood the role of simple liking in his ties to others. He liked Jay and Wenlocke and the others, Finch, Swallow, and Robin. And he liked his grandfather, too. With them, he shared experiences. Though they never spoke of feelings, he understood that his friends saw the world much as he saw it.

They laughed at the things that made him laugh, and frowned at the things that made him frown.

Hugh sauntered off to see what he could do about making the outing happen, and Amabel turned to Raven on their couch.

"We've been so dull here," she pleaded.

"Have we?" Raven asked. "We've had tennis and picnics and riding."

"You don't like the idea of going to the races, do you?" she asked.

"But you do," he said. He would make the best of it. As long as Cassie was not there.

"You don't like it because it is Hugh's idea." She pursed her lips in the little pout Raven had so much wanted to kiss for weeks. "He is my brother, so you ought to respect him and treat him decently. He's a little wild, but he will have my father's place someday, and I intend to be on good terms with him always."

"I know," he said. "We'll go. Amabel wills it so." He managed a smile.

"Then I will talk to Mama. She will listen to me."

Amabel had no trouble convincing her mother to support the scheme, so Hugh was sent ahead to find accommodations in the town, and the ladies began packing. Raven would make it his first object on arrival to warn Jay Kydd of Hugh's presence.

CHAPTER TWENTY-ONE

THE HOUSE CASSIE'S grandmama took in Chichester's St. Martin's Square was a plain cream-colored affair of three stories, five bedrooms, and a basement kitchen area, conveniently placed near the elaborate sixteenth-century market cross at the center of town and with a view of the unmistakable cathedral spire. Cassie discovered that it was but a short walk to the old priory green. The race course where Hermes was already stabled was a little over three miles away.

The morning after their arrival, Grandmama whisked Cassie off in her landau to see Hermes. Honoria was left to explore the town. Sky and clouds were brilliantly blue and white while ripening grain gave a golden cast to the fields. Dust lay on the hedgerows. Twisting to look behind her from the carriage Cassie could see the blue expanse of the sea below the cathedral's spire.

The Duke of Richmond's house was imposing, and the stables, very grand, with a large grassy courtyard, and room for dozens of horses. The steady clop of hooves accompanied them as Grandmama led Cassie to Hermes's roomy stall. Jay and Dick Crockett were there, deep in a conversation of hands. Both turned to Cassie with grins. Hermes saw her and stretched out his neck to be petted. She rubbed his sleek coat with gentle strokes.

"You all look well. What is the worry that made you send for me?"

"We are generally right and tight," Jay said, "but Hermes has had so many disturbances to his routine, we thought it would help to have you here."

"Then, I'm glad to be here." She brushed Hermes's forelock, and he tossed his head. "How are his prospects?"

"Good, I'd say," Jay offered. "He's ready, but a lot depends on the ground. He's best on hard ground, and he's agile enough to handle the downhill. If the ground is loose on top after the early heats, he may have some trouble."

"You've been out walking the course?" Cassie asked. Jay Kydd knew his business and wanted Hermes to run well. Jay was his usual jaunty self with his blue-dotted neckerchief and riding boots.

"Very early in the morning. Getting a feel for it, you know. He's going to do the six-furlong dash for three-year-olds and older."

"And is every other owner as secretive as you are? Or do you know who the competition is?"

A look passed between Jay and Grandmama that made Cassie instantly suspect that they were up to something.

"There will be twelve entries, and a couple of them have won before," Jay said.

"And what are you not telling me?" Cassie asked.

"Well, girl, you are the listed owner," Grandmama said.

"Me?"

"C. J. Lavenham," said Jay. "That way no one will think of Verwood. We don't want any other jockey setting his sights on Hermes as the one to beat."

"So that's why you sent for me, Grandmama."

"I sent for you because you started Hermes on this path, and you will see him through. I expect you to walk him to the paddock tomorrow."

Under the gaze of Grandmama, Jay Kidd, and Dick Crockett, Cassie could hardly say no. They had put such effort into preparing Hermes for his day. She could walk the mile easily enough, though she did not like the idea of so many eyes upon her as she walked. "Very well," she said. "I'll do it."

"Good for you, Bluebell," Jay said. "It's only right that you should be part of Hermes's triumph."

"Oh, is he going to win then?" Cassie grinned at Jay. She did like his confidence.

THE DAY OF the race exactly answered Amabel's desire for excitement. It was easy, after all to please her, Raven thought. At the Anchor where they were staying, she encountered friends from London. Rolling along to the track in a smart landau, wearing an equally smart hat, and catching the notice of the crowd suited her. She laughed and smiled and waved. She did not enjoy the walk up to the enclosure, as much, for along with people of rank, were vendors of beer and sandwiches, and fellows who would pitch their tents to offer dancing dogs and games of chance.

She had only one complaint to make as a group of London friends passed by them eager to get to the enclosure set aside for fashionable guests in a prime spot on the rail.

"Gentlemen don't notice me the way they used to," she said.

"I notice you," Raven replied.

"But it's not the same, is it?"

"You mean because you are an engaged woman? Wouldn't it be ungentlemanly for other men to think of you as … unattached?"

"Of course. I belong to you now, don't I?" She smiled up at him from under her frothy hat.

Raven found them seats near the rail inside the enclosure marked for the highest-ranking guests. He procured lemonade for the ladies and went in search of his brother-in-law to be. There was no sign of Hugh at the betting stands.

CASSIE PARTED FROM Grandmama and Honoria at the entrance to the large stable compound, more of a palace for horses, she thought, but Verwood, on a smaller scale, could measure up. Jay was with Lester Oakley seeing the jockey weighed and ready and would return to meet Cassie at the stall for Hermes's walk to the paddock where the jockeys would mount. Trainers passed Cassie on their way out of the stable compound with their horses, and she admired the glossy coats and easy walks of horses who had probably raced before. She tried to notice which of them looked especially fit and prepared to run and at ease in spite of the hum of excitement in the air. It would all be new to Hermes, and she understood the importance of helping him keep his composure.

As she approached Hermes's stall, she heard sounds of a scuffle, grunts and thuds, and Hermes snorting and squealing in distress. She dashed forward and flung open the stall door. Hugh Haydon and Dick Crockett lurched about in a tangled clinch. Hermes reared and came down hard, blowing, his ears back.

Cassie rushed forward to calm the horse. "Hugh, stop," she cried. "Stop!"

Her cry had no effect. The two men reeled, and banged into the wall. Dick tried to free his arms from Hugh's hold. Abruptly, Hugh pushed back, shoving Dick off of him. Dick's head hit the wood with a crack. The youth slid down the wall, and slumped against it.

Hugh panted and pointed at Dick. "He was interfering with the horse."

Cassie shook her head. "That's not possible, and you know it."

"Look in his hand. You'll find a nail. He was going to drive it into your horse's hoof." Hugh nudged Dick's hand with his boot. The boy's palm opened, and a nail, a short, sharp bit of iron, just long enough to penetrate the hoof through the shoe, rolled out of his slack hand.

Cassie knelt at Dick's side. The youth groaned and opened his eyes. He tried to stand, but Cassie held him down. His throat made agonized sounds. His eyes pleaded with her.

From behind her, a sharp, cold voice demanded, "What's going on?"

Cassie spun round. Raven stood in the doorway, outlined

by the light. She blinked as if his very solid presence were a mere illusion. In her mind he was miles away with Amabel at Ramsbury Park, lost to Cassie forever. Now the distance between them had shrunk to the narrow width of a horse stall. With a little leap her heart broke free of the hold she'd kept on it for weeks.

Then Hugh turned to Raven. "Mind your business, Cole. This man was interfering with the horse."

"Let me summon one of the stewards." Raven looked as composed as ever, with that arrogant assurance Cassie had seen in him at their first meeting.

"No," Cassie protested. "Dick would never harm Hermes."

Raven flashed her a warning glance. She could not read his expression. He would not look directly at her. She thought he was on Dick's side as he had been that first day, but Hugh was to be his brother-in-law.

Footsteps pounded outside. Jay and three stable hands showed up at the stall door.

"You," Jay shouted at Hugh. He lunged for him, but Raven held him back.

"Get a steward, Jay." Jay wrenched himself out of Raven's grip, his mouth open to protest, but when he met Raven's gaze, he nodded. He stepped outside the stall. More running footsteps sounded.

Hugh brushed straw off of his jacket. "My work is done, here. I'll return to my friends."

"I think not." Raven's voice was cool and unyielding. "You'll want to repeat your accusation for the steward."

Hugh glanced at the stall door, as if he would try to push

his way past Raven. Behind Raven stood the three stable hands. "Very well, but my sister will be wondering where her escorts are."

Jay returned with a steward, a stout, ginger-haired fellow, with a bristling beard in the top hat and coat of his position. "Mr. Jennings," Jay announced.

"What's amiss here?" Jennings asked.

Raven pointed to Hugh. "Lord Farnley here accuses this man, Dick Crockett of interfering with Lady Cassandra's horse."

Cassie wanted to protest that nothing of the kind could possibly have happened, but she caught a look from Jay.

Jennings looked at Hugh. "What did you see, my lord?" he asked.

"I found this fellow trying to drive a nail into the horse's hoof. You can see it in his hand."

"And were you here, my lady?" asked Jennings.

"I came in as the two men fought," Cassie answered.

"So you did not see the lad attempting to harm the horse?"

"I've known Dick Crockett for years. He would never harm an animal. He is Hermes's farrier," Cassie said.

Jennings turned to Dick, still sprawled against the wall, looking dazed. "What do you have to say for yourself, lad?"

Cassie took Dick's hand and gave him the sign to speak. He gave her an agonized look. Like her, he hated to admit what others regarded as a limitation. She nodded.

Dick pushed himself upright, turned to Jay, and began to make hand gestures.

"What's this?" Jennings asked.

"The lad can't hear," said Raven. "He communicates with hand gestures. Jay Kydd, the trainer, knows the lad's hand language. He can interpret."

"Never heard of a deaf farrier." Jennings paused a moment, and looked at each of the persons in the room. "So, you," he indicated Kydd, "are the trainer." Jay nodded. "The boy is the farrier. And, you," he looked at Cassie, "are the owner."

Cassie nodded.

Jennings had another look at Hugh, a look at the nail, and a look around the stall. Then he turned to Jay. "What's the boy saying then?"

"He says that he found Lord Farnley attempting to hammer that nail into Hermes's rear off-side hoof, sir. He tried to take the nail from Farnley. They fought, and Farnley slammed him into the wall."

"Nonsense," said Hugh. "You can't believe the word of a freakish lout over the word of a gentleman."

There was a stir at the stall door. "Let me through," came a cool voice. Viscount Tyne pushed aside the stable hands to enter the stall. "Having some trouble, Farnley?" he asked.

"For God's sake, Tyne, this fellow Jennings is trying to stitch me up here. Can't get anyone to take the word of a gentleman."

Tyne turned to Jennings. "I can vouch for Lord Farnley."

Jennings nodded. "That may be, my lord, but as you were not present when the incident occurred, your word is not needed. Not the way we do things here." Jennings turned back to Cassie.

"Is the horse harmed?" Jennings asked.

Cassie stood and went to Hermes's head, stroking his neck and murmuring reassurance. Jay checked the horse's hooves. "He looks sound," he said.

"And he's to race today?" Jennings asked.

"Yes," Cassie said. "But we must take him up to the paddock now."

Jay helped Dick to his feet. The youth went straight to Hermes and laid his head against Hermes's crest. The horse turned and nuzzled him.

"You may take him, my lady," said Jennings. "As for you two," Jennings gestured to Hugh and Dick, "you two will be locked up until further investigation."

"Not Dick!" Cassie cried.

"Locked up!" Hugh exclaimed. "You can't do that." He spun to Raven. "This is your doing. You will not please my sister by having me detained. If you think she'll marry you after this, you're mad."

"Mr. Jennings," said Raven, "I think it will shorten your investigation considerably if you ask Lord Farnley to remove his coat."

Hugh's face reddened. "If you think I'm removing my coat on your say so, Cole, you *are* mad."

"On my say so, then," said Cassie, "as the owner of the horse."

Jennings turned to the three stable hands standing by. "Lads, his lordship is reluctant. Please assist him. My lord, these fellows can be as nice as your best London valet, or not."

Hugh made a sudden lunge for the door. Raven stepped in his path. Hugh swung at him. In the process, an object tumbled to the ground. At the thud, everyone stopped. Jennings reached down and picked it up. He held it aloft for everyone to see, a slim-handled, triangular-headed shoeing hammer.

"Lock his lordship up." Jennings shook his head. "Not well done, sir. We'll see what the duke has to say about a gentleman interfering with a horse."

CHAPTER TWENTY-TWO

THERE WAS NO time for a word with Raven, to thank him, to understand the meaning of his being there and taking Dick's side again.

Cassie, Dick, and Jay started up the hill to the paddock with Hermes. Jay held Hermes's lead, while Dick and Cassie walked on either flank. At first, Hermes tossed his head fretfully, his ears pinned back, his gait choppy. Cassie walked as near him as she could, patting his shoulder, and speaking to him, hoping her voice would soothe him. She told him that no harm had come to Dick. She told him that he was going to enjoy running as he was meant to run. She told him that Lester Oakley would keep him safe. As they approached the paddock, Hermes began to calm, his walk became steady, his ears came up and a little forward. Cassie shot Jay a relieved glance.

They were almost the last horse to arrive, and Lester broke into a wide smile when he saw them. In no time Lester, in Verwood's dark-blue silks, mounted and joined the parade around the paddock. There Hermes drew attention with his glossy coat, strong muscles, and tucked-in belly. He looked like a horse ready to run. People around them took note.

"Excuse me, miss," one of the blacklegs asked, "is that

your horse?"

Cassie nodded.

"His first time out, is it?"

"Yes."

The man turned back to his race card. "He has the outside position."

"He'll do well there," she said. "Where he can see the field and not get boxed in. He loves to run."

Once the parade finished, the gate was opened, and the horses moved onto the track itself. Cassie stepped into the owner's enclosure, largely dominated by men, but with wives and daughters there as well. She spotted Grandmama in the grandstand, her usual imperious self, talking to the Duke of Richmond. Whatever happened in the race, they had broken through things that had held them back for three years. In minutes the flag would drop, and Hermes would have his long-delayed chance to run.

RAVEN SLIPPED BACK into the enclosure where Amabel sat in urgent conversation with her friends. He felt the difference in the conversation at once. Tyne glanced his way with a look of smug triumph. Amabel jumped up when she saw Raven.

"Where's Hugh? Tyne says the stewards have taken him and locked him up." She clung to Raven's arm.

"It's true." Raven held himself very still. Conscious of hostile looks from everyone around them. Tyne was holding up Lady Ramsbury. Raven was the outsider that he had been all along. He had not broken the barrier he'd set out to break all those years ago.

"But Hugh's a gentleman," Amabel protested. "How dared they. You must get him released."

Raven shook his head. "Your brother attempted to interfere with a horse."

"You can't believe that," she said, stepping back from him.

"There is a witness."

"A witness? Oh, the deaf boy with the donkey. Tyne said he was there. No one will believe him."

"Why shouldn't they?"

Amabel stared at him as if she thought him particularly dense. She lowered her head, so that he stared briefly at the frothy lace and rose-colored silken bows of her hat. When she lifted her face to him again, she gave him one of the pretty glances that had so often dazzled him. "Hugh is my brother. If you love me, you must tell the stewards that he was not at fault. They will believe you."

"I can't do that, Amabel." Raven spoke as gently as he could. On the track, the flag dropped and the horses thundered past the enclosure. The crowd erupted in cheers. He hoped Cassie's horse had a good run.

"Hugh was right about you," Amabel said bitterly. "You are not a real gentleman." She stepped back, tugged his ring from her finger, and threw it at him. It landed somewhere in the grass at his feet.

It was the truth. He was not a gentleman in her eyes. "Are you releasing me?" he asked.

Tyne stepped to Amabel's side and took her arm in his.

"She's dismissing you, Cole. You have no place here. You will find London's doors closed to you, and you will hear from Lord Ramsbury's solicitor."

Raven gave Amabel a parting look. Her English femininity, like a spring garden had drawn him in London in the winter after the fire, but he was, perhaps, a man with a taste for autumn, for a garden tested and shaken by blasts and vivid with warmth.

"My best wishes for your happiness, madam," he said. With a quick bow, he turned away. He squeezed through the crowd straining toward the rail as the horses drew near again. As he passed from the enclosure, the crowd exploded in cheers.

CHAPTER TWENTY-THREE

IN THE END Hermes pulled away from the pack, finding his pace, something clicking in his brain about the speed he possessed, a surge of the joy of running, a need to lead the pack, not follow. The outside position had been a lucky draw for him. He was never boxed in, and he pounded down the final stretch, moving easily.

Cassie looked up to find her grandmother beaming down on her as she headed to the winner's enclosure. It was vain to hope that she would see Raven, but she looked anyway. Nowhere in the crowd could she spot him. They owed this moment to him, and she had not thanked him. Jay and Dick led Hermes into the winner's enclosure. Lester Oakley jumped down and did a couple of handsprings before removing Hermes's saddle. Cassie accepted congratulations from the duke who told her he hoped they would see more of Hermes. Hermes himself appeared cool and composed under the attention. He and Dick had a moment of closeness, Dick communicating with the horse by touch, and Hermes nudging the youth.

Once Lester was weighed and the victory confirmed they returned to the stables and everyone fussed over Hermes, washing him down, giving him a nibble of grass, telling him how well he did, until Grandmama called a halt.

"Stop fawning over that horse. He did what he trained to do. I won't have him spoiled."

Dick stubbornly refused to leave the horse, telling Jay with agitated hands that he feared some retribution from Hugh. Jay told him that Hugh was locked up, but Dick remained adamant about not leaving.

Grandmama demanded to be told what was going on. Cassie related the details of the fight not leaving out Raven's role. Grandmama sought out Jennings, questioned him about the likelihood of Hugh's release, and secured his assurance that two stable hands would share a night watch over the horse. She strode off for her carriage. In the carriage, she fumed, her eyes snapping, declaring her intent to write to the authorities, including the duke and the local magistrate, with her expectation that whatever decision was made regarding Hugh's behavior utterly unbefitting either a gentleman or a sporting man, he would be kept away from her granddaughter's horse. And, she told them, she would write to Ramsbury himself about his disgraceful offspring. With a final flourish of energy, she told Cassie to find and thank Sir Adrian.

At the house on St. Martin's Square, Grandmama retired to write her letters, sending Pindock scurrying for pens and paper.

Cassie turned to Honoria in the entry as her aunt untied her bonnet. "Fancy an outing?"

Honoria looked confused. "Now? Aren't you tired?"

"I am, but didn't you have somewhere you wanted to show me? What was it?"

"Oh." Honoria brightened, resettling the bonnet on her

head. "Well, if you're not too tired. The house where the poet John Keats wrote *The Eve of St. Agnes* is hereabouts."

"Excellent. Let's go, shall we? And then I've one more errand for us to do."

At Eastgate Square they stood in the twilight, a little awed at being close to a bit of history. Cassie was content to stand as long as Honoria wanted. Honoria had been dragged from London, plunged in crowds, and rather ignored for two days. The plain brick house, its only ornamentation a pedimented door flanked by two white columns, had none of the poem's medieval atmosphere, but Cassie figured that was a testament to the poet's imagination, and to the strength of his feeling about the woman from whom he had been parted. Honoria recited a passage from the poem and sighed.

"I do think Keats captured the atmosphere of the town," she said. "Thank you for coming with me."

"Glad to. Are you ready for another errand?" Cassie asked.

With one more sigh, Honoria turned away. "Where are we going?"

"To the Anchor."

"What's there?"

"I hope to find Sir Adrian to thank him." She did not know where the Ramsbury party had taken rooms, but she would start with the best-known inn in town.

The Anchor was the newer of a pair of rivals well-established in the town, and crowded in the aftermath of the day's races. It took some time to gain even a minute of the proprietor's attention. Cassie inquired directly after Sir Adrian. The man looked at her suspiciously, and she explained that she was Lady Cassandra Lavenham, and that Sir Adrian was her tenant at Verwood Hall.

The name Verwood seemed to relieve his suspicions, but the proprietor only shook his head. "He's left for London, I believe. Paid handsomely for the nights he won't be staying. Not like the rest of the party."

"The rest of the party?" Cassie asked.

"The Ramsbury party. They made a special request for rooms, and then up and left without paying the full shot."

"The Ramsburys have left?"

"All gone, my lady, and good riddance to 'em."

He was summoned by one of his waiters. "Your pardon, my lady."

"Thank you, you've been most helpful."

Cassie stood in the midst of the noise and confusion with a single thought in mind—how to interpret Raven's abrupt departure in the middle of the race meeting, which still had two days to go.

"So, he's gone," said Honoria. "How strange. And to London, the man said?"

"Yes. I meant to thank him for his aid in dealing with Hugh this afternoon. Without his insisting on Hugh removing his coat, Dick would have been locked up."

They made their way back to St. Martin's Square. Along the way nothing occurred to Cassie to explain Raven's departure for London. She had not thought in time to ask whether the proprietor knew where the Ramsburys themselves had gone. The family would not be happy with Raven, and she wished she knew what that meant for him. Everything he had done at Verwood he had done for Amabel's sake.

At supper, Grandmama read them a note from the duke. Hugh had been released, but had received a summons from the magistrate. A further witness, another of the stable hands, had seen and described the timing and suspicious manner of Hugh's entry into the stall. The duke assured Grandmama that he would personally see that Hugh would no longer be welcome at any respectable turf in England.

"Will Hugh attempt some revenge?" asked Honoria.

Grandmama put aside the duke's letter and gave Honoria a quelling glance. And then she laughed. "Are you still scribbling that rubbishy book about the war? The one I told you stop writing?"

Honoria looked wounded, but she straightened and gave Grandmama a stubborn look. "I am."

"Good. You have my blessing and you may call your villain Horrible Hugh, if you like, and make him as vile as possible. Now there's just a bit more from the duke. He says, I HAVE WRITTEN TO RAMSBURY TO INFORM HIM THAT HIS SON'S NAME NOW HAS SUCH A STINK TO IT THAT HE WOULD DO WELL TO SEND HIS HEIR ABROAD FOR A TIME. THE AMERICAS MIGHT SERVE." Over her letter, Grandmama gave them her most indomitable look.

"I doubt Hugh will attempt revenge, but Verwood will be prepared."

RAVEN REACHED LONDON by nightfall. He wanted to be in Verwood, but he knew he was not truly free of Amabel. He found his grandfather in his favorite leather armchair, wrapped in a maroon silk banyan, his feet on a Kilim-covered ottoman, brandy at his side, perusing *The Times*. Grandfather Cole looked up and lowered the paper.

"This is unexpected," he said. "Are you feeling guilty for fawning off those three imps of yours on me?"

Raven had sent his trusty messengers to his grandfather. "Are they much trouble?"

"I'm no nursemaid, boy. They need a woman to look after them," his grandfather grumbled.

Raven heard the affection under the mild complaint. "What have you been doing with them, Grandfather?"

"Teaching them about engines. They ask a plaguey lot of questions." He fell silent, and said nothing for longer than Raven had ever known him to keep silent. He felt the old man's gaze.

At last, his grandfather asked, "Need a drink, do you, lad?"

"I do." Raven poured himself a brandy and took a seat. He swirled the amber liquid in his glass and thought about how to begin his tale of what? Lost love, lost hopes, or sheer folly. He didn't know which. Had he ever loved Amabel? There was no good answer to that question. If he had loved her, he had let himself fall out of love, hardly the act of a gentleman. If he had never loved her, if he had pursued her for entry into the bright, glittering world she inhabited, he was still no gentleman.

"You've broken with Lady Amabel?" his grandfather asked.

"She broke with me." Raven stared into the glass. "But—

"

"They want a fight, don't they?" The paper slipped from his grandfather's lap as the old man sat up. "We can give them a fight. We can buy and sell them. See if we don't. I will not let that puffed up fellow Ramsbury get the best of us."

Raven looked up at that. It would take time, but he would get untangled from Amabel. Verwood, he hoped, would be waiting when he returned.

"Now tell me everything, lad."

WHEN THE THREE ladies of Verwood reached home, it was the week for getting in the grass. Though the summer had been dry, there was always a bit of trepidation in August that rain could spoil the harvest. Verwood hall was closed, its servants scattered, and no messenger boys about. Raven's army of gardeners continued their work, and the stables buzzed with new energy in the wake of Hermes's triumph, while Grandmama's estate manager oversaw the home farm harvest.

The three women in the dower house returned to their separate spheres. Cassie wrote a long letter to cousin Marianne, thanking her for taking them in and apologizing for their abrupt departure. Honoria went to work on her Peninsular War novel, freely making her villain Horrible Hugh, and reading the parts of his comeuppance aloud to Cassie and Grandmama at night. Grandmama, herself, returned to her stables full of plans for training more horses.

Jay Kydd had gone to London, but promised to return.

Cassie walked and thought. Something had happened to Raven. If she had understood what passed between them at the ball, he must love her. But there was only silence from wherever he had got to in the world. When she looked at the hall, a rather large reminder of his absence, her heart wavered between two possibilities. He could not be free because how could he be free and not come to her. Or he did not love her at all, and she had again been mistaken as she had been years ago about Torrington.

The first word of him burst on her on a bright Sunday morning when Miss Montford began a conversation outside of St. Andrews under the elms.

"It is quite sad to have the hall shut up, isn't it?" she commented. "You must miss the activity, Lady Cassandra."

"We do. My aunt especially misses our tenant's messenger boys."

Miss Montford stared as if Cassie had not understood her.

Cassie tried to make herself clear. "You have brothers, so you understand how their energy livens a place."

"Oh, I hadn't thought of that. I was thinking what a fine ball Sir Adrian gave. Do you know when he will return?"

"I don't," Cassie admitted, very much wishing that she did.

Miss Montford sighed. "Maybe he will never come again now that his engagement to Lady Amabel has ended." She drifted off toward her mother.

Cassie stood rooted to the spot, the same spot outside the church under an old elm where he had told her he would court Amabel. He was free, and he had not come. Around her, neighbors chatted, and their children, released from the good behavior demanded in church, ran about, chasing each other and laughing.

Honoria came to her side. "Are you unwell?" she asked. "Lottie is waiting."

Cassie made herself walk to the carriage, allowed herself to be assisted inside, and faced her relations.

"So you heard," Grandmama said.

Cassie nodded.

"There was an announcement in the papers last Sunday," said Grandmama. "You know the usual thing that Lady Amabel Haydon is no longer betrothed to Sir Adrian Cole."

"You knew?" Cassie asked.

Grandmama looked a little embarrassed, as nearly as it was for her to be so. "I thought he would have come by now."

"You thought Sir Adrian was in love with me?" Cassie asked.

"I have suspected as much since we invited him to tea." Her grandmother spoke with her usual maddening assurance that she was right.

"Tea? We hardly knew him."

Cassie tried to remain calm. He was free. If he loved her, he would come to Verwood, but she distrusted his history. He had been a lost boy. The world had regarded him as beneath its notice, and his proud spirit had rebelled against those who rated him so. He might not trust her love. The next moment another thought occurred. Why should she wait? She could return to London. She could show him how to face the world. She could show him that for her he had risen above them all. She would write another letter to cousin Marianne.

WITHIN A WEEK Cassie returned to Brunswick Square. Within two days she left her card with the Duchess of Wenlocke. On the following day, the duchess returned the call.

Marianne was awed almost to silence by the presence of such a person in her small drawing room. She apologized for her tea and cakes and offered them repeatedly. The duchess was dressed with quiet elegance, and wore an unusual fragment of a man's military medal and ribbon pinned to one shoulder. Her grace appeared cool and self-contained, except for smile lines around her blue eyes. Cassie suspected that the duchess was amused. She inquired after Marianne's children and mentioned her own interest in the Foundling Hospital.

When the customary visit came to an end, she asked whether Cassie was willing to take a turn about the square with her. Cassie found a bonnet, and off they went.

"I gather," the duchess said, "that you have something to communicate of a more private nature."

Cassie steadied herself. This was her opportunity. "I want first to ask whether you have seen Raven, or whether you know how he is faring after the breakup of his engagement."

The duchess stopped and turned that warm, sympathetic gaze on Cassie. "Ah," she said. "He is *Raven* to you, too. I have always thought the name suited him better than Adrian. Adrian sounds a bit like putting on the posh, if one can do such a thing. And our Raven is … cheeky, clever, proud, fearless."

The duchess slipped her arm in Cassie's and gave the arm a little squeeze. "It's an airy park, isn't it?"

Cassie's heart leapt. She might not know how to explain her feelings or what she thought Raven's might be, but her companion understood. The dry summer had dulled the grass, but the plane trees were still green overhead.

"Shall I begin?" the duchess asked.

"Please."

"Very well. Raven has been meeting with my husband regularly since his return to London. He put an announcement in the papers immediately upon his return on the advice of solicitors—his grandfather's and my husband's. Since then, there have been a series of lawyerly exchanges between Ramsbury's solicitors and Raven's."

They reached the far end of the square and turned back. Above them in the hazy distance lay Hampstead.

"If you are wondering, Lady Cassandra, I don't believe Raven feels free yet."

Cassie felt the heaviness lift from her heart. There was a reason he had not come to Verwood. "Do you know what happened? May I ask? Did she end it?"

"Oh, she did!" said the duchess with a laugh. "Dramatically and publicly. She threw his ring at his feet at the races, and it has hindered her cause."

Cassie stopped cold. Instantly the scene was before her, Amabel with her mother and friends in the fashionable enclosure, choosing her moment to inflict the most humiliation on her rejected lover.

"May I tell you a bit of our history?" The duchess gently tugged Cassie back into motion.

"Of course, I must be the most self-absorbed of companions," Cassie replied.

"Not at all. I am glad you have confided in me. My husband spent years in court fighting for his inheritance. He has excellent solicitors as does Raven's grandfather. Both men know how to deal with Ramsbury's legal maneuvers. And you must not fear the Ramsburys too much. The facts of the case will be more damaging to their reputation than to Raven's. Isn't there a saying about being tarred with one's own brush?"

"I'm glad Raven has such friends," Cassie said.

"Raven and the others were my pupils once, which is a story for another day, but what may I do for you? Do you doubt Raven's love?"

Cassie felt her cheeks redden.

"Am I too frank?" the duchess asked. "You did not come to London simply to talk about him."

"No, not at all," Cassie admitted. "What I hope, what I have been thinking, is that there might be a way for me to meet him. I don't know where, a party, a ball, though it is hardly the season, but somewhere where I could show the world my ... respect for him."

"I see. I admire your courage. The world has rated him far below his worth, and that has always chafed at him, but you could show him that the world's opinion means nothing next to the good opinion of the woman he loves."

"Can it be done?" Cassie asked.

"Oh yes. I know just the thing. We must make it very public. Are you game?"

Cassie nodded.

"Good. Then Sunday's the day. You and your cousin Mrs. Howarth must put on your finery and prepare to drive with me in the park at the fashionable hour. Maybe a new hat is in order?"

"The park? Will he be there?" Cassie thought it unlikely. The park on a Sunday was Amabel's world.

"Getting Raven there will be my husband's work. Trust me, he is up to it."

They reached the front of Marianne's house, and Cassie was fairly certain that her cousin was peeping out her front window as the duchess bid Cassie farewell and entered her carriage. In any case, Marianne met Cassie as she came in.

"How extraordinary! I suppose she is doing some looking about here in Brunswick Square for one of the duke's charities."

"Not at all, Marianne. She has invited us to go driving in the park with her, and recommends that we treat ourselves to new hats."

CHAPTER TWENTY-FOUR

BY THE TIME the duchess's smartly turned-out landau, with a pair of high-stepping matched bays and a footman behind, passed through the crowd of equipages entering Hyde Park, Cassie knew they had been noticed. Though neither Amabel nor her circle would be in town in August, the year-round denizens of London who took note of the duchess and her companions would fuel London's tireless gossip machine.

Around them phaetons, cabriolets, a barouche or two, and even one lumbering old closed coach streamed through the screen at the entrance to the park heading for the Ring, the place for the fashionable to see and be seen. Marianne looked about, as the duchess discreetly identified some of the more prominent members of the elite, the renowned beauty, Lady Blessington among them. An enormous gray horse carried a military gentleman. An old lord of Falstaffian proportions dwarfed his rather delicate phaeton. A daring boy in a sailor suit dashed across the line of carriages in pursuit of a small dog.

Once they entered the long line of carriages winding through the park, they became part of an unhurried scene in which voices and laughter mixed with bird cries and a band playing somewhere, and always the steady clop of horses' hooves and the crush of wheels against gravel. The grass had a golden hue, and a few leaves of stately elms showed the autumn yellow to come. The lake was a steely patch of blue, fringed with reeds. Cassie readied herself to meet Raven. The duchess insisted that Cassie sit in the forward-facing seat so that she would be spotted. She wore a gown of serene glacial blue for a calm she was far from feeling with just a dash of garnet silk ribbons on her hat for boldness.

The duchess smiled encouragement. "He will be here."

In the crush of vehicles, they had not gone far when there he was, on horseback, coming along the parallel track. At his side, also mounted on a fine horse, was the Duke of Wenlocke. Raven's face when he saw her told Cassie how ill-prepared he was for the moment. His roan horse did a little dance until he brought it under control. His stunned gaze did not leave Cassie's face.

The duchess's own carriage came to a halt. There was a moment's confusion, and then Raven slid from his mount, and the duchess's footman went to take charge of the horse. An exchange of satisfied glances passed between the duke and duchess, Marianne directed a questioning look at Cassie, and then Raven opened the carriage door, letting down the steps, and offering Cassie his hand to aid her descent. Cassie, her spirits dancing, took that hand.

He was as she remembered him from that first day, tall and elegant, with a defiant flash in his dark eyes that she now understood. He was a raven among lesser birds, no fearful barnyard fowl preening and squawking and getting his feathers ruffled. He was haughty and cheeky, too.

He took her arm in his, and they began to walk, headed

anywhere and nowhere in the rich ripe summer of sun-warmed earth and drying grass. As they sauntered on, he adjusted his stride to the rhythm of hers.

"I see that my friends have conspired against me, but you should know that I was on the point of returning to you," he said.

"Were you?" She slanted him an amused glance. He could have no idea of her impatience. "A word would have been nice. I did not know the state of your feelings."

"You must have guessed," he said, gazing warmly at her.

"I did not know that your engagement had ended until last week." She nudged him with her elbow.

He gave her a quick comprehending look. "So, you came for me."

"Are you shocked?"

"Merely a little frustrated that this is not the place for all that I want to say to you." He looked about. "Who are all these people? I thought London was deserted in August."

"Those people are our ambassadors," she said. "We must keep walking so that they will see us together and … talk."

"Ah," he said. "That's your plan. You will restore me to some sort of acceptance. It won't be easy. I've made enemies now. There will be people who choose to believe Hugh, and whatever ill-repute sticks to him, he still has friends, like Tyne."

"But you have friends, too. This afternoon show, the duchess tells me, is the ladies' battleground, where we go to outdo our rivals and lay siege to manly hearts."

"You have no need to lay siege to my heart. You won it long ago."

She smiled at that. "But you did not know, did you, until the night of the ball?"

His expression turned serious. She quite liked this freedom to study him.

"Yes, that disastrous night. It serves me right for my single-mindedness and determination to have everything go according to plans I made months earlier. And I was angry with you, that is I *thought* I was angry with you. I told myself that if I worked only for Amabel and planned for her, I would forget you."

"Did you?"

"Not for a minute. Custom required me to open the ball with you, and your grandmother let me know that she expected nothing less. But I knew that for Amabel, who was, after all, expecting my proposal, to see me open the ball with you would be difficult." He gave a rueful laugh. "Possibly, the worst proposal ever offered a woman. I rushed it so that she could have her moment."

He fell silent, and Cassie reflected how this talking and sharing of feelings was new to her. She had done nothing of the kind with Torrington. She would have confessions of her own to make sometime in their future, now that they had a future.

"You think that if you had danced with me first, you would not have proposed? You were in a very difficult place. I knew that you had raised expectations that it would be most ungentlemanly of you to disappoint."

"If her sentiments were as deeply engaged as I had led her to believe mine were, I was bound."

He looked out over the park. "We came here sometimes

as boys, at night, or very near night, in summer, just to play in the woods and climb trees. Wenlocke, before he was kidnapped, lived in his mother's house, not far from here. He knew his way around. Sometimes there were fetes and fireworks or music. I wanted to be like the people we saw from our hiding places. Courting Amabel was a way to enter that glittering world."

There was disillusionment there, and Cassie understood. She, too, had been dazzled by someone from that world. Raven was opening his heart to her, unburdening himself of wounds that lay there.

Oarsmen rowed their boats on the lake, boys launched tiny sailboats from the shore, and a very small girl and her mother fed the ducks.

"Do you think of me as a gentleman?" he asked abruptly, turning to her. The question was earnest, pressing even. Her heart lurched. She could guess what had been said to him, the wound it made.

Cassie stopped. Slowly, gently she put her hand on that wounded heart. "Unquestionably," she said. "I have never met a finer."

He covered her hand with his. They stood still as others passed around them on the path. They would certainly get themselves talked about. At last one rude comment compelled them to walk again.

"Ramsbury was quite determined to prove I was not a gentleman, but a cad who had wronged his daughter. However, Amabel does not want to marry me. She merely wants compensation for having been engaged. Their lawyers prolonged the argument as long as they could, but in the end, they didn't have a winning case."

"The duchess told me that her duke and your grandfather are formidable opponents."

"They are, and I am grateful to them. It is only right that it took some time to become disentangled from my own folly." He turned to her. "And until I did, I could not come to you."

"Do you call it folly?" she asked.

"It kept me from you," he said. "It took me long enough to know my feelings. I suspected myself of terrible disloyalty to Amabel."

"So you quarreled with me in the rain?"

"Yes. And wanted to kiss you at the same time. Now I've shocked you."

"Ah," she said.

"What struck me the night of the ball, and it flashed upon me almost like this comet everyone's going on about, was that I liked you. I liked you before I loved you. What hurt the afternoon of our quarrel was thinking that I had been wrong to like you, that you did not like me."

"I wonder that you did not see how much I liked you, more than I should have liked a man intent on winning another woman's love." She paused. "You know about my foot, but you don't know how I made such fool of myself in London over Torrington, a man everyone but me could see was going to marry another. I thought I could never love again."

He stopped walking abruptly and hauled her up a short bank to an ancient tree with drooping branches, ducking, he pulled her into a green space apart from the crowds below.

"I can see that this hat of yours," he said, tilting her chin up, "is the height of fashion." It was a little joke about the silk flowers piled on the hat's crown. In his eyes was a curious, almost disinterested expression, a man facing the mysteries of a woman's dress. He tugged the end of the wide garnet ribbon under her chin and the bow gave, letting the ribbons flutter down her bodice. An answering flutter started low in Cassie's belly. He brushed the ribbons back over her shoulders and rested his hands there. "You don't need to wear fine gowns or fashionable hats for me. I had to learn how to see you. I caught a glimpse that first day, but until the ball I did not see you ... whole."

His eyes grew solemn. "I love you, Cassie. I have been calling you Cassie in my head since the day of our quarrel in the rain. I quarreled with Jay because he was happily calling you Bluebell when I had lost any chance of speaking to you at all."

Cassie reached up and lay her hand against his cheek and brushed that cheek with her thumb. "I love you, Raven."

His kiss when it came was sudden and impassioned, the end of holding back and waiting, the end of the advance and retreat of the dance they had been doing from the beginning. Cassie returned it with all the fierceness she possessed. He had invited her into this other dance, in which her damaged foot could not hold her back, a joyful dance of soaring spirits. And yet even as he claimed her, and she him, Cassie knew they would fly higher into an endless sky.

When he released her, to hold her lightly in his arms, their hearts still thundering, she remembered that they were not alone, but in the middle of the most crowded park in

London.

She leaned her head against his chest. "We must turn back, you know. There is one more part of this afternoon's plan."

"And that is?" He showed no inclination to move, his voice a low, lazy rumble.

"For the duchess to take us both up in her carriage. We must be seen together for the plan to work." She pulled against his hold, and smiling, touched her fingers to his lips, a promise of other times.

CHAPTER TWENTY-FIVE

From the south entry, Raven surveyed Verwood, for perhaps the hundredth time since he first stood on its steps, vowing to make it his. He might not own the place, but he belonged to it now. A week earlier he sent Cassie ahead from London in his traveling carriage with the three messenger boys who had been plaguing his grandfather. In her absence from London, he had found a ring for her, one for her taste and her character, with its steady radiance rather than Amabel's glittering surface.

Nearly a year had passed since fire destroyed the Houses of Parliament. His memories of that night remained vivid. The burning of the old wooden tally sticks in a furnace meant for the lower temperature of burning coal had melted the copper flues running under the House of Lords. Cracks in the brickwork from frequent repairs had allowed the fire to send smoke and heat into the closed chamber full of ancient tapestries until the whole room had spectacularly burst into flame. A strong wind blowing from the west had whipped the fire to monstrous heights.

From all over London, fire companies responded, two of them with new Cole engines, marvelous machines of iron and brass, sprung wheels, oaken tanks, and leather hoses with copper rivets, capable of sending gallons of water per minute as long as hearty, twelve-man crews pumped the horizontal bars that drew water from London's plugs, and sent it cascading onto the burning fuel. He had been at the heart of the fire, standing knee-deep in water, supervising the changing of the crews and directing the hoses. The heaving of those pumps, the roar of the fire, the crackling of red-hot timbers never stopped until eleven when the wind shifted, and the hall was saved. Beating that fire, maybe that was the thing that made him feel unstoppable.

Even as the ashes smoldered, invitations had come for him from hostesses eager to claim a firefighter as a guest. At first the ladies in their silks were a blur of names and faces until his old friend Ned Farrington introduced him to Amabel. She eclipsed the others, and he pursued her the way he pursued any object he had in mind to win. Only when he accomplished his dream did he realize it was the wrong dream for him. Now he was awake, clear-headed, and in pursuit not of a dream, but of a woman, a wonder made of the ordinary elements out of which all women were made. Miraculously, she was his. He strode down the drive toward the dower house and Cassie.

When the bend in lane opened on the grass in front of the house, he stopped short. His three young messengers rolled and tumbled over each other on the lawn, fists flying, arms flailing, tearing at each other's clothes and hair, kicking and shouting. Honoria stood over them, wringing her hands, and calling on them. "Stop, boys. Stop this minute. You shall have no tea."

Raven simply waded into the fray and lifted Ben and Joe by their torn and sweaty jackets. Tim lay in a heap in the grass, panting and pointing an accusing finger at the others.

"They started it," he said.

"That's a lie," said Joe, squirming and dangling in Raven's hold.

"'oo's callin' me a liar?" Tim sprang to his feet, ready to charge.

"Enough," Raven said. "You lot are coming with me, but first, you must apologize to Miss Thornhill for not listening to her when she has charge of you."

"Wot's 'pologize'?" asked Joe.

Raven set the two boys in his hold down on the grass. He gestured to Tim to join the lineup and faced the small troublemakers. "Apologizing is begging pardon when you've offended someone. It's tricky because it only works if you are sorry for the harm you did. And it helps if you name the harm you did." As he spoke, he shed his coat, waistcoat, and tie. The boys watched him with wide eyes. He kept his face as grave as he could and handed his discarded clothing to Honoria.

"We didn't mean no 'arm to Miss T," Ben said.

"She's a good 'un," added Joe.

Raven nodded and stepped aside. "Your apology, now."

The boys studied the grass, drawing imperceptibly closer together. Then Joe looked up. "We're sorry, Miss T, that we spoiled the scene. We liked the fightin' part."

"And we forgot our lines," added Ben.

"Sorry we didn't listen," said Tim.

Honoria smiled at them and thanked them for their apology. They turned warily to Raven.

"With me, now," he snapped. "Leave your coats here."

The boys exchanged worried glances but did as they were told.

"I'll bring the miscreants back shortly, Honoria," he said. "Could you find Cassie for me?"

"They'll be fine, won't they?" Honoria twisted the ends of her shawl as if she feared for their lives, so Raven's stern face must be having an effect. Raven leaned close and whispered to her, "They will be wet, very wet." He saw the comprehension dawn in her eyes.

"March, lads," he said.

He herded them to the edge of the lake. "Shoes off," he ordered.

"Are ye goin' to drown us?" Joe looked resigned to his fate.

"Like they does to dogs?" Tim's chin quivered.

Raven recognized in the small shaking voice, his own small voice as an unwanted boy, lost in London, to be used for the most disagreeable work and then discarded, until Wenlocke had invited him into a gang of hearty survivors. He laughed at himself. He was turning into a Wenlocke himself these days.

"You can swim, right?" Raven looked at each in turn.

Three heads nodded.

"Good," he said, moving to the edge of the lake. "It's wise to cool off after a fight. Who's first?"

Ben shoved Joe forward. Raven swooped, lifting the boy high in the air, and tossing him into the lake. He landed with a great splash and came up sputtering and laughing and swimming. Then the other two came forward. In minutes they were flinging water at each other, and Raven, thinking of Cassie, missed the moment when they decided he would be their target.

With a sudden flurry of action, they sent great scoops of water his way, and left him soaked from his chin to his knees, his shirt clinging.

"Out now," he roared. It was a mock roar, but it did the trick. He led them back to the dower house. They chatted and laughed, describing moves in their water battle, their friendship restored.

Cassie stood at the door with Honoria beside her. Cassie smiled at him with the sort of smile that said she saw through him, and he wanted her so intensely, that it stopped him in his tracks.

"Oh dear," Honoria said, "Let's go round to the kitchen, boys."

"Are there cakes, Miss T?" asked Joe.

"Once you dry off." Honoria herded her small charges away.

Raven's throat was dry, his body barely held in check in its desire for her. "Meet me," he said in a voice roughened by his body's need, "at the fountain in an hour?"

He could live an hour without her, couldn't he?

"Yes," she said.

RAVEN FOUND CASSIE sitting on the stone parapet that surrounded the sunken fountain, dipping a sprig of lavender in the water. The golden light of an early autumn afternoon streamed down on her, and her inner light shone out, sweet and unwavering. Again, he had that experience of seeing her, really seeing her. He stopped to catch his breath. Her dark hair was wound in a low knot at her nape, her lashes lay across her smooth cheek with its faint flush of warmth, and her nose, that slightly upturned, slightly damaged nose spoke of her sense and her fearlessness. Insects caught in the light shimmered in the air, and the edge of her white collar and the brim of her bonnet shown bright with a hint of the passion in her that he had just begun to discover. She did not hear his approach over the sound of the fountain.

As he came nearer, she looked up and smiled a welcome. He came and stood before her. She patted the stone beside her. He sat.

"I've been thinking," she said, her expression turning grave. "That I should tell you the true story of my dreadful Season."

He took the lavender sprig and tossed it in the water, and took her hand in his. "And you think this because?"

She gave him an earnest gray gaze. "Because you should know that I deserved the things people said about me."

He doubted that. "Do you think my knowing your history will alter my feelings for you?"

She shook her head. "No. I don't doubt your love. You are constant, but..." She patted the stone rim of the fountain, and he sat beside her. She folded her hands in her lap, drew in a breath, and began in her usual forthright way. "I was infatuated. I'm sure everyone else could see it, but I could not. I let my world narrow to him. I never really saw him for who he was. I just floated on a little cloud of his attentions for weeks, ignoring everyone else. Honoria tried her best to wake me up to my folly, but I wouldn't listen. Even when we returned to Verwood, I could think only of myself, of my hurt, and so I rode Hermes too far, too often."

For a moment she seemed lost in the past, then she turned to him, her eyes clear again, shining. "You see, I think love, genuine love, is meant to connect us to others."

"Done?" He stood, and dropped down to his knees in front of her in the grass. Taking hold of her injured foot, he gently unloosed the boot, and slid it from her foot.

"What are you doing?" she asked, trying to pull the captured foot from his grip.

"I am making love to you, in the only way I can until you are truly mine."

She stopped tugging.

He held her damaged foot in his hands. "My turn," he said. "I, too, was infatuated, with a perfect picture, an artificial creation. I had no true interest in knowing Amabel. I wanted to be accepted by her world, and she seemed to invite me in. Then I came to Verwood, and you were before me every day, but I didn't, couldn't see you at first. What you are is yourself, strong and gentle. You are *you* perfected, and if this, this poor foot helped you become the woman I love, then I must love it, too."

"Oh."

He laughed. He rested her white-stockinged foot against his thigh. The touch of her foot there sent a bolt of desire straight to his groin. He steadied himself and slowly drew her pale blue muslin skirts up over her knees. He felt her hands settle on his head, her fingers slipping into his hair. Again, he paused to collect himself.

"Prepare to be shocked," he said.

"Shock me," she whispered.

He slid his palms up her thigh to the garter that held her stocking in place against the softest, silkiest of skin. She stiffened and then relaxed. He was crazy, but he meant to show her how perfect she was for him. His pulse hammering, he untied the garter and brushed it aside. Slowly he rolled the stocking down her leg, letting his thumbs trail along the smooth muscled flesh. She began to tremble, but she didn't stop him until he reached her ankle. Her grip tightened on his head.

He looked up and met her gaze. "I love you, Cassie," he said.

She nodded, and he peeled away the stocking to examine the foot, the trim ankle, the perfect toes, and in the middle a bony hump, gnarled and twisted like a tree stump. He did not look away. That lump was a sign of the hurt and shame of her past. He knew she had looked at it every day since her accident. Slowly, he dipped his head and planted his kiss there. His kiss could not melt away the misshapen bone, but he hoped it would melt away the old sense of unworthiness that haunted her.

When he looked up, he saw her eyes shining with tears.

He leaned back and got to his feet, pulling her up into his arms, pressing her head to his chest. She sobbed quietly, clinging to him. A breeze blew drops from the fountain over them as it had the day of their tea when she'd let her hat be carried away. She lifted her face to his and let him kiss her as deeply as he wished.

Only the ring in his pocket stopped him, but at last, he

drew her back to their stony seat. "I have something to ask you," he said.

"Do you? May I put my shoe back on?"

He nodded, watching as she deftly restored her stocking, shoe, and skirts to order. "You know this proposal business is harder than I imagined."

"Perhaps it only works when one is truly in love."

He took her hand and knelt again. "I love you, Cassie, will you do me the honor of becoming my wife?"

"Yes, Raven.

CASSIE KEPT THE secret of her betrothal as a special bouquet of happiness that was hers alone to enjoy for about two hours. Over tea that evening, lost in thoughts of Raven, she was called to attention by Grandmama. She looked up, and knew at once that she'd given the thing away.

Grandmama and Honoria demanded to see the ring, and Grandmama immediately began to order and arrange wedding clothes, guest lists, wedding breakfast menus, and wedding trip plans. Cassie only laughed and said that she and Raven could manage, thank you.

"Well," said Grandmama, "Don't forget that I had a hand in all this when I said he had to have your approval for his improvements."

Cassie crossed the room and gave her grandmother a quick kiss, the most affection her stiff nature ever allowed. "And we are most grateful, Grandmama."

"I suppose the big house will be full of all and sundry for

the wedding," she said.

"At least Grandfather Cole will be here…" Cassie began.

Honoria looked up from her tea. "Oh, I didn't think he liked the country much."

"I think he misses the boys." Cassie did not reveal that Raven had told her that Grandfather Cole had asked lots of questions about Honoria.

Grandmama rose. "You've done well, girl, better than you ever would have in London. I suppose I may tell your Sir Adrian now that you will one day inherit the hall."

"Not too soon, Grandmama, I hope," said Cassie.

CASSIE AND RAVEN emerged from the last patch of woods on the Wormley side of road. They had been to see Mr. Montford about their wedding plans. Mr. Montford would call the banns for three weeks, and they would be married on the third, the first Sunday of October in St. Andrews Church among their family and friends. Wenlocke was to give Cassie away.

In the blue September sky overhead, clouds massed for a storm, so they hurried a bit. But coming to the road, a pair of unmistakable voices raised in argument stopped them on their side of the hedge. Raven caught Cassie's hand, and she threw him a glance over her shoulder.

"Don't be tiresome, Bel. You must get down." Cassie recognized Tyne's voice.

"Why? It's not my fault we're in the ditch."

"Your silly little ponies have landed us here."

"Don't you blame my ponies, Tyne. I should never have let you drive."

"Get down, Bel."

"I won't."

"Fine, be stubborn. It's going to rain."

Cassie turned to Raven. They had to cross the road, so a meeting was unavoidable. She knew he would never choose to see Amabel again, but Amabel and Tyne were no threat to the happiness Cassie and Raven had. "We should help," she whispered to him. He nodded a tight-lipped agreement and helped her up the embankment through an opening in the hedge and onto the road.

There, a cream-colored phaeton, with its top folded back, and pulled by two stocky golden ponies with yellow manes, stood, its body on a tilt, its left rear wheel in the ditch.

"Can we offer any assistance?" Raven asked.

Amabel and Tyne whipped around to face them. Both faces flashed shock, annoyance, contempt, and chagrin.

"No," Tyne said.

"Yes," Amabel said. "We'll be soaked, and my hat will be ruined. Make him help you, Tyne."

"I think, you misunderstand your circumstances, Lady Amabel. Sir Adrian has offered to help. Lord Tyne may accept if he chooses." Cassie went to the ponies' heads. They looked heated and distressed. The weight of the stuck carriage must be pulling at them. She rubbed the soft muzzles and reassured them that they would soon be home.

Raven crossed to Amabel and lifted a hand. "Dismount. Your ponies will have a better chance of pulling the carriage out of the ditch."

"Oh, very well," she said, and offered her hand. Raven helped her to descend. "Now," he said to Tyne, "What's your thinking?"

"My thinking is that this is a bloody mess," Tyne said, throwing up his hands.

Cassie suspected that Tyne, a man of a light willowy build had never lifted anything heavier than a tennis racket or a cricket bat. He didn't want to admit he needed Raven's help, and she could see his distaste for the actual work of lifting the wheel out of the ditch.

"If my hat is ruined, Tyne, I blame you," Amabel said. The clouds were closing fast now, the bright sunlight dimming. That seemed to stir Tyne to action. He marched round the rear of the carriage and peered into the ditch.

"It's simple mechanics, Tyne," said Raven. "You and I put our backs to the carriage and push, while the ponies pull."

Tyne glared at him. Raven pulled his coat off and handed it to Cassie. She stood at the ponies' heads, ready to give them the signal to walk.

Amabel watched the two men, her head tilted under a lovely lilac-ribboned bonnet. Cassie tried to find some sympathy in her heart for the girl. Amabel had thrown away a good man's love for the company of a man of mere rank and position in the world. Cassie figured that if Amabel had not already realized it, this moment would teach her that she'd made a bad bargain. Maybe the two of them would find some happiness, but it would be a paltry sort of happiness compared to the one Cassie and Raven shared.

Cassie wanted to laugh aloud. Everything that had threatened that happiness was just this, a petulant, cross girl who wanted her own way in the world.

With the two men in position, though clearly, Raven would bear more of the weight than Tyne ever could, Cassie signaled the ponies to pull. At first, they strained and the phaeton rose and hung on the lip of the roadway. Then with a final pull, the wheel rolled back onto the road. Cassie praised the ponies.

Raven turned to Cassie at once and shrugged back into his coat. Amabel stood sending him covert glances. Tyne strolled up to her, putting on his own coat. "That's over then."

She gave him a cold glance. "Help me up, Tyne. I'm driving."

Cassie exchanged a glance with Raven, managing a straight face. They left the fuming couple on the road to sort out who was more to blame.

Raven pulled Cassie through the hedge on the opposite side of the road on Verwood property and stopped abruptly, turned her to face him, holding her by the shoulders, a clear intent in those dark eyes of his.

"You were going to show me a raven's nest you found," he said.

"We'll be soaked," she protested.

"I like you soaked," he said.

He kissed her then, a kiss full of hair-ribbon curling heat and promise. She stood dazed by it for a moment, before she recovered enough presence of mind to say, "The nest it is."

EPILOGUE

MARIANNE HOWARTH READ with great disappointment the London papers' account of her cousin's wedding. Really, it had been a most unconventional affair with an extraordinary guest list such as had probably never assembled in a little country church. And she, Marianne, had been there, mingling in London's best company, the wittiest, most elegant people. She resolved to set the record straight. She took up her pen to write to her dear friend Eloise.

Dear Eloise,

You must have seen the shabby account of my cousin, Lady Cassandra Lavenham's nuptials in our papers. I must tell you how really remarkable the whole affair was.

First, Lady Cassandra and Sir Adrian Cole married on a glorious October morning in the little church of St. Andrews in the village of Wormley. In attendance were the bride's paternal grandmother, Her Grace, the Dowager Duchess of Verwood, the Duke and Duchess of Wenlocke, the groom's grandfather Jedediah Cole, and the bride's aunt, Miss Thornhill. Standing up with the groom was Mr. Jay Kydd of Kydd Brothers Horse Auction House in London.

The dignitaries present were too numerous to name,

but Peel was there, and who knows how many of our members of Parliament. I met so many "sirs" you will hardly credit it, even your Sir William Jones and his Lady Helen. The Duke of Wenlocke gave the bride away, and in a break from custom, three young male attendants served to strew the flowers in the bride's path.

It is fair to say that St. Andrew's was packed with both dignitaries and villagers and ever so well-adorned. I think they must have emptied the hot houses at Verwood to supply the roses. And then when the bride and groom emerged from the church, the bride's horse, much beflowered, waited in the church yard. He was a recent winner at Chichester. Her groom lifted her onto its back, her satin cascading down. With Sir Adrian leading the horse, they led a parade of the most elegant carriages from the church to Verwood itself for a breakfast al fresco on the northern terrace, overlooking the recently restored formal garden.

Do let me know when you can come for tea. There is so much more to tell.

Your friend,
Marianne

The End

If you enjoyed *The Raven's Lady*,
you'll love the other books in…

The Duke's Men series

Book 1: *The Lady and the Thief*

Book 2: *The Raven's Lady*

Available now at your favorite online retailer!

About the Author

Kate taught English Literature to generations of high school students, who are now her Facebook friends, while she not-so-secretly penned Romances. In Kate's stories an undeniable mutual attraction brings honorable, edgy loners and warm, practical women into a circle of love in Regency England or contemporary California. A Golden Heart, Golden Crown, and Book Buyers Best award winner and three-time RITA finalist, Kate lives north of San Francisco with her surfer husband, their yellow Lab, toys for visiting grandkids, and miles of crowded bookshelves.

Thank you for reading

The Raven's Lady

If you enjoyed this book, you can find more from all our great authors at TulePublishing.com, or from your favorite online retailer.

Made in United States
North Haven, CT
22 October 2024